T5-DHD-939

Atlantic Sea Stories

John Bell, editor

Pottersfield Press

Lawrencetown Beach, Nova Scotia

Printed in Canada

Copyright © Pottersfield Press 1995

Introduction, headnotes and "Further Reading" copyright © John Bell, 1995

All rights reserved. No part of this publication may be reproduced or transmitted in any form by any means, electronic or mechanical, including photocopying, or by any information storage or retrieval system, without permission from the publisher.

Canadian Cataloguing in Publication Data

Main entry under title:

      Atlantic Sea Stories

      ISBN 0-919001-91-2

1. Sea stories, Canadian (English) — Atlantic Provinces. I. * Bell, John, 1952-

PS8323.S4A75 1995   C813'.010832162   C95-950041-3

PR9197.5S4A75 1995

Cover photo: "Starboard Lookout" by Wallace R. MacAskill, courtesy of the National Archives of Canada.

Pottersfield Press gratefully acknowledges the ongoing support of the Nova Scotia Department of Education, Cultural Affairs Division, as well as the Canada Council and Department of Canadian Heritage.

Pottersfield Press

R.R. 2 Porters Lake

Nova Scotia, Canada, B0J 2S0

CONTENTS

INTRODUCTION

Although it is a truism to say that the North Atlantic has shaped the history and culture of the Maritimes and Newfoundland, not all aspects of Atlantic Canada's relationship with the sea have been fully explored. One important area that has been largely overlooked during the past sixty years is the depiction of seafaring life in regional literature, particularly prose. This neglect has led some critics to misread the place of the sea in regional literature. Janice Kulyk Keefer, for instance, in *Under Eastern Eyes* (1987), an influential survey of Maritime fiction, remarks on "the surprising rareness with which the sea makes any major appearance in works sprung from a region in which no writer can live more than a few hours' drive from salt water." The fact is, the Atlantic region can boast a significant sea-story tradition.

In the latter part of the nineteenth century, a number of Atlantic-Canadian authors turned to the writing of sea fiction, most of it intended for juvenile readers. Typical works of the era included James De Mille's *Lost in the Fog* (1870), Charles W. Hall's *Adrift in the Ice Fields* (1877), James Macdonald Oxley's *The Wreckers of Sable Island* (1894), B. Freeman Ashley's *Dick and Jack's Adventures on Sable Island* (1895), and Charles G.D. Roberts' *Reuben Dare's Shad Boat* (1895). During this period the region's maritime life was also portrayed by foreign writers such as R.M. Ballantyne, Kirk Munroe, and Rudyard Kipling.

In the 1890s, two notable Atlantic authors of sea non-fiction were also active. Joshua Slocum, an expatriate Nova Scotian living in New England, and John Taylor Wood, a former Confederate naval officer exiled in Halifax, both contributed maritime memoirs to major American magazines. Slocum's third autobiographical narrative, *Sailing Alone Around the World* (1900), has long been regarded as one of the greatest classics of sea literature. Wood's exploits were later celebrated in *The Tallahassee* (1945), a ballad by the Halifax poet Andrew Merkel.

The sea story has also figured prominently in modern Atlantic prose. Since the 1930s, many of the region's leading writers — including Thomas H. Raddall (who actually began publishing sea stories in the late twenties), Will R. Bird, Evelyn Richardson, Farley Mowat, Alistair MacLeod, Silver Donald Cameron, and Antonine Maillet — have depicted the experiences of fishermen, sealers, rum-runners, and other mariners in fiction or non-fiction. At the same time, Atlantic Canada has continued to be portrayed in the writing of maritime authors from outside the region, such as the Canadian Victor Suthren, the Americans Edmund Gilligan and Marsden Hartley (who also painted Lunenburg County maritime life), and the British authors Frank Knight and Patrick O'Brian.

The most significant era in the history of Atlantic-Canadian maritime writing, though, was the period from 1900 to 1930. Not only was the region and/or its mariners depicted in works by Jack London, James Connolly, George Allan England, and other foreign writers, but, more importantly, these years saw many Atlantic authors draw inspiration from the seafaring traditions of the Maritimes and Newfoundland. The best Atlantic sea stories of the era were produced by ten writers who were particularly committed to maritime writing: Wilfred T. Grenfell, Colin McKay, Norman Duncan, W. Albert Hickman, Theodore Goodridge Roberts, Frederick William Wallace, Archibald MacMechan, Arthur Hunt Chute, Erle R. Spencer, and Frank Parker Day. The sea tales (both fiction and non-fiction) of these authors represent an unjustly forgotten chapter in regional literature: the golden age of the Atlantic sea story. It is this era which is the focus of *Atlantic Sea Stories*.

Even though the heyday of the group as a whole was during the first three decades of this century, a few of the Atlantic sea-story writers did publish work before 1900 or after 1930 (for bio-bibliographical information see the notes preceding the selections). Within the 1900-1930 period, they tend to fall into two groupings: those whose principal work appeared before 1920 and those who were active primarily between 1920 and 1930. Grenfell, McKay, Duncan, Hickman, Roberts (who was also an accomplished poet of the sea), and Wallace comprise the first group; MacMechan, Chute, Spencer, and Day, the second. Grenfell and Roberts, of course, continued to publish after 1920, but most of their best sea tales appeared before the end of the First World War. As for Wallace, who was active throughout most of the 1900-1930 period, the focus of his writing began to shift, following the war, from the sea story to maritime history.

While it would be presumptuous to speak of these writers as a formal literary group — one might be tempted to refer to them as the Seaward School — there were connections between several of them. Duncan, for instance, was initially sent to Newfoundland by *McClure's Magazine* to report on the good works of Dr. Grenfell. Grenfell, who later contributed a foreword to one of Duncan's posthumous collections, also likely had contact with Spencer and Roberts. McKay was a contributor to Wallace's *The Canadian Fisherman*, and MacMechan corresponded with both Day and Wallace. Other links probably remain to be uncovered.

The three decades during which these writers, as a group, produced close to forty volumes of sea-related prose were a time of profound change in Atlantic Canada. The golden age of sail was becoming a memory (although many schooners continued to be built for the fisheries and local and international coastal trade). Especially in the Maritimes, these were years shaped by urbanization, modernization, industrialization, and progressive reform, including prohibition. Furthermore, the impact of these new social forces was heightened after the First World War by a severe economic depression, which led to a substantial exodus from the region, political and social unrest, and the strengthening of a regional consciousness that had begun to take shape at the turn of the century.

In the Maritime provinces, this regionalism was eventually manifested politically in the Maritime Rights movement, which sought to increase the region's influence within Confederation. Not surprisingly, regional sentiment also found strong expression in culture, much of it centring on the most crucial aspect of Atlantic Canada's identity — its relationship with the sea. It was, after all, an era when a fishing schooner, the *Bluenose*, came to serve as a symbol of regional pride following her victories in the 1921 and 1922 International Fishermen's Trophy races.

Although the writing of the sea-story authors represented one of the most important aspects of the seaward thrust of much Atlantic culture during the 1900-1930 era, other cultural producers were equally intent on recording the region's maritime experience. Among those active in this movement were the folklorists James Murphy, Gerald Doyle, Roy Mackenzie, and Helen Creighton; the narrative poets Robert Norwood (a leading member of the Halifax-based Song Fishermen poetry group) and E. J. Pratt; the artist Rockwell Kent (who lived in the Newfoundland outport of Brigus from February 1914 to July 1915); and the photographer Wallace R. MacAskill. As well, Atlantic seafaring life was portrayed in at least four films: *The Doctor of Afternoon Arm* (1916), based on a short story by Duncan; *Blue Water* (1922) and *Captain Salvation* (1927), adapted from novels by Wallace; and *The Viking* (1931), which featured an on-screen appearance by Grenfell.

While the sea-story writers were encouraged by — and, in turn, helped to foster — the development of regional consciousness, their interest in fishermen and other seafarers can also be attributed, at least in part, to the dictates of the literary marketplace. From 1900 to 1930, there was an enormous demand for fiction. Not only did general-interest magazines in Canada, the United States, and Britain regularly publish short stories and serials, but there was also, in

North America, a proliferation of pulp magazines (named for their cheap paper stock) devoted mostly to fiction. In addition to a growing market for fiction in general, there was a particular interest in stories featuring local colour or adventure. Especially successful were genres that combined both, such as the western and the northern-adventure story.

Between them, the sea-story writers appeared in most of the leading American, Canadian, and British periodicals of their day. To readers of *McClure's Magazine, Blackwood's, Canadian Magazine,* and some of the other more staid magazines of the era, stories about fisherfolk living at the northeastern edge of North America made for exotic reading. To the readership of pulps such as *Adventure, Blue Book,* and *Argosy,* the relative primitiveness of the region's maritime environment represented a perfect setting for the two-fisted heroism which they had come to expect in fiction. Of course, by the turn of the century, tales of the sea had become a mainstay of adventure fiction, as evidenced by Stephen Leacock's spoof of such writing in *Nonsense Novels* (1911).

In short, the widely published Atlantic sea stories had much to recommend them: local colour, stirring drama and adventure, and the elemental struggle of man against the sea. It was a combination that was especially appealing for male readers. Which is not to say that women were entirely absent from the work of the writers represented in *Atlantic Sea Stories*; however, the primary focus of the sea story was on the male-dominated world of seafaring. The only book of sea-related stories by an Atlantic woman writer of the period is Lucy Maud Montgomery's posthumous collection *Along the Shore: Tales by the Sea* (1989), the very title of which reflects the distance from life on the sea that most women in the region experienced during the first three decades of the twentieth century. It was not until the publication of Martha Banning Thomas' *Stormalong Gert* (1936) that a female mariner would figure as the main character in an Atlantic novel of the sea.

Despite the strong elements of masculine adventure found in much of the work of the sea-story writers, their writing is not merely conventional adventure fiction. Nor is it primarily a nostalgic evocation of a lost golden age of wooden ships and iron men, which is how social historians have tended to describe the post-war work of Frederick William Wallace and Archibald MacMechan. Actually, Wallace himself was wary of the temptation to romanticize the past. In a letter to MacMechan dated 6 February 1928 (found in the latter's papers in the Dalhousie University Archives), he observed that "...the romance in seafaring is in retrospection — seldom when one is actually engaged in it. Nobody thought much of the sailing ship when they were common."

While interest in the region's marine history did increase as Atlantic Canada's economic and social crisis deepened in the 1920s, a significant portion of the work of the Atlantic sea-story writers appeared in the more prosperous, forward-looking period that preceded the First World War. And even after the war, much of their writing dealt with what was for them contemporary seafaring life during the final decades of the age of sail.

For the most part, these writers — several of whom worked as journalists — were not given to lyrical explorations of the sea's eternal mysteries. Instead, the focus of the Atlantic sea story was largely on the region's mariners and the quiet courage and fortitude which they displayed as they routinely pitted themselves against the sea's dangers. And while some of the sea-story writers obviously made concessions to the demands of the literary marketplace, they all strove for authenticity in their depiction of seafaring. As a result, several are regarded as early realists.

A key factor contributing to the accuracy and immediacy of the group's portrayal of maritime life was their ability to draw, to varying degrees, on first-hand experience. Wilfred Grenfell, Colin McKay, and Frederick William Wallace were all veteran sailors. Frank Parker Day, as a young man, had worked on fishing schooners. Arthur Hunt Chute was the proud owner of an able seaman's certificate. W. Albert Hickman was a professional marine engineer. Norman Duncan spent several summers living with fishermen and their families in Newfoundland outports. Erle R. Spencer had grown up in a fishing community and had made a voyage on a schooner from Newfoundland to Portugal. Theodore Goodridge Roberts had explored the coasts of Newfoundland and Labrador and had spent time sailing in the West Indies and South America. Even Archibald MacMechan, the least experienced sailor of the group, had voyaged to Europe on a cattleship in 1883 and later sailed on yachts out of Halifax harbour. Moreover, MacMechan compensated for his own inexperience by seeking out the mariners of the golden age of sail and hearing their stories first hand.

Certainly in their day the Atlantic sea-story writers were viewed as sympathetic chroniclers of the authentic maritime culture of Atlantic Canada. Not only did editors, publishers, and the reading public respond favourably to their work, but so did contemporary critics. From 1920 to 1930, five major surveys of Canadian literature appeared. Between them, these works discussed most of the writers represented in *Atlantic Sea Stories*. The most sustained examination of the Atlantic-Canadian sea story was found in Lionel Stevenson's *Appraisals of Canadian Literature* (1926), which included a chapter entitled "Down to the Sea in Ships." Stevenson's perceptive essay dealt with five of the sea-story authors: Duncan, Wallace, Roberts, Grenfell, and MacMechan. Stevenson attributed the success of these writers to both their commitment to authenticity and the "simplicity of the situation" encountered in their work.

In spite of the recognition that the sea-story writers achieved in the late 1920s, the golden age of the Atlantic sea story was nearly over. Grenfell was approaching the end of his writing career. Duncan had died of a heart attack. McKay had stopped writing sea tales. Hickman had given up literature for a successful marine business. Roberts was working mostly in other genres. Wallace had turned to maritime history. In 1929, Chute was killed in a plane crash. Four years later, MacMechan died and Day was forced by ill health to retire.

By the time of Spencer's death in 1937, the sea-story writers were drifting into obscurity. Most of their *oeuvre* was out of print, a significant portion of it buried in difficult-to-obtain magazines. A variety of factors contributed to this neglect, including the rise of realism and modernism in Canadian literature and the increasing marginalization of regional culture.

This situation continued until the late 1960s and early 1970s. The first sign of rediscovery came in 1968, when Malcolm Ross included Roberts' *The Harbor Master* in the New Canadian Library series. Three years later, Hickman's *Canadian Nights* was reissued in the United States. In 1973, Day's *Rockbound* finally appeared in its first Canadian edition. Since that time, works by Grenfell, McKay, Duncan, Wallace, MacMechan, and Spencer have been reprinted by various publishers (see the note on "Further Reading" for more information on these reprints).

While only a fraction of the total output of the Atlantic sea-story writers has been resurrected to date, it is obvious that interest in individual members of the group has gradually been increasing over the course of the past two decades. This renewed attention has coincided with the rebirth of Atlantic-Canadian regionalism and the attendant growth of Atlantic studies. Today, researchers in various fields are attempting to recover the region's lost cultural heritage.

Hopefully, these efforts will result in a broadening of the Atlantic literary canon to include the work of the main sea-story writers of the 1900-1930 period. For there is still much of relevance for contemporary readers in the writing of these authors who devoted themselves to the portrayal of the Atlantic-Canadian seafaring experience. Their largely forgotten stories offer a passionate — even defiant — celebration of the particular at a time when regional identity is increasingly beset by the powerful forces of homogenization that drive technological society and mass culture.

Atlantic Sea Stories will have served its purpose if it helps to rekindle at least some interest in the golden age of the Atlantic sea story, a time when some of the region's best writers took their readers on voyages into a vanishing maritime world.

* * * *

The compilation of this anthology could not have been completed without the generous assistance of a number of people in Canada and the United States. I would particularly like to thank the staff of the National Library in Ottawa, Goose Lane Editions in Fredericton, and the following individuals: Charles Armour, Richard Bleiler, Lesley Choyce, Donald Day, Fred Farrell, Mary Flagg, Anne Goddard, Donald M. Grant, John Leisner, Audrey Ogilvie, Norman Peterson, Joan Roberts, the late Peter G. Rogers, Sue Rogers, and Rena Van Dam.

John Bell

NORMAN DUNCAN

Norman Duncan was born in North Norwich Township, Ontario in 1871 and grew up in Brantford and other Ontario communities. After spending four years at the University of Toronto, he became a journalist in the United States, first in Auburn, New York and then in New York City. In 1900 McClure's Magazine *sent him on the first of several trips to Newfoundland to document life in the outports. From 1901 to 1906 he taught at Washington and Jefferson College in Washington, Pennsylvania. In 1907, he moved to the University of Kansas. Although Duncan's later travels took him to the Middle East, Southeast Asia, and Australia, it was his time in Newfoundland that had the most profound effect on his writing. Between 1903 and 1916 — the year of his death — he published numerous books about Newfoundland and Labrador, including* The Cruise of the Shining Light *(1907) and the Billy Topsail series of juvenile novels. Two more books, the sea-story collections* Battles Royal Down North *and* Harbor Tales Down North, *appeared posthumously in 1918.*

"The Strength of Men" first appeared in McClure's Magazine *(September 1903) and was then collected in* The Way of the Sea *(1903). Like all the stories in Duncan's first sea-fiction collection, it is written in the powerful documentary style that won him many admirers, including the noted British sea writer Frank T. Bullen, who observed that "with the exception of Mr. Joseph Conrad and Mr. Rudyard Kipling no writing about the sea has ever probed so deeply and so faithfully its mysteries as his. The bitter brine, the unappeasable savagery of snarling sea and black-fanged rock bite into the soul..."*

Norman Duncan

The Strength of Men

It may be that there comes a time in the life of the Newfoundlander when chance flings him into the very vortex of the unleashed, swirling passions of wind, night, and the sea. That event, to be sure, never disturbs the course of the pallid days of the city men, the fellows with muscles of dough and desires all fed fat, who, as it were, wrap the fruits of toil in pink paper, tie the package with a pretty string and pass it over the colony's counter. It comes only to the brawny, dogged men of the coast, to whom cod and salmon and seal-fat are the spoils of grim battles. In that hour, it is to be said, being of a sudden torn from the marvellous contrivance of hewn wood and iron and rope and canvas, called a boat, with which the ingenuity of all past generations has equipped him, the Newfoundlander pits his naked strength against the sea: and that fight comes, to most men, at the end of life, for few survive it. Most men, too, have to face this supreme trial of brute strength in the season when they go to hunt the hair-seal which drift out of the north with the ice to whelp—but that is an empty phrase; rather, let it be said that it may be set down in significant terms, when, each with the lust of sixty dollars in his heart, they put forth into the heaving, wind-lashed waste of ice and dusk and black, cold seas, where all the hungry forces of the north are loosed as for ravage. It came upon Saul Nash, of Ragged Harbour, this fight did, when in temperate lands mellow winds were teasing the first shy blossoms in the woods and peopled places were all yellow and a-tinkle and lazy.

At break of day — a sullen dawn which the sky's weight of waving black cloud had balked for an hour — the schooner was still fast in the grip of the floe and driving sou'west with the gale. Then the thin light, flowing through a rent at the horizon, spread itself over a sea all dull white and heaving — an expanse of ice, shattered and ground to bits, fragments of immeasurable fields, close packed, which rose and fell with the labouring waves. There was a confusion of savage noises, each proceeding from the fury and dire stress of conflict; for, aloft, where every shivering rope and spar opposed the will of the wind, the gale howled its wrath as it split and swept on, and, below decks, the timbers, though thrice braced for the voyage, cried out under the pressure and cruel grinding of the ice; but these were as a whimper to a full-lunged scream in the sum of uproar — it was the rending and crashing and crunching of the wind-driven floe, this thing of mass immense, plunging on, as under the whip of a master, which filled all the vast world with noise. The light increased; it disclosed the faces of men to men — frozen cheeks, steaming mouths, beards weighted with icicles, eyes flaring in dark pits. It disclosed the decks, where a litter of gaffs and clubs and ropes' ends lay frozen in the blood and fat of slain seal, the grimy deck-house and galley, the wrecked bowsprit, the abandoned wheel, the rigging and spars all sheathed with ice; and, beyond, as it pushed its way into the uttermost shadows, the solid shape of Deadly Rock and the Blueblack Shoal lying in the path of the wind.

"Does you see un, men?" said the skipper.

They were seven old hands who had gathered with the skipper by the windlass to wait for the morning, and they had been on the watch the night long — big, thick-chested fellows, heavy with muscles and bones — most with forbidding, leathery faces, which were not unused, however, at other times, to the play of a fine simplicity — men of knotty oak, with that look of strength, from the ground up, which some gnarled old tree has; and they were all clothed in skin boots and caps, and some coarse, home-made stuff, the last in a way so thick and bulky that it made giants of them.

"Does you see un — the Blueblack — dead ahead?" the skipper bawled, for the confusion of ice and wind had overwhelmed his voice.

They followed the direction of his arm, from the tip of his frozen mit to the nearing shoal, dead ahead, where the sea was grinding the ice to slush. Death, to be died in that place, it might be, confronted them; but they said nothing. Yet they were not callous — every man loved his life; each had a fine regard for its duties and delights. But the schooner was in the grip of the pack, which the wind, not their will, controlled. There was nothing to be done — no call upon strength or understanding. Why talk? So they waited to see what the wind would do with the pack.

"Well, men," the skipper drawled, at last, "she'll wreck. Seems that way t' me — it do."

"Eh, b'y?" ol' Bill Anderson shouted, putting one hand to his ear and taking a new grip with the other, to keep his old hulk upright against the wind.

"She'll wreck," the skipper shouted.

"Iss," said ol' Bill, "she'll wreck." A pitch of the ship staggered him. When he had recovered his balance, he added, in a hoarse roar: "She'll strike well inside the easter' edge o' the shoal."

Thereupon there was a flash of discussion. The precise point — that was a problem having to do with the things of their calling: it was interesting.

"Noa, noa, b'y," said a young man, who had lurched up. "She'll strike handy t' the big rock west o' that by a good bit."

"Is you sure?" retorted ol' Bill, with a curl of the lip so quick that the pendant icicles rattled. "Ben't it Ezra North I hears a-talkin' agin?"

"Iss, 'tis he," North growled.

"Tell me, b'y," Anderson shouted, "has you ever been wrecked at the ice?"

"I 'low I were wrecked twice in White Bay in the fall gales, an' 'tis so bad —" A blast of wind swept the rest of the sentence out of hearing.

"At the ice, b'y, I says," ol' Bill cried. "Has you ever been wrecked *here*?"

Some fathoms off the starboard-bow a great pan of ice lifted itself out of the pack, as though seeking to relieve itself of a pressure no longer to be endured. It broke, fell with a crash, and crumbled. North's sulky negative was lost in the clap and rumble of its breaking.

"Has you ever been caught in the pack afore?" ol' Bill pursued.

"You knows I hasn't," North snapped, in a lull of the gale.

"Huh!" ol' Bill snorted. "You'll know moare about packs nex' spring, me b'y. I — *me*, b'y — *I* been swilin' (sealing) in these seas every spring for fifty-seven years. An' I says she'll strike inside the easter' edge o' the shoal a bit. Now, what says you?"

North said nothing, but he looked for support to Saul Nash, who was braced against the foremast — a hairy man of some forty-odd years, with great jaws, deep-set eyes, and drawn, shaggy brows; mighty in frame and brawn, true enough, but somewhat less than any there in stature.

"Maybe she will," said he, "an' maybe she woan't. 'Tis like us'll find out for sure."

"'Twill prove me right when us do," said young North.

"'Tis is not so sure," Nash returned. "'Tis like she'll strike where you says she will, an' 'tis like she woan't, but 'tis moare like she woan't. But wait, b'y — bide easy. 'Twill not be long afore us knows."

"Oh, *I* knows where," said North.

But in half an hour he slunk aft, ashamed: for it was beyond dispute that she would strike where the old sealer had said. The shoal lay dead ahead in the path of the schooner's drift. In every part of it waves shook themselves free of ice and leaped high into the wind — all white and frothy against the sky, which was of the drear color of lead. Its tons were lifted and cast down — smashed — crunched: great pans were turned to finest fragments with crashing and groaning and hissing. The rocks stuck out of the sea like iron teeth. They were as nothing before the momentum of the pack — no hindrance to its slow, heavy onrush. The ice scraped over and between them, and, with the help of the waves, they ground it up in the passage. The shoal was like some gigantic machine. It was fed by the wind, which drove the pack; it was big as the wind is big. Massive chunks came through in slush. The schooner may be likened to an egg-shell thrown by chance into the feeding-shute of a crusher. The strength of the shoal was infinitely greater than her strength. Here,

18

then, as it appeared, was a brutal tragedy — a dull, unprofitable, sickening sight, the impending denouement inevitable and all obvious. The seal hunters of Ragged Harbour, mere sentient moles, hither driven by the wind of need, were caught in the swirl of the sea's forces, which are insensate and uncontrolled. For the moment, it was past the time when sinew and courage are factors in the situation.

"Sure, men," said the skipper, "'tis barb'rous hard t' lose the schooner — *barb'rous hard t' lose her*," he bawled, with a glance about and a shake of the head.

He looked her over from stem to stern — along her shapely rail, and aloft, over the detail of her rigging. His glance lingered here and there — lingered wistfully. She was his life's achievement: he had builded her.

"Iss, skipper, sir — sure 'tis," said Saul Nash. He lurched to the skipper's side and put a hand on his shoulder.

"'Twere a good v'yage, skipper," ol' Bill Anderson said, lifting his voice above the noise of the pack.

"'Twere a gran' haul off the Grey Islands — now, 'twere," said the skipper.

"'Twere so good as ever I knowed from a schooner," said Anderson.

"I hates t' lose them pelts," said the skipper. "I do hate t' lose them pelts."

"Never yet were I wrecked with bloody decks," said Anderson, "that I didn't say 'twas a pity t' lose the cargo. Never, b'y — never! I says every time, says I, 'twas a pity t' lose the pelts."

Just then Saul's young brother John approached the group and stood to listen. He was a slight, brown-eyed boy, having the flush of health, true, and a conspicuous grace, but dark eyes instead of blue ones, and small measure of the bone and hard flesh of his mates. Saul moved under the foremast shrouds and beckoned him over.

"John, b'y," the man said, in a tender whisper, leaning over, "keep alongside o' me when — when — Come," bursting into forced heartiness, "there's a good lad, now; keep alongside o' me."

John caught his breath. "Iss, Saul," he whispered. Then he had to moisten his lips. "Iss, I will," he added, quite steadily.

"John!" in a low, inspiring cry.

"Saul!"

The swift, upward glance — the quivering glance, darting from the depths, which touched Saul's bold blue eyes for a flash and shifted to the dull sky — betrayed the boy again. He was one of those poor, dreamful folk who fear the sea. It may be that Saul loved him for that — for that strange difference.

"Come alongside, John, b'y," Saul mumbled, touching the lad on the shoulder, but not daring to look in his face. "*Close* — close alongside o' *me*."

"Iss, Saul."

It began to snow: not in feathery flakes, silent and soft, but the whizzing dust of flakes, which eddied and ran with the wind in blasts that stung. The snow came sweeping from the northeast in a thick, grey cloud. It engulfed the ship. The writhing ice round about and the shoal were soon covered up and hidden. Eyes were no longer of any use in the watching: but the skipper's ears told him, from moment to moment, that the shoal was nearer than it had been. Most of the crew went below to get warm while there was yet time — that they might be warm, warm and supple, in the crisis. Also they ate their fill of pork and biscuit and drank their fill of water; being wise in the ways of the ice, each stuffed his stomach, which they call, at such times with grim humour, the long-pocket. Some took off their jackets to give their arms freer play in the coming fight, some tightened their belts, some filled their pockets with the things they loved most: all made ready. Then they sat down to wait; and the waiting, in that sweltering, pitching hole, with its shadows and flickering light, was voiceless and fidgety. It was the brewing time of panic. In the words of the Newfoundlander, it would soon be every man for his life — that dread hour when, by the accepted creed of that coast, earth is in mercy curtained from heaven and the impassive angel's book is closed. At such times, escape is for the strong: the weak ask for no help; they are thrust aside; they find no hand stretched out. Compassion, and all the other kin of love, being overborne in the tumult, flee the hearts of men: there remains but the brute greed of life — *more life.* Every man for his own *life* — for his life. Each watched the other as though that other sought to wrest some advantage from him. Such was the temper of the men, then, that when the skipper roared for all hands there was a rush for the ladder and a scuffle for place at the foot of it.

"Men," the skipper bawled, when the crew had huddled amidships, cowering from the wind, "the ship'll strike the Blueblack inside o' thirty minutes. 'Tis every man for his life."

The old man was up on the port-rail with the snow curling about him. He had a grip of the mainmast shrouds to stay himself against the wind and the lunging of the ship. The thud and swish of waves falling back and the din of grinding ice broke from the depths of the snow over the bow — from some place near and hidden — and the gale was roaring past. The men crowded closer to hear him.

"'Tis time t' take t' the ice," he cried.

"Iss, skipper!"

"Sure, sir!"

Young John Nash was in the shelter of Saul's great body: he was touching the skirt of the man's great-coat — like a child in a crowd. He looked from the skipper's face, which was hard set, and from the deck, which was known to him, to the waste of pitching ice and to the cloudy wall of snow which shut it in. Then he laid hold of a fold in the coat, which he had but touched before, and he crept a little closer.

"Is you all here?" the skipper went on. He ran his eye over them to count them. No man looked around for his friends. "Thirty-three. All right! Men, you'll follow Saul Nash. When you gets a hundred yards off the ship you'll drift clear o' the shoal. Now, over the side, all hands!" In a lull of the wind the shoal seemed suddenly very near. "Lively, men! *Lively!*"

The schooner was low with her weight of seal-fat. It was but a short leap to the pack in which she was caught — at most, but a swinging drop from the rail. That was all; even so, as the crew went over the side the shadow of the great terror fell — fell as from a cloud approaching. There was a rush to be clear of this doomed thing of wood — to be first in the way of escape, though the end of the untravelled path was a shadow: so there was a crowding at the rail, an outcry, a snarl, and the sound of a blow. The note of human frenzy was struck — a clangourous note, breaking harshly even into the mighty rage of things overhead and roundabout; and it clanged again, in a threat and a death-cry, as the men gained footing on the pack and pushed out from the schooner in the wake of Saul Nash. The ice, as I have said, was no more than a crust of incohesive fragments, which the wind kept herded close, and it rose and fell with the low, long heave of the waves: the very compactness of these separate particles depended, from moment to moment, upon the caprice of the wind and the influences at work within the body of the pack and in the waters beneath, which cannot be accounted for. Save upon the scattered pans, which had resisted the grinding of the pack, but were even then lifting themselves out of the press and falling back in pieces; save upon these few pans, there was no place where a man could rest his foot: for where he set it down there it sank. He must leap — leap — leap from one sinking fragment to another, choosing in a flash where next to alight, chancing his weight where it might be sustained for the moment of gathering to leap again — he must leap without pause; he must leap or the pack would let him through and close over his head. Moreover, the wind swept over the pack with full force and a stinging touch, and it was filled with the dust of snow: a wind which froze and choked and blinded where it could. But in the lead of Saul Nash, who was like a swaying shadow in the snow ahead, thirty men made the hundred yards and dispersed to the pans to wait

— thirty of thirty-three, not counting the skipper, who had lingered far back to see the last of the work of his hands.

"Leave us — wait — here," said Saul, between convulsive pants, when, with John and ol' Bill Anderson, he had come to rest on a small pan. He turned his back to the wind to catch his breath. "Us'll clear — the shoal — here," he added.

Ol' Bill fell, exhausted. He shielded his mouth with his arm. "'Tis so good as any place," he gasped.

"'Tis big enough for seven men," said John.

Bill was an old hand — an old hand; and he had been in the thick of the pitiless slaughter of seals for five days. "Us'll let noa moare aboard, b'y," he cried. He started to his elbow and looked around; but he saw no one making for the pan, so he said to Saul, "'Tis too small for three. Leave the young feller look out for hisself some other—"

"Bill," said Saul, "the lad bides here."

Bill was an old hand. He laughed in scorn. "Maybe," said he, "if the sea gets at this pan — to-morrow, or nex' day, Saul — if the sea gets at un, an' wears un down, 'tis yourself'll be the first t' push the lad off, an' not — "

"Does you hear me, Bill! I says the lad — "

John plucked Saul's sleeve. "'Tis goain' abroad," he said, sweeping his hand over the pack.

Then a hush fell upon the ice — a hush that deepened and spread, and soon left only the swish of the gale and the muffled roar of the shoal. It came creeping from the west like a sigh of relief. The driving force of the wind had somewhere been mysteriously counteracted. The pressure was withdrawn. The pack was free. It would disperse into its separate parts. A veering of the wind — the impact of some vagrant field — a current or a tide — a far-off rock: who knows what influence? The direction of the pack was changed. It would swerve outward from the Blueblack shoal.

"Back, men! She'll goa clear o' the shoal!"

That was the skipper. They could see him standing with his back to the gale and his hands to his mouth. Beyond, in the mist of snow, the schooner lay tossing; her ropes and spars were a web and her hull was a shadow.

"Back! Back!"

There was a zigzag, plunging race for the schooner — for *more life*: for the hearth-fires of Ragged Harbour and the lips of wives and the clinging fingers of babies, which swam, as in a golden cloud, in the snow the wind was driving over the deck. The ice went abroad. The pack thinned and fell away into its fragments, which then floated free in widening gaps of sea. The way back was vanishing — even the sinking way over which they had come. Old James Moth, the father of eight, mischose the path; when he came to the end of it he teetered, for a space, on two small cakes, neither of which would bear him, and when his feet had forced them wide he fell back and was drowned. Ezra Bull — he who married pretty Mary o' Brunt Cove that winter — missed his leap and fell between two pans which swung together with crushing force in the trough of the lop; he sank without a cry when they went abroad. It was then perceived that the schooner had gathered way and was drifting faster than the pack through which she was pushing. As the ice fell away before her, her speed increased. The crew swerved to head her off. It was now a race without mercy or reproach. As the men converged upon the schooner's side their paths merged into one — a narrow, shifting way to the ice in her lee: and it was in the encounters of that place that three men lost their lives. Two tumbled to their death locked in each other's arms, and one was bested and flung down. When Saul and John, the last of all, came to that one patch of loose ice where the rail was within reach, a crowd of seven was congested there; and, with brute unreason, they were fighting for the first grip; so fast was the schooner slipping away, there was time left for but four, at most to clamber aboard. They had no firm foothold. No single bit of ice would hold a man up. It was like a fight upon quicksand. Men clawed the backs of men to save themselves from sinking; blows were struck; screams ended in coughs; throats were thick; oaths poured from mouths that were used to prayers. . . .

24

"Saul! Saul! She'll slip away from we."

She was drifting faster. The loosened pack divided before her prows. She was scraping through the ice, leaving it behind her, faster and faster yet. The blind crowd amidships plunged along with her, all the while losing something of their position.

"Steady, John, b'y," said Saul. "For'ard there — under the quarter."

"Iss, Saul. Oh, make haste!"

In a moment they were under the forward quarter, standing firm on a narrow pan of ice, waiting for the drift of the schooner to bring the rail within reach. When that time came, Saul caught the lad up and lifted him high. But she was dragging the men who clung to her. They were now within arm's reach of John. Even as he drew himself up a hand was raised to catch his foot. Saul struck at the arm. Then he felt a clutch on his own ankle — a grip that tightened. He looked down. His foot was released. He saw a hand stretched up, and stooped to grasp it; it was suddenly withdrawn. The face of a man wavered in the black water and disappeared. Saul knew that a touch of his hand was as near as ol' Bill Anderson had come to salvation. Then the fight was upon him. A man clambered on his back. He felt his foothold sinking — tipping — sinking. But he wriggled away, turned in a rush of terror to defend himself, and grappled with this man. They fell to the ice, each trying to free himself from the other; their weight was distributed over a wider surface of fragments, so they were borne up while they fought. The rest trampled over them. Before they could recover and make good their footing, the ship had drifted past. They were cut off from her by the open water in her wake. She slipped away like a shadow, vaguer grew, and vanished in the swirling snow. But a picture remained with Saul: that of a lad, in a cloud of snow, leaning over the rail, which was a shadow, with his mouth wide open in a cry, which was lost in the tumult of wind and hoarse voices, and with his hand stretched out; and he knew that John was aboard, and would come safe to Ragged Harbour. They would count the lost, he thought, as he leaped instinctively from cake to cake to keep himself out of the water; they would count the lost, he thought, when they had cleared the pack and were riding out the gale under bare poles.

"For'ard, there — stand by, some o' you!"

It was the skipper's voice, ringing in the white night beyond. There was an answering trample, like the sound of footfalls departing.

"Show a bit o' that jib!"

The words were now blurred by the greater distance. Saul listened for the creak and rattle of the sail running up the stays, but heard nothing.

"Sau-au-l-l!"

The long cry came as from far off, beating its way against the wind, muffled by the snow between.

That was the last.

Now, the man was stripped to his strength — to his naked strength: to his present store of vigour and heat and nutriment, plenteous or depleted, as might be; nor could he replenish it, for a mischance of the lifelong fight had at last flung him into the very swirl of the sea's forces, and he was cut off and illimitably compassed about by the five enemies. Grey shades, gathering in the snow to the east, vast and forbidding, betrayed the advance of the night. The wind, renewing its force, ran over the sea in whirling blasts; and to the wind the snow added its threefold bitterness. The open water, which widened as the pack fell away, fretted and fumed under the whip of the wind; little waves hissed viciously and flung spume to leeward, foreboding the combing swells to come. The cold pressed in, encroaching stealthfully; touching a finger here, and twining a tentacle there; sucking out warmth all the while. He was cut off, as I have said, and compassed about by the five enemies. He was stripped of rudder and sail. It was a barehanded fight — strength to strength. Escape was by endurance — by enduring the wind and the waves and the cold until such a time as the sea's passion wasted itself and she fell into that rippling, sunny mood in which she gathers strength for new assault. Even now, it was as though the fragments of ice over which he was aimlessly leaping tried to elude him — to throw him off. So he cast about for better position — for place on some pan, which would be like a wall to the back of an outnumbered man. After a time he found a pan, to which three men had already fled. He had to swim part way; but they helped him up, for the pan was thirty-feet square, and there was room for him.

"Be it you, Samuel?" said Saul.

"Iss, 'tis I — an' Matthew Weather and Andrew Butts."

Saul took off his jacket to wring it out. "Were it you, Matthew, b'y," he said, making ready to put it on again, "were it you jumped on me back — out there?"

"Sure, an' I doan't know, Saul. Maybe 'twere. I forgets. 'Twere terrible — out there."

"Iss, 'twere, b'y. I were just a-wonderin'."

They sat down — huddled in the middle of the pan; the snow eddied over and about them, and left drifts behind. Soon the pack vanished over the short circumference of sight. Then small waves began to break over the pan to windward. The water rolled to Saul's shoes and lapped them.

"How many does you leave t' hoame, Matthew?" said Saul.

"Nine, Saul."

"Sure, b'y," Matthew's brother, Samuel, cried, impatiently, "you forgets the baby. 'Tis ten, b'y, countin' the baby."

"Oh, iss — 'tis true!" said Matthew. "Countin' the last baby an' little Billy Tuft, 'tis ten. I were a foster father t' little Billy. Iss — 'tis ten I left. 'Tis quare I forgot the baby."

It was queer, for he loved them all, and he had had a doctor from Tilt Cove for the last baby: maybe the cold was to blame for that forgetfulness.

"You leaves moare 'n me, Matthew," said Saul. " I leaves oan'y one."

The snow cloud darkened. Night had crept near. The shadow overhung the pan. More, the wind had a sweep over open water, for the pack was now widely distributed. Larger waves ran at the pan, momentarily increasing in number and height. One swept it — a thin sheet of water, curling from end to end. Then another; then three in quick succession, each rising higher.

"Iss — a lass, ben't she?" said Matthew, taking up the talk again.

"A girl, Matthew," said Saul. "A girl," he repeated, after a moment's silence, "just a wee bit of a girl. 'Tis like John 'll look after she."

"Oh, sure, b'y — sure! 'Tis like John will."

"Does you think he'll see to her schoolin', b'y?" said Saul. "She do be a bright one, that lass — that wee girlie." He smiled a tender, wistful smile — like a man who looks back, far back, upon some happiness. "'Twould be a pity," he went on, softly, "t' leave she goa without her schoolin'."

The wind was at the sea. It gathered the waves — drove them along in combing swells. It tore off their crests and swept spume with the snow. Great waves broke on every side — near at hand with a heavy swish, in the distance with a continuing roar. It was but a matter of chance, thus far, that one had not broken over the pan.

"Does you know what I thinks, Saul?" said Matthew. "Does you know what I thinks about that b'y John? He's a clever lad, that. He does well with the lobsters, now, doan't he, for a lad? Iss — "

"Iss," said Saul, "he does that, b'y. Iss he does."

"He'll have a cod trap some day, that lad. They's nothin' ol' Luke Dart woan't do for un; an' they's noa better trader on these shores than Luke. He'll be rich, John will — rich! An' 'tis like he'll send that little maid o' yourn t' school t' Saint John's. That's what I thinks about it — 'tis."

"Does you?" said Saul. "Does you think that? May be. He've a terrible fancy for that wee girl. He brings she mussels an' lobsters, do John, an' big star-fish an' bake-apples an' — "

28

"Sure, he do," said Matthew. "B'y," he added, impressively, "'twould surprise nobody if he'd give she music-lessons t' Saint John's."

"That lass!" said Saul. "Does you think he'll give she music-lessons — that wee thing?"

"Iss, sure! An' she'll play the organ in the church t' Ragged Harbour — when they gets one. She'll be growed up then."

"Iss, maybe," said Saul.

There was a long time in which no word was spoken. A wave broke near, and rose to the waists of the men. No one stirred.

"Does they l'arn you about — about — how t' goa about eatin', t' Saint John's?" said Saul. "All about — knives — an' forks?"

"Eh, b'y?" said Matthew, spurring himself to attend.

"I always thought I'd like she t' know about they things — when she grows up," said Saul.

Soon, he stood up: for the waves were rising higher. In the words of the Newfoundlander, he stood up to face the seas. The others had so far succumbed to cold and despair that they sat where they were, though the waves, which continuously ran over the pan, rose, from time to time, to their waists. It was night: the man's world was then no more than a frozen shadow, pitching in a space all black and writhing; and from the depths of this darkness great waves ran at him to sweep him off — increasing in might, innumerable, extending infinitely into the night. All the concerns of life — deeds done, things loved, tears, dreams, joys: these all melted into a golden, changing vision, floating far back, which glowed, and faded, and came again, and vanished. Wave came upon the heels of wave, each, as it were, with livelier hate and a harder blow — a massive shadow, rushing forth; a blow, a lifting, a tug, and a hiss behind: but none overcame him. Then a giant wave delivered its assault: it came ponderously — lifted itself high above his head, broke above him, fell, beat him down; it swept him back, rolling him over and over, but he caught a ridge of ice with his fingers, and he held his place, though the waters tugged at him mightily. He recovered his first position, and again he was beaten down; but again he rose to face the sea, and again a weight of water crushed him to his knees. Thus three more times, without pause: then a respite, in which it was made known to him that one other had survived.

"Be it you, Matthew?" said Saul.

"Noa — 'tis Andrew Butts. I be fair done out, Saul."

Saul gathered his strength to continue the fight — to meet the stress and terrors of the hours to come: for it was without quarter, this fight; there is no mercy in cold, nor is there any compassion in the great Deep. Soon — it may have been two hours after the assault of the five great waves — the seas came with new venom and might; they were charged with broken ice, massed fragments of the pack, into which the wind had driven the pan, or, it may be, with the slush of pans, which the Blueblack Shoal had discharged. The ice added weight and a new terror to the waves. They bruised and dazed and sorely hurt the man when they fell upon him. No wave came but carried jagged chunks of ice — some great and some small; and these they flung at the men on the pan, needing only to strike here or there to kill them. Saul shielded his head with his arms. He was struck on the legs and on the left side; and once he was struck on the breast and knocked down. After a while — it may have been an hour after the fragments first appeared in the water — he was struck fair on the forehead; his senses wavered, but his strength continued sufficiently, and soon he forgot that he had so nearly been fordone. Again, after a time — it may now have been three hours before midnight — other greater waves came. They broke over his head. They cast their weight of ice upon him. There seemed to be no end to their number. Once, Saul, rising from where they had beaten him — rising doggedly to face them again — found that his right arm was powerless. He tried to lift it, but could not. He felt a bone grate over a bone in his shoulder — and a stab of pain. So he shielded his head from the ice in the next wave with his left arm — and from the ice in the next, and in the next, and the next. . . . The wave had broken his collar-bone.

And thus in diminishing degree, for fifteen hours longer.

The folk of Neighborly Cove say that when the wind once more herded the pack and drove it inshore, Saul Nash, being alone, made his way across four miles of loose ice to the home of Abraham Coachman, in the lee of God's Warning, Sop's Arm way, where they had corn-meal for dinner; but Saul has forgotten that — this and all else that befell him after the sea struck him that brutal blow on the shoulder: the things of the whirling night, of the lagging dawn, when the snow thinned and ceased, and of the grey, frowning day, when the waves left him in peace. A crooked shoulder, which healed of itself, and a broad scar, which slants from the tip of his nose far up into his hair, tell him that the fight was hard. But what matter — all this? Notwithstanding all, when next the sea baited its trap with swarming herds, he set forth with John, his brother, to the hunt; for the world which lies hidden in the wide beyond has some strange need of seal-fat, and stands ready to pay, as of course. It pays gold to the man at the counter in Saint John's; and for what the world pays a dollar the outport warrior gets a pound of reeking pork. But what matter? What matter — all this toil and peril? What matter when the pork lies steaming on the table and the yellow duff is in plenty in the dish. What matter when, beholding it, the blue eyes of the lads and little maids flash merrily? What matter when the strength of a man provides so bounteously that his children may pass their plates for more? What matter — when there comes a night wherein a man may rest? What matter — in the end? Ease is a shame; and, for truth, old age holds nothing for any man save a seat in a corner and the sound of voices drifting in.

W. ALBERT HICKMAN

Born at Dorchester, New Brunswick in 1877, William Albert Hickman grew up in Pictou, Nova Scotia. Descended from a ship-building family, he studied marine engineering at Harvard University, receiving a B.Sc. in 1899. After working for the New Brunswick and Canadian governments, he was forced by illness late in 1903 to give up active work for two years. During this period he began to contribute short stories to some of the leading periodicals of the day, pursuing the literary career that he had launched in 1903 with a well-received maritime novel, The Sacrifice of the Shannon. *Starting in 1906, he combined writing with work as a marine engineer, experimenting at Pictou with speedboat technology. His first boat design, the Viper, was followed by the revolutionary Sea Sled, which featured an inverted-V bottom. Not long after the publication of his first story collection,* Canadian Nights *(1914), the success of Hickman's marine business ventures led him to move to New England, putting an end to his literary career. He died in Massachusetts in 1957.*

"The Goosander" *first appeared in two parts in* The Canadian Magazine *(November-December 1904). It is one of two stories that Hickman wrote about Donald McDonald, the Caribou engineer who first made his appearance in* The Sacrifice of the Shannon. *Like the latter work, which was partly written aboard the icebreaker Minto, "The* Goosander" *is set among the yachting set on the Gulf of St. Lawrence.*

W. Albert Hickman

The Goosander

Mr. Montgomery Paul sat on the broad verandah of his bungalow and, through his cigar smoke, looked up the harbour at Charlottetown, Prince Edward Island. Mr. Paul's business lay chiefly in following the fluctuations of Twin City and C.P.R. and Dominion Steel and Sao Paulo and Grand Trunk and such like commodities. He had followed with considerable foresight and, as a result, had had a comfortable feeling for some years. His base of operations was Toronto. Five years before he had discovered that Muskoka and the Georgian Bay lacked coolness, and various other things which a man from Toronto seeks in a summer holiday, and simultaneously discovered that in the five continents and seven oceans there is, in all probability, no such summer climate as that of Northumberland Strait and the southern light of the Gulf of St. Lawrence. So he built a bungalow on Hillsborough Bay, and every summer he transported his family thither and sat on the white sand watching the sparkling water and the fifty miles of Nova Scotia coast beyond, and went cod and bass and mackerel fishing outside and forgot how the heat came up in waves from the asphalt on Yonge Street and on King Street West.

For the first four summers he had cruised about a good deal in a twenty-five-foot launch he had bought in Charlottetown, and had found it such a delightful pastime that he had ordered a bigger boat from a Toronto firm. She was to be a fine, seaworthy craft with a steel hull. She was to have power enough to enable her to steam away from any boat of double her size in the Gulf. She was finished by the time he was ready to leave, and he had come in her by lake and river and open gulf all the way from Toronto to Charlottetown. If his stories counted for anything she must, indeed, be a marvellous boat in a sea. She was fifty feet over all, and though she had a comfortable beam her lines were as pretty as those of a destroyer. She had a pair of locomotive-type boilers, a low-set, short-stroked, big-pistoned, triple expansion engine, which swung a long-bladed wheel at a very respectable speed, and from her low house projected a short, stumpy, businesslike funnel. Altogether, to the trained eye, she looked well balanced and formidable. Mr. Paul's tastes were somewhat luxurious, and he had fitted her up with all sorts of shining brass yacht jewellery and innumerable blue plush cushions. So, from Charlottetown's point of view, the *Niobe*, as she was called, was a wonder on the face of the deep.

For that matter, she was not much less in the eyes of her owner, who had just been explaining her virtues to Mr. Robert Hunter, also a follower in the fluctuations of things, and resident in Montreal. Mr. Hunter had a yacht, too, a red cedar boat a foot or two longer than the *Niobe*, and with her engines set away aft along with the water-tube boiler fired with oil. She was called the *Mermaid*. In magnificence the *Mermaid* surpassed even the *Niobe*. Her boiler and funnel blazed and scintillated crimson and gold, for they were covered with rose-lacquered brass. Yes, and rose-lacquered brass was in all her parts, and her cushions were crimson plush instead of blue. Mr. Hunter had said a good deal as to the *Mermaid's* capabilities during the previous season, and this was one of the chief reasons why Mr. Paul had had the *Niobe* built with plenty of power. There were boats belonging to other magnates in other parts of the Island and on the near mainland, but Mr. Paul felt sure of his position.

"Yes, sir," he was saying to Mr. Hunter, "she'll beat any boat in the Gulf under seventy-five feet in length!"

"Don't believe it!" said Mr. Hunter.

"You don't, eh! Well, I believe it so much that I'll put a thousand dollars to be raced for, and they can all come; but it's got to be a good, long, open course — say from Charlottetown to Caribou. How does that strike you? Will you come?"

"Will I come!" said Mr. Hunter, and he became reminiscent and thought of the quiet way the *Mermaid's* engine turned two hundred and fifty, "will I come! Yes, I'll come — and I'll give you a drink out of that thousand when we get to Caribou."

"Nice Christian spirit," said Mr. Paul, and he laughed and lit another cigar.

"And you're going to throw it open?"

"Oh, what could you do? If you didn't, every tug-boat captain, every man in the Strait who owned any kind of a scow with a portable sawmill boiler and a single-cylindered junk heap in her would say that if 'they'd 'a' let him in he'd 'a' showed 'em.' But it'll be a circus, anyway. The thousand dollars ought to bring out pretty nearly everything with wheels in it," and Mr. Paul smiled complacently, and blew a smoke ring in which he framed a picture of the *Niobe's* triumphant rush across the line in Caribou Harbour.

The next harbour up the Strait from Caribou is called North Harbour. On its south shore is a deep cove with its east side a steep, spruce-covered bank, and the west sloping away into a sandy beach. Down by the beach is a long, white lobster factory. One day in August a young lady of about fourteen summers was sitting on a rock at the foot of the bank and swinging a bare foot in the water. The sky was without a cloud, and, as usual, as blue as that of the Mediterranean. The Strait rippled and sparkled, and every white house about Wood Islands, on Prince Edward Island, could be seen with perfect distinctness through the fifteen miles of crystal-clear air. It was a perfect Nova Scotia summer day — and there was nothing beyond. But it was evident that the young lady was not happy. Her golden hair — and it was golden, and glinted like polished gold in the glare of the sun — blew down across her glowing cheeks and freckled nose, and she brushed it back petulantly and wearily, and scowled. Then a sculpin swam lazily up to the rock and settled down to rest, and the girl threw a quohog shell at him. "Go away, you ugly beast!" she blurted, and the sculpin accepted the advise and kept on going until he found a hole four feet deep under a friendly bank of eel grass. Before the sculpin reached the eel grass — though he went so fast that his tail ached for some time afterward — the change had come, the inevitable reaction with all her sex from six to sixty, and the young lady was weeping. Finally she heard the shingle crunch and she faced round defiantly, while she rubbed the tear stains away with the edge of her skirt. A small boy, a year or two younger than she, was coming toward her, piloting a man with grizzled hair, who was smoking a little black pipe. The two were followed by a portly black cocker spaniel. The girl raced over the rocks.

"Hello, Mr. McDonald," she cried, "where did you come from? Where did you find him, Dick?"

"He walked down," said Dick, "and I saw him comin' in the gate," and he swung the big hand he was holding with vigour. Donald McDonald, the old engineer of the Caribou Fire Department, used to walk over to North Harbour periodically on an informal visit to Aleck Morrison's lobster factory. When he came the children knew there was sure to be something interesting happen. Donald could make the most wonderful boats with stern wheels, which were driven by rope belts and a treadle that you worked with your feet. Once he came down on Campbell's team with some iron bars and pieces of brass, and in a few days had turned a leaky dory into a treadle boat with a real screw propeller. Donald's most communicative moments were while he was with Aleck Morrison's two children, and then he was nothing less than a revelation to the black spaniel. On this particular occasion Donald smiled his most ingenious smile.

"A joost looked't Conoondrum theyre," indicating the spaniel with a wave of the three-inch pipe, "'n' a thocht: Weel, y're gettin' so fat that y' won't ha' hair t' coover y're skin een a leetle while, 'n' a'll ha't be gettin' old strips o' buffalo robes 'n' dyin' them black an' cementin' them over th' theen places, 'n' a don't know that a'd make mooch of a job o' ye then. So a joost thocht a'd walk heem doon hear for exercise, y'see." The three laughed, and the black spaniel took the joke pleasantly and wagged his tail.

"Ees y're father better, Maisie?" Donald went on.

"Some," said the girl. Then she remembered her troubles again. "But he says he's goin' to sell the colt, 'n' he won't let me 'n' Dick go to th' circus in New Glasgow, 'n' he won't let me go in 'n' get the wool to knit a shawl for Grandma's birthday, 'n' he won't—" and the girl's lip trembled again.

"Noo y' needn' cry," said Donald hastily, "a've na doot we can—"

"I don't care, it's my colt anyway; Papa said so when it was born, 'n'—" and there were further signs of a breakdown, as well as of another in sympathy on the part of Dick. Donald was in a difficulty for a moment.

"Y' see," he finally said, "y're father's been seeck a long time, 'n' he mayn' be sure aboot sellin' th' colt, 'n' ye see he hasn' had a chance t' get t' th' bank, 'n' maybe he deedn' ha' th' money f'r y' t' go t' N' Glaisga. Y' know," he went on confidentially, "people when they're seeck often get so worrked up aboot themsel's thut they never theenk o' leetle things. Here, noo, here's five dollars for the two o' y', 'n' a'll see him aboot th' colt, 'n' a've got a gran' plan on foot thut when y' hear aboot 't y' won't want t' go t' N' Glaisga or onywhere. Y' musn' tell onyone a gave y' th' five dollars." The lack of logical sequence in it all was splendid, but it had the desired effect. Aleck Morrison had put a good deal of money into additions to the lobster factory and into new gear, and the season had been poor. All the summer he had been sick, and now ought to be well on the road to recovery. But he didn't seem to mend as he should, and Donald knew that worry had as much to do with it as anything else. His wife thought he was well off, and the children thought him rich, and so it might prove ultimately; but now things were running pretty close, and the proposed selling of the colt was, in all probability, only a method for raising a necessary hundred dollars or so to bridge over the hard time. Aleck had always said, with a good deal of pride, that he had never owed a man a cent for more than two weeks in his life, and Donald knew Aleck, and knew that he would object to breaking his record now. After all, two or three hundred dollars would make everything easy again.

Maisie had brightened up wonderfully, and Dick had become sympathetically cheerful.

"Tell us what y're goin' t' do?" he said. Donald made up the trio of smiles.

"Coom up 'n' we'll see y're father firrst," he said. "Thees plan," he went on, as they started, "ees a great plan. Eets goin' t' beat th' dory wi' th' propellor all t' pieces. No, y'll joost wait! Y'll know all th're ees t' know soon enough." Maisie and Dick ran ahead, and left Donald and the black spaniel to follow more slowly. They rushed into the room where their father was sitting.

"Here's Mr. McDonald comin', papa, 'n' he's goin' t' make something new for us, maybe a new kind of a boat."

"He's a great Donald!" said Aleck, half to himself. "He's always able to keep the two of y' quiet, anyway."

"Well, Donald, I'm glad to see y'. I get pretty dull sometimes. Maisie says you've got some new plan on hand. What are y' going t' make now — a real steamboat, I suppose?" Donald got comfortably settled, with the girl on his right knee and the boy on his left. He stowed the black pipe in a pocket reserved for it alone.

"A want y' t' lend me th' *Goosander!*" he said solemnly. It may be explained that the *Goosander* was a long, black launch that Aleck had bought two years before from the Dominion Government for use in towing out loads of traps and for general service about the factory. The Government had used her as an auxiliary to their revenue boats, in preventing smuggling from St. Pierre and Miquelon, but she was not well adapted to their purposes and they had disposed of her.

"The *Goosander!*" said Aleck, with a look of surprise, "yes, y' can have her and the whole factory if y' like. But what are y' goin' to do with her?" Donald drew forth from his pocket a copy of the *Caribou Courier*, and pointed to a paragraph. Aleck read as follows: —

"Owing to a discussion as to the relative speed of certain steam yachts which has arisen among a number of the wealthy Toronto and Montreal men who are summering on the Island, Mr. Montgomery Paul, the owner of the splendid yacht *Niobe*, has generously put up a thousand dollars to be raced for by steamers of any type up to seventy-five feet over all. Entries are confined to boats owned by summer or other residents of the Maritime Provinces. The course is to be from Charlottetown to Caribou, and the date, weather permitting, September 12." The paragraph gave various other details, and ended up with the assertion that the proposed race was already exciting great interest. Aleck finished and looked at Donald.

"Y' don't mean to say that y' want to go into that with the *Goosander*!" he said.

"O' coorse a do!" was the reply; "a'm needin' soom recreation 'n' a dare say y'll be able t' fin' soom use for th' thoosan' dollars."

"Yes, we could find plenty of use for a thousand dollars if we got it, though y' would have to take the half of it. But there's not much danger of gettin' it. The *Goosander* would be somewhere off here when those fellows got in. They've got some fine boats over there now: boats they've brought down from Upper Canada."

"Aye!" said Donald, "so a've heard. Howefer, eef y' theenk we'll not get th' thoosan' y' needn't mind sayin' y'll tak' 't eef we do. A don't want th' money, y' know; a'll get more th'n a thoosan's worth o' recreation oot o' th' beezness; so between us we'll be makin' a clear two thoosan'," and Donald smiled. Aleck grinned at the argument, and submitted the more readily because his faith in the *Goosander's* chances was exceedingly small. Donald thought a moment.

"Aleck," he said, "d'y' know wheyre a cud buy a nice young horse?" Maisie's eyes had been sparkling at the thought of the *Goosander* racing the yachts across the Strait; now she became very solemn, and flashed a bewildered glance at the old engineer. She felt the big hand tighten for an instant on her shoulder, and knew that in some inscrutable way it was all right. Aleck was silent, and looked doubtfully at Maisie. He was surprised to see that young lady very cheerful.

"What do you want with a horse?" he said.

"What a wanted t' know wiz wheyre a cood get one," was the

reply. Aleck knew it was no use to ask for further information. He hesitated.

"I've got a fine colt that might suit y'," he said finally; "Maisie, y' bring the colt round, like a good girl."

Still more to his surprise Maisie ran off willingly enough, accompanied by the boy, and in five minutes the colt was at the door. Donald made a critical examination of him, and finally offered a hundred and twenty-five dollars, which was promptly accepted. He wrote a cheque and handed it to Aleck.

"Theyre!" he said, "Noo, a'm goin' doon t' look ofer th' *Goosander*; coom on, Dickie. A'll be up t' dinner, Aleck," and the three started for the shore, leaving Aleck Morrison surprised, but more comfortable than he had been for some time. They had not gone far when Maisie looked up inquisitively at Donald, who smiled.

"A suppose y' want t' know aboot th' colt," he said; "weel, a'll joost be needin' a horse for a leetle, 'n 'ts fery likely a'll be willin' t' sell een a month or two — 'n y' may be wanting' t' buy one yersel' aboot thut time. Y' never can tell what will happen. A — a tak' fery good care o' my horses," he added, as he got the black pipe underway again. Maisie laughed and was satisfied, and, of necessity, Dick was satisfied, too.

The *Goosander* lay at the wharf below the factory. As has been recorded, she was once the property of the Dominion Government, and for a number of years she had come and gone by night, and had hung just over the edge of fog banks, and had travelled betimes without lights, and had escorted one or two brigs and several small, slippery-looking schooners into Sydney or some other port, and had lain still amid the sound of axes on full casks, and had floated in a sea that reeked of Cognac. In those days many a good, fast fore-and-after knew that she was not to be despised. But she had too little freeboard and she was too fine, lacked the beam that makes a good sea boat, and the Government had finally sold her to Aleck Morrison. The *Goosander* had never been beautiful, and Aleck had added to her freeboard by putting a gunwale plank all round her. The gunwale plank made her too high, and took away all the torpedo-boat appearance she formerly had. Then it had not been put on very artistically, and had left her with a magnified sheer, so that she didn't look unlike a gigantic dory. Aleck finished by painting her black. Altogether, the effect was not pleasing. She had a fine, steeple-compound engine and a new boiler that Aleck had put in under Donald's advice shortly after he got her. Donald had often cruised in her, and had apparently a vast belief in her capabilities. "A'd like t' ha' her for aboot a week!" he often said, "a'd show y' what she cud do. All she'd need'd be t' get a string o' kelp tangled up een her rudder for a tail 'n' they'd theenk 'twas th' Great Sea-Serpent coomin'.'"

Just at present she looked particularly disreputable. Below the waterline she was grown over with weed; her black paint was blistered and peeled; her gunwale was split and splintered in many places along its fifty-seven feet of length; the engine was covered with a scant, dirty tarpaulin, and the boiler and long funnel were streaked with yellow rust. Maisie and Dick went out to the end of the wharf to spear flounders, the black spaniel retired to the shore and found a shady spot under a bush, and Donald climbed aboard the *Goosander*. He looked over her slowly, then lifted up a hatch over the shaft and sniffed at the oily, iridescent, black water that was sluicing about with the slight motion of the boat.

"Y' dirrty, deesgraceful old hoolk! Y' shood be ashamed o' yersel' for not keepin' yersel' clean. Beelge water! Beelge water! Y' can't help havin' a leetle, but no self respectin' steamer allows't to accumulate like thut!" After this rebuke the old engineer rummaged around for pieces of oily waste and kindlings and soon had a fire underway. Then he opened up the lockers and got out hammers and monkey wrenches and spanners and oil cans and boxes of packing and laid them all in order. While the steam was getting up he swept her from stem to stern. He caught the sound of a slight hiss, "Pop valve leakin'!" he commented, and made a mental note. "Aye, 'n' a try cock, too." He swung his weight on each of the eccentric rods, and felt a hardly noticeable jar. "Pairfectly deesgraceful!" he said. "Aye, nuts on th' straps loose." He studied the inside of the fire-box. "Tubes tight; thut's good, disteenctly good!" A little later he examined the gauge. "Seventy poon." He opened the throttle and immediately closed it again. "Not packin' enough een th' three boxes for one. Magneeficent gland!" and he began measuring and cutting, packing and sliding it into inaccessible places with a jack knife. Bye and bye he looked to his moorings and opened the throttle again. *Bump-siss-bump-siss-bump-siss* went the *Goosander's* engine, with a lot of little *psp-clicks* in between, which, to the uninitiated, mean nothing. Donald turned on the bilge water ejector and sat down to listen. For a diagnosis his ear was as good as an indicator any day. It came in muttered comments. "Low press' valve set too high — cut off too late — guides bindin' a leetle — th' cross-head soonds like a wire nail machine — a cood leeft out thut crank pin," and he aimed a dexterous blow at it as it flashed past. "Weel, een coomparison wi' soom o' them y're not bad! A'd like a leetle more vacuum, tho', eef a cood get 't. Howefer, a'm not goin' t' poot a surface condenser 'n' a circulatin' poomp 'n' an air poomp een y' for 't." So the comments went on until he drew the fire, and a little later there were rods and bolts and nuts and valves lying about on all the lockers, and the Goosander's engine was an apparent wreck. In the midst of the wreck, filing and hammering and fitting and testing, sat Donald McDonald, late engineer of the MacMichael boat *Dungeness*, the craft which, for some mysterious reason, used to do twelve knots while he was in her, and never before or since.

When the time came Donald went up to the house to dinner, during which meal he was uncommunicative. Immediately after dinner he went back to the *Goosander* and worked until they blew the horn for supper. Again after supper he went back and worked until darkness came down. After the children went up to bed the black spaniel came aboard for company, and Donald lighted a lantern and kept at it. When Aleck went to bed about eleven he could see the faint light down by the wharf and hear the sound of hammering of steel on steel coming up on the quiet night air. He knew that it was useless to interfere. Donald knew where to find his bed, and when he was ready he would come to it, and not before. The fact that the bed bore marks of having been slept in was the only evidence that he had been near the house during the night. No one heard him come in, and when Aleck first looked out in the morning, when the sun was coming up over the Gulf, the old engineer was aboard the *Goosander*, smoking like a locomotive and still hammering, and the spaniel was slumbering on his jacket on the wharf.

That day Donald worked steadily; and again brought the lantern into use and knocked off at midnight. The following day by eleven o'clock he had the engine assembled again. He filled the boiler and started a fire. When the steam was up and he opened the throttle it was easy to see that the *Goosander's* engine had seen magic. The piston rod glided up and down noiselessly; not a breath of steam showed anywhere; and never a hiss or a sigh could be heard; the eccentrics slid around, oil-bathed in the straps, and the straps never varied the width of a hair; and the cross-head and crank, no matter how fast they were swung, were perfectly silent.

Then Donald cast off the *Goosander's* moorings and started out into the harbour alone, and the way the *Goosander* ploughed up and down North Harbour astonished the inhabitants of the surrounding country. Aleck watched through the glass and could see the old man studying his watch while he raced back and forward between the buoys. After a little while he came into the wharf, tied up, drew the fire, covered the engine, and came ashore to dinner. During the progress of the meal he spoke very seldom, and then his remarks referred chiefly to smelt fishing, to an incident that occurred on the *Dungeness*, and to the probable weather. On the last subject he was noncommittal. After dinner he departed, leading the colt and followed by the black spaniel, and said that he would be back in a day or two.

Late that afternoon he took the Island boat, and that evening he stepped ashore at Charlottetown. The next day was devoted to research. He wandered about the wharves and got various and unreliable opinions on to the capabilities of the *Mermaid* and the *Niobe* and other boats in the vicinity. His only generalisation from the information he gathered was that the *Niobe* was the best of them all. Then he went to headquarters for fuller details. He got a small boat and rowed down slowly past Mr. Paul's bungalow. The *Niobe* was at anchor, and Mr. Paul was aboard, pottering about and offering advice to his engineer. Donald stopped rowing and cast a glance of evident admiration at the steam yacht. Incidentally, the admiration was perfectly sincere. The bait was too seductive to Mr. Paul, who liked to dissertate on the *Niobe*, and was fond of a new and sympathetic audience.

"Fine day!" he remarked, "having a look at the boat?"

"Aye!" said Donald, ingenuously, "she's a gran' craft."

"One of the finest! one of the very best! Would you like to come aboard?" Donald accepted with apparent reluctance.

"That's right. Come right up here. I suppose you belong about here? Other shore. Do you fish?"

"A've feeshed a little — Weel! This ees a magneeficent boat. A'd think 't 'd be deeficult t' keep all th' brass clean. She's beautifully feeted up — A — does she burrn wood or coal?" The question was uttered with the innocence of a little child.

"Coal," was the reply, "all these steamers burn coal, you know. Don't know whether you'd like to see the engine or not. It's down here." Donald signified his willingness, and Mr. Paul proceeded to dilate on machinery in general, in passing mentioning the fact that the *Niobe's* boiler was so strong that it stood the strain when the steam inside pressed one-hundred-ninety pounds on every square inch of it, that that type of engine was called a triple expansion engine for various complicated reasons, and that it had driven the boat seventeen measured miles in one hour. Donald asked if the seventeen miles would be considered fast, and Mr. Paul answered "Very. Faster, in fact, than any other boat of the size in Canada can do." Donald said "No doot" with perfect sincerity, adding: "A'd like t' see her goin' t' full-speed." Mr. Paul appreciated the interest.

"I was just getting up steam to take her out when you came along. She'll be ready in a few minutes now. If you're not in a hurry perhaps you'd like to have a turn in her." "A'd be fery glad," was the reply.

"Have a cigar?" said Mr. Paul.

"No, thank y'; a'll joost smoke thees," and he produced the black pipe. A little while later Donald's boat was tied to Mr. Paul's wharf and the *Niobe* was steaming out toward Charlottetown Light. At the light her engineer opened her up and she came in at full speed, while Donald sat by the wheel with Mr. Paul and marvelled. Several times he seemed to have difficulty in getting the black pipe going properly, and had to resort to holding his coat over it. A close observer would have noted that he surreptitiously looked at his watch on each occasion. When they got back and Mr. Paul had been duly thanked, he asked Donald if he expected to be in Caribou on September 12.

"A hope t' be theyre parrt o' th' day," was the reply.

"The reason I asked," said Mr. Paul, "is that we're going to have a steam yacht race from here to Caribou. I thought you might like to see this boat when she's at her best. You ought to be there in time to see the finish."

"A'd like t'," said Donald, "a'll try t' be theyre een time. A'm sure a'm mooch obliged t' y'," and he climbed into the little boat and rowed away toward Charlottetown.

"That's a queer old cuss," said Mr. Paul to the engineer. The engineer admitted that he seemed to be.

As Donald tied up his boat he smiled drily. "Seventeen mile," he murmured; "more like thirteen, a theenk. Howefer, a'll soon see." He went up to the nearest bookstore and bought a chart of Charlottetown Harbour. Then he went back to the wharf and sat down to it with a pencil and a foot rule. When he had finished he began smoking with unusual vigour.

"Good! fery good!" came between puffs. "Better than a thocht. She's not so bad, th' *Niobe*," and he smiled. As he spoke there came over him an almost imperceptible change. Perhaps only those who had been with him in the *Dungeness*, or those who had stood beside him on the night he screwed down the pop-valve of the old Ronald fire engine and spoiled the reputation of the new double-cylindered machine, or those who had seen him work in the number six compartment or at the centrifugal pumps of the *Shannon* before she sank, would have been able to interpret the meaning of the change. To the uninitiated it was only that his smile was a little more bland than common. But the light of battle was in his eye. As usual, when the odds against him suddenly loomed up heavier than he expected, he became more imperturbable than ever.

He went back to Caribou by the next boat, and on the following afternoon appeared at North Harbour. He was exceedingly uncommunicative, stating merely that he had been "doin' a leetle explorin'." He got a fire going in the *Goosander* as soon as possible, and started out into the harbour again to race against time between the buoys. When he came back he told the black spaniel, and him alone, that the trial was not satisfactory. The rest of the morning he spent in making all sorts of measurements of the old boat, and in figuring and making complicated drawings on a piece of planed pine board. At dinner he said he was going away in the *Goosander* for a few days, and about three he took the black spaniel aboard, cast off his moorings, hauled on his wheel-ropes until his tiller was hard-a-port, threw open his throttle, and the *Goosander* boiled out through the little entrance to the Strait. He turned once and waved his cap to the children. The last they saw of him the *Goosander* was heading south and he was sitting motionless in the stern.

Four days passed without a sign of Donald; but on the fifth morning the black launch appeared around the point of the Little Island and came in through the Wide Entrance. In her there were four men instead of one, and over her gunwale protruded various things, including, apparently, a good deal of dimension lumber. That morning Aleck had managed to walk down to the wharf, and he gasped with amazement as the *Goosander* tied up.

"Hello, Jim McIntyre," he said, "have you come too? Donald, for heaven's sake, what have y' got there? It looks as if you'd been robbin' a junk heap." Donald grinned.

"Y' look as eef y' were feelin' better," he said, irrelevently. "A'm glad o' thut." He surveyed the load with complacency. "A've brought McIntyre 'n' Carswell 'n' Beely Dunn," he went on, "'n' we're goin' t' make some leetle temporary alterations een th' *Goosander*." Aleck was speechless for some time while he carefully looked over the collection.

"It looks as if y' were goin' to make something," he said finally. The remark was quite justifiable. It may be said the *Goosander's* boiler and engine were compact, and there was plenty of room fore and aft of them. At present in forward, and lying on its side, was a very short, very stout and apparently very rusty upright boiler. Beside it lay a firebox, equally rusty, which had evidently been built for a boiler of larger size. There was also a great variety of old iron tyres off cart and waggon wheels of all sizes, together with a full thousand feet of iron wire off hay bales, and perhaps a thousand superficial feet of spruce boards. In aft there was a long-cylindered, deliberate looking old horizontal engine, which bore the marks of having already accomplished a life-work. Donald confessed later that it had spent twenty-two years in a sash and door factory. Then over the *Goosander's* stern there projected a battered, rust-pitted funnel, a dozen feet in length. Besides these things there were boxes containing innumerable bolts and spikes and staples and nails; a long, new, somewhat ponderous bit of shafting, with a double crank; most of the portable tools from Donald's little machine shop, and a great unclassified residüum, which to a less ingenious mind than Donald's would have been nothing more than what Aleck called it — junk. Aleck had been studying the load carefully.

"Look here," he finally said, "what are y' goin' to build, anyway?" Donald smiled.

"A'm goin' t' beeld what y' might call 'n accelerator," he said.

"And what's an accelerator?"

"Thut's what a'm goin' t' beeld!" was the reply, and there the conversation stayed.

Ten minutes later the old man and his crew had brought down a couple of piles, and were erecting them as shears over the *Goosander* as she lay at the wharf. The spaniel viewed the operations from a distance and inferred some permanency; so he retired to his bush and slumbered. With tackle rigged to the shears the ancient boiler and engine were hoisted on to the wharf along with the rest of the junk. Then ways were laid and the *Goosander* was hauled up ready for operations to begin. Her bottom was cleaned and painted with copper paint until it looked as in the days of her youth. At supper the accelerator was discussed at some length, but as neither McIntyre nor Carswell nor Billy Dunn seemed at all certain as to its precise construction, and Donald refused to give any further details, the result was not satisfactory. The next day two timber bases were built in the *Goosander*, one forward of her machinery and one aft, and in the former was set the newly acquired fire-box. Donald's plan was unfolding. Now there began, along lines new to marine engineering, the construction of a pair of remarkable paddle wheels. Both in diameter and in width their size was considerable, but their chief glory lay in their strength. Their construction occupied nearly ten days, and would be extremely difficult to describe. It is sufficient to say that, in the end, if analysed and their component parts traced, they would be found to embody portions of the following: three derelict wind-mills, a worn-out mine-ventilating fan, and a cotton loom, together with practically all the spikes, staples, bolts, iron tyres and wire before mentioned, and a goodly part of the unclassified junk and the spruce boards. During their building Maisie and Dick watched every movement, and would stay until Donald and the others knocked off in the evening.

Finally the *Goosander* was launched again. The long shaft was fitted into the old horizontal engine, which was swung aboard and bolted down to the base. Great bearings were bolted to the gunwale, and the paddles were slid into place and keyed. The short boiler was dropped on to the fire-box, and stayed with a forest of iron wires and a few lengths of chain. Then came the fitting and connecting up of the new main steam pipe, and the setting up and guying of the twelve-foot funnel, and the *Goosander* was complete.

The result was somewhat incongruous. When Donald had tightened the last nut he walked along the beach for fifty yards or so and sat down on a rock to look at her. When he came back he said: "What a ha' been tryin' to fin' oot wiz whayther she looked more like a paddle boat wi' a screw, oor a screw boat wi' paddles. We'll ha' t' get a fire een th' two booylers 'n' see what she'll do." So they filled the boilers and started the fires, while Donald reached into inaccessible places with a long-nosed oil can and drowned all the new bearings with oil. In a few minutes the steam began to show in the gauges. The old man smiled.

"McIntyre," he said, "y' can fire th' fore booyler 'n' look after th' wheel; Beely, y' can fire th' aft booyler; Carswell, y' tak' th' screw engine, 'n' a'll look after th' paddle engine mysel'. Bein' unaccoostomed t' th' worrk eet may ha' soom leetle peculiarities." Aleck came down and sat on the wharf with Maisie and Dick to see the start. The black spaniel thought over the matter and decided to superintend in person, so he went aboard and sat in the stern with Donald. Carswell looked at his gauge.

"I've got a hundred and sixty," he said, "what have you got, Jim?"

"Hundred and thirty!"

"Y' might cast off that line, Beely," said Donald. In a moment the *Goosander* was floating free. Carswell swung over his lever and opened his throttle. There was a swirl under the stern and the ripples clacked against the bow. The paddle wheels stirred uneasily. Maisie danced up and down on the wharf, and Dick shouted: "Look, Pop, she's goin'!" Donald opened his cylinder cocks and started his throttle, and the long-cylindered engine heaved a profound sigh, spluttered out a stream of mixed steam and water, and started. *Pap —pap—pap-pap-pap-pap-pa-papapapapa* went the floats of the paddles, as Donald opened the throttle wider, and the *Goosander* gathered way and moved majestically out into the harbour. McIntyre brought her round until she was broadside to the wharf, and they stopped her for Aleck to inspect. It was the first time he had had a good look at her since the transformation. He was immediately seized with a convulsion of unseemly merriment, and lay on the wharf with his knees drawn up and laughed until he was red in the face.

"Take her away!" he gasped, "she looks like a suction dredge. Say, Donald y' want to be careful not to get the two engines goin' opposite ways or Dick and Maisie 'll have to take the dory out after y'. If y' want any more funnels on her I've got a lot of old stove-pipe up at the house. Go ahead and let's see if y' can make the new wheels go round." Donald suddenly opened her up. The long-cylindered engine evidently looked upon Aleck's remarks as personal, and the way it handled the new wheels was a sight to see. There was a tremble, a roar as of the noise of many waters, a rush of foam, and a great cloud of flying spray that enveloped Donald and the stern of the *Goosander*, and caused the black spaniel to sneeze violently and finally to crawl into an open locker, where he remained during the rest of the voyage. Aleck expressed his satisfaction. Carswell opened up, and the *Goosander* boiled off towards the buoys on Donald's trial course, leaving a wake like a Fall River boat. McIntyre kept urging his fire, and for an hour they ran back and forward from buoy to buoy while Donald studied his watch. When they got ashore he said he was pleased, and spent the rest of the afternoon wrapping pieces of old carpet and jute bags around the whole length of the new main steam pipe "t' prrevent excessive coondensation." He finished the dressing with a coat of marine glue, and from that time forward, wherever the *Goosander* was, that steam pipe was a notable object in the landscape.

Now the fateful twelfth of September was only two days off. The time between was spent in putting on finishing touches and in testing and retesting everything from stem to stern. The afternoon before the race the whole Gulf was flooded with sunshine. Aleck and the children and Donald and his crew lay on the bank above the lobster factory and looked out over the Strait toward Charlottetown. The *Goosander* lay below at the wharf. Donald had Aleck's long telescope balanced across a log, and was sweeping the Island shore. Everywhere there hung lines of smoke along the horizon, and they were all converging on Charlottetown Harbour. Donald's smile was constant.

"Joost's a thocht!" he murmured, "they're all comin'; efery towboat from Sydney t' Miramichi! 'n' steam yachts 'n' launches, too. Theenk o' th' wheesky 't 'll tak' t' droon their recollection o' th' resoolt!" Carswell was studying the blotches of smoke.

"There's Long Rory's *Susan Bell*, the one he built for a pilot boat and put an engine in afterward. She's doin' about four miles an hour; an' there's the boat Johnnie Lawson brought from the States. He says she can do fourteen knots. That one up to wind'ard is the old *Micmac* that Henry Simpson runs to Cape Breton. She's listed to starboard, as usual. That one right off the Island Shoal is Colonel Dan McPherson's yacht round from Halifax. That's all I can make out. There's lots of them, anyway!" This was evident, and Aleck came to believe less than ever in the *Goosander's* chances. But every addition to the fleet seemed only to add to Donald's complacency. "Eets goin' t' be a gran' race!" he would say. Then he would sit in silence while the rest talked.

"When are you going to start?" they finally asked him.

"Oo, we'll joost wait 'n' ha' supper, 'n' go ofer by night. A'm fery modest; 'n' besides, a don't want to make any o' them jealous or t' scare th'm oot o' th' race. Eef they saw th' *Goosander* they might'n' care t' stairt."

"By George! if they knew who was in her a lot of them wouldn't!" said Billy Dunn, warmly. The old man winced under the compliment.

"A'll trry not t' frighten them!" he said suavely.

After supper they built a fire under the *Goosander's* new boiler. As a final test, Donald was going to take her across with the paddles alone. By the time they were ready the sun had been down an hour and the stars were out. Across the Strait they could see the light on Wood Islands and catch the blaze of Point Prim Light away up to the northward. Maisie and Dick were on the wharf to watch the departure, and were trembling with excitement.

"Y' mus' watch us wi' th' glass, Maisie," said Donald, as he climbed aboard with a suit of oilskins under one arm and the spaniel under the other, "'n' when we go ahead y' mus' cheer, d' y' see? A' can't hear y', but a'll know y're cheerin', 'n' that'll make us beat them." The children promised to do their best. The old man opened the throttle, the long-cylindered engine churned the water into froth, and the *Goosander* glided off under the stars, out toward the Gull Rock Light, leaving a trail of glittering phosphorescence behind. The two small figures on the wharf watched the dark cloud of smoke go out through the Wide Entrance. Then they ran up to give their father a circumstantial account of the departure.

By midnight, in the bungalow on Hillsborough Bay, Mr. Montgomery Paul was sleeping peacefully, entirely oblivious of anything that the calm waters of Northumberland Strait might be bearing on toward his discomfiture. In the morning his friend, Mr. Hunter, strolled over for breakfast.

"Well, what do you think of them?" said Mr. Paul. "I told you they'd come!"

"Never saw such a collection of craft in my life!"

"It's going to be tremendous!"

"It is!"

"Look at the smoke of them up there now!"

"Yes, looks like a picture of the battle of the Nile. That's the advantage of having a boat fired with oil."

"Humph!" said Mr. Paul, "stinking nuisance."

"Stink be hanged!" said Mr. Hunter. "But say, your engineer told me that one with paddles came in about two o'clock this morning."

"Paddles?"

"Yes, paddles; and he says she had two funnels." Mr. Paul laughed.

"He must have been taking something to brace him up. Maybe a torpedo boat came in, and made such a row he thought it was paddles. Well, we'd better get some breakfast."

The race was to start at ten o'clock, and from dawn boats of all kinds had been up at the wharves getting water and preparing generally. The day was clear, and a stiff north-west breeze was making the harbour choppy. Spectators were everywhere; on the wharves and in row-boats and sailboats. Every lobster fisherman in the vicinity had sailed in with his family, and the sails, from white to tan brown, were all over the harbour. But the steamers were the overpowering feature. There was the Caribou boat and six others loaded with spectators lying at the wharves. There were smaller steamers of all shapes and descriptions rushing about and dodging each other, and the chorus of shrieks from their whistles was indescribable. It was as if a steam caliope, such as circuses carry, was being abused. A deep-sheared tug would roll by, low set, and with her circulating pump hurling a jerking stream of water eight feet from her side. Then would follow a long, smooth-polished craft with a striped awning and an engine that sounded like a sewing machine. Then *bang—bang—snap bang! puff—puff—bang!* and a gasoline yacht would pass and recall a militia company after the order "Fire at will!" had been given. She would be followed by a bluff-bowed tug, high forward and low in the stern, piling up a great wall of water in front of her. She had spent most of her life towing about a big dredge, and her owner said that if she could do that he didn't see why she couldn't keep up with the best of them. Down in the opposite direction would come a beautiful little schooner-bowed yacht, white, and with polished spars and shining brass, slipping along with hardly a ripple; while out beyond, with her skipper solid in his convictions as to what she could do in a seaway, would loom a two-masted ocean-going tow-boat. Then a top-heavy passenger boat from the Bay Chaleur would come down, letting herself out, and loosening up just to be sure that nothing was wrong; then two more launches, followed by another tug. And so they went. Over the rails of the open ones, and from doors amidships in the others, protruded heads of men with grimy faces and with hands holding bunches of waste or oil cans or spanners, each studying the bewildering array of his enemies, and each reasonably certain that, given favourable conditions, he "could lick the whole lot o' them."

About half-past nine Mr. Hunter's *Mermaid* came up the harbour. The sunlight was glinting on her varnished sides and glaring red and gold from the rose-lacquered brass of her funnel and boiler. A quarter of a mile behind her came the *Niobe*, hardly less dazzling, and looking very formidable with her low set hull and big stubby funnel. She was at once recognised as the boat of the man who was willing to risk the thousand dollars, and was greeted by all the whistles. Then came a gun from one of the big passenger steamers that served as the judge's boat. It was the preparatory signal. In fifteen minutes the race would start. The crowd on the wharves and on the boats commenced to shift uneasily. The steamers circled and began to draw up into a long uneven line that stretched away across the big harbour; ocean tugs, harbour tugs, passenger boats, yachts and launches, each with its boilers fired up to the blowing-off point, and each after the thousand dollars offered by Mr. Montgomery Paul. Mr. Paul himself was excited, there was no denying that. He was trembling as he sat at the little brass wheel and swung the *Niobe* in alongside the *Mermaid*. He made a remark to Mr. Hunter concerning the weather. Then his engineer spoke up:

"Now will y' say I was drunk!" he said. "Look there!" and he pointed up the harbour.

"Well, I'm blowed!" said Mr. Paul. Mr. Hunter gasped.

"What in — ;" then he stopped. Coming down from far up the harbour was something that looked not unlike a Tyne tug. Above a narrow black hull, crammed with machinery, towered two long, rusty funnels of unequal height, which were pouring out volumes of black smoke. Below were two broad paddles without boxes — paddles that were now being swung so viciously that the after part of the apparition was half hidden in clouds of flying spray that glittered in the morning sun. The boat's speed seemed to be marvellous, and her ugly black bow, with its copper-red bottom, sat on a cushion of seething foam. Behind her stretched a wide white wake. Other eyes were turned in her direction, and, as she came closer, still others, until nearly everyone in the fleet was watching her approach.

> "On she came, with a cloud of (coal dust),
>   Right against the wind that blew,
>   Until the eye could distinguish
>   The faces of the crew."

The said crew

> "— stood calm and silent
>   And looked upon the foes,
>   And a great shout of laughter
>   From all the vanguard rose."

Mr. Paul's engineer spoke.

"Look at her machinery!" he gasped, "she's full of it. I'll be hanged if she hasn't got a screw, too! And Lord! look at her paddles! That beats anything I've ever seen!" The *Susan Bell* happened to be near, and Long Rory stood up.

"*Great Eastern* ahoy!" he yelled, and the crowd roared. Rory began to see who comprised the *Goosander's* crew.

"Hi, Donald," he shouted, "can y' lend us a boiler?" Donald stood up and smiled blandly.

"A'd be pairfectly weelin' t' lend y' th' two o' them 'n' row her ofer eef a wiz racin' th' *Susan Bell* alone," he said, and the crowd laughed again. The word went down the line that it was Donald McDonald, and those who knew him said: "We might have known he'd be here." Henry Simpson said: "Donald McDonald — that settles some of us!" Donald came up astern of the *Niobe*, and the paddles stopped.

"Good day, Mr. Paul," he said.

"Good day," said Mr. Paul, "that's a great boat you've got there."

"Aye," was the solemn answer, "a like th' design mysel'."

"By George!" said Mr. Paul to his engineer, "that's the old chap we had aboard the *Niobe!*" The engineer grinned unsympathetically. The *Susan Bell* was near and Mr. Paul turned to Rory and said quietly:

"Who is he?"

"Donald McDonald," said Rory.

"And who's Donald McDonald?" Rory laughed.

"Oh, he belongs to Caribou; y'll likely know something about him before night," he said. Mr. Paul turned to the *Goosander* again.

"Aren't you coming up into line?" he shouted.

"Not 't present."

"There's only four minutes before the starting gun."

"A'm afraid o' gettin' my paddles broken. A'll trry 'n' coom up ootside wheyre th're's plainty o' sea room." Rory chuckled. "He's got blood in his eye this morning," he said to himself.

The *Goosander* hung back of the line and the big boats ranged up behind her. The Caribou boat was crowded with Caribou people, and they all seemed to recognise Donald at once, and yelled simultaneously. The old man sat in the *Goosander's* stern with the black spaniel beside him and his eye on his watch.

"Carswell," he said, softly, "y' needn't open up for a while. A'll run her wi' th' paddles." Now there was only a minute to spare. All down the line pop valves were blowing off, while clouds of steam were floating to leeward and the boats were rocking uneasily. For a moment everyone watched everyone else. Then came the boom of the gun from the judge's boat, followed by the throb of many engines and the spattering rifle fire from three gasoline launches; then the boil and rush and swirl of white water being hurled back by many screws, and the movement of the boats as they felt the thrust and started forward. The light launches got under way quickly and darted ahead, and the line swept on. Donald let them get fifty yards away. He looked up at the Caribou boat, which was bearing down on his stern.

"Don't hurry!" he said, "we've got feefty miles t' catch them."
Then he opened the throttle of the long-cylindered engine. The
paddles pounded the sea into smoke and disappeared in the spray,
and the spray made the black spaniel sneeze violently. The crowd on
the Caribou boat howled with enthusiasm, and a howl of derision
came back from the fleet. The great race was started. The boats
swept down Charlottetown Harbour and out past the light, leaving
the water white behind them. Already they were beginning to sort
themselves out.

A gasoline launch had caught fire and was burning briskly,
while lobster boats from every direction were going to the rescue of
her crew. Her owner was standing on her counter and swearing, and
his language was fearful beyond description. A boat from Antigonish
had run aground on a shoal on the far side of the harbour, and her
skipper was following the example of the owner of the gasoline
launch with a fluency bred of a lifetime of practice. A boat from
Newcastle had run into a boat from Chatham, and they went on
shoulder to shoulder, trying to shove each other out of the channel.
Drawing out ahead were Col. Dan McPherson's yacht, the ocean tug,
a tug from Charlottetown, one from Sydney and two from Halifax,
with the *Mermaid* and the *Niobe* on pretty even terms just behind
them. Astern straggled out a long line, of which the last two were
Long Rory's *Susan Bell* and the *Goosander*. So they passed out into
the Bay and bore away for the buoy off Point Prim. The *Goosander*
crept up on the *Susan Bell*, and Carswell began to give the screw
engine steam. Now they had plenty of sea room, and he opened her
wider. The boats felt the first sweep of the seas coming down from the
north-west, and rolled and wallowed ahead, throwing clouds of spray
from their bows. A wave would come up and hit the *Goosander*, and
her whirling starboard paddle would pulverise it and heave it aloft
in bucketfuls and drench Carswell and Billy and Donald and the
spaniel impartially. In the meantime McIntyre was getting wet over
the bow, so the crew of the *Goosander* donned oilskins. The spaniel

wanted to see everything that happened, and, bathed with salt water, sat up and wagged his tail and sneezed. In five minutes the *Goosander* was alongside the white yacht, and in two minutes more she had passed her. Then she crawled up between two tugs and pulled ahead until she left them in her wake. Every time she passed a boat a cheer would come from the Caribou enthusiasts astern. Some few who knew Donald's record well noticed that so far neither of the *Goosander* boilers had blown off. "Pop valves screwed down, as usual, I s'pose," said one, and the others nodded.

The *Goosander* was extremely persistent. She worked up gradually, and passed other and still other boats. The leaders were doing magnificently. Between the big two-masted tug and Col. Dan's yacht and the *Mermaid* and the *Niobe* there seemed but little to choose. But there was a good deal of a sea running, and the big tug was at her best.

One of the tugs from Halifax was holding on well and having a little private race with the boat from the Bay Chaleur. The other Halifax tug was a few lengths behind, and the *Goosander* was slowly coming up with her. Then they hung side by side for a few minutes. Finally Donald motioned to Carswell, and at the same time swung his throttle wide open. The *Goosander* trembled and seemed to fairly leap the seas. She passed the Halifax tug as though the latter were moored, and bore down on the other Halifax boat and the boat from the Bay Chaleur. She rushed in between them with her stern low and her paddles whirling halos of foam, and she left them and bore down on the van. She passed within twenty feet of the ocean tug and hauled across her bow; then she drove past the *Mermaid* and the *Niobe* and Col. Dan's yacht and pounded on ahead. Her boilers and funnels were white with crusted salt, and every time the spray hit them would send a great cloud of steam off to leeward. With the driving water slashing into his face and running down his oilskins, McIntyre crouched low in the bow, Billy Dunn and Carswell fired vigorously, and the old man sat motionless in the stern, smiling grimly. So the flotilla went past Point Prim Light, with the *Goosander* always gaining. Mr. Paul and Mr. Hunter were beyond talking, but their thoughts were stupendous; and Col. Dan was grinding out through his teeth something about "slab-sided coal scows," and freely damning a well-known builder of marine engines.

Now, anyone who knows Northumberland Strait knows that the worst place for an ugly, piled-up sea, that seems to come from everywhere at once, is just off Point Prim. In this case the wind, though not heavy, was brisk, and an occasional white comber came down from the direction of Cape Tormentine. The *Goosander* was doing splendidly. The long-cylindered engine's cross-head was rushing up and down the guides at a rate that satisfied Donald — and that is saying much — and one bearing that had threatened to get hot had been flooded with oil and had decided to cool down again. The *Goosander* now led the van by a quarter of a mile. Altogether, things looked propitious. Just at this stage a big roller gathered itself together and bore down on the boat's starboard side, breaking and hissing as it went. For a moment it towered, and then dashed into the starboard paddle. The *Goosander* staggered over to port, righted again and went on. Carswell pointed to starboard. The paddle was swinging two pieces of wood like flails. Donald signalled to stop her, and shut his throttle.

"Y' might breeng the hatchet, Meester Carswell," he said, slowly, "'n' joost tell Beely 'n' Jim t' coom aft 'n' breeng a bar to hold th' wheel." In a few moments the *Goosander* was drifting side to the sea and rolling violently. Carswell and Billy and McIntyre jammed a bar into the wheel and held it steady, while Donald climbed out on it with the hatchet. Two of the floats were split, and one of them was started away from the frame. The old man hacked and hammered and clung to the wheel as the *Goosander* rolled it half under water. In the meantime the *Niobe* and the *Mermaid* came boiling up astern with the big tug and Col. Dan's yacht pressing them hard.

"Beely," said Donald, "y' might joost coom out here 'n breeng a few spikes." Billy climbed out warily, and together they hammered and chopped while the *Goosander* rolled prodigiously and soused them up and down in the waters of the Gulf of St. Lawrence. They were still hard at it when the *Mermaid* came up, sometimes lifting her screw half out of the water and sending the spray forty feet. The *Niobe* wasn't thirty yards behind her, and was visibly gaining. Mr. Hunter looked round and kissed his hand to Donald as he drove past, and Donald stopped work expressly to admire the *Mermaid*.

"She looks fery nice, a' must say," he said appreciatively, "'n' look 't thut boat; eesn' she pretty?" waving the hatchet at the *Niobe*. The *Niobe* took it as a friendly greeting and whistled as she passed.

"For heaven's sake, hurry up," said Carswell.

"Oo, th're's no hurry," was the slow reply. Col. Dan's yacht rushed past.

"Making some repairs?" asked the Colonel pleasantly.

"No," shouted Donald, "we're joost goin' t' cut away th' paddles; we've foond we don't need them." The big tug *poomp-poomped* past and offered a tow, and the rest of the fleet began to come up. Billy hammered in the last spike and the two, very wet, climbed hastily aboard. A moment later both engines were going at full speed again, and the *Goosander* was boiling along after the leaders. The whole episode only lasted three or four minutes, but it was enough to give her a long, hard chase. Donald and Carswell moved around with oil cans, Billy flitted from fire-box to fire-box, and McIntyre sat immovable, with eyes shifting from the compass to the Nova Scotia coast, and prayed. The combination was too strong for fate, and before long the *Goosander* was again beside the big tug. As she was crossing her bow, which McIntyre did with elaborate ostentation, Donald, without looking up, hung a rope over the stern. They passed Col. Dan silently and came up on Mr. Hunter, who was trying to light his oil fire, which had blown out for the fifth time. McIntyre went close to him and Donald threw aboard a lobster can with a bunch of matches in it. The *Niobe* was still eighty yards ahead, and as the water was getting smoother was going faster than ever. But at last even she had to succumb, and the *Goosander* splashed up beside her. Donald talked pleasantly to Mr. Paul, and told him that, aside from the *Goosander*, the *Niobe* was the finest boat of her size he had ever seen. Then, as the *Goosander* drew ahead, he said he was sorry to leave, but he wanted, if he could, to be in Caribou in time to see the finish of the race.

By this time the head of the long procession of boats was between North Harbour and the west end of Pictou Island. The old man smiled as he thought of Maisie and Dick and Aleck seated on the high bank and watching with the long telescope. "Na doot they're cheerin' noo," he said to himself. He tied a pair of spare overalls to the end of the boat hook and hoisted them up in the stern. The black spaniel got up to superintend, sneezed, slipped, sprawled, and silently went overboard. Donald jumped to the paddle engine.

"Stop her 'n' back up," he roared to Carswell. In a few moments the *Goosander* was stopped again and was slowly backing. The black head and shoulders would be seen on the top of a sea and then would disappear in the trough again. Donald would say "Coom on, old mon, y're doin' gran'!" and the tail would appear and agitate the water violently. Finally the *Niobe* came up and went past, followed by Col. Dan, and later by the big tug. The white yacht with the polished spars was within fifty yards when, at last, Billy leaned far over, grabbed the black spaniel by the back of the neck and hauled him aboard. He immediately proceeded to shake himself over Donald, coughed for half a minute, and went back to his seat wagging his tail and evidently much pleased with the whole business.

Twenty seconds later the *Goosander* was boiling along again in the wake of the big tug. Carswell's hand shook as he tried to twist his throttle open beyond the thread. He looked ahead at the tug, with Col. Dan's yacht beyond, and the *Niobe* away beyond her. It seemed a fearful distance.

"Donald," he said despairingly, "we'll never catch her. We can't do it!"

"She's joost off th' Skinner's Reef buoy?"

"Yes."

The old man took off his oil-soaked cap and scratched his head.

"Weel," he said, "we can only try. A don't know thut we can eemprove her speed much. Y' might break up thut half barrel o' peetch thut's een th' for'd locker 'n' feed her w' thut." So the pitch was sacrificed, along with the barrel and a box that McIntyre had been sitting on, and the *Goosander's* long funnels took to vomiting fire, much to the awe of the crew of the big tug, which was passed again at McDonald's Reef. Col. Dan's yacht passed Cole's Reef buoy, and the *Goosander* passed Col. Dan's yacht at the same time, and still the *Niobe* was a long way ahead. Now they were heading straight into Caribou Harbour, with the finish line not four miles away. Ahead, the end of the lighthouse beach was black with people. The *Niobe* rushed up against the tide, and as she passed within twenty yards of them they cheered. The cheer that was on their lips for the second boat died away when they saw her, and they were silent with amazement. The speed of the extraordinary craft forbade laughter. They watched her in utter surprise, the black dory hull, the high, white, fire-vomiting funnels, the mass of machinery and the whizzing paddles hurling water over everything.

"She swings a wicked wheel," said one of them. Others had their eyes fixed on an old man in oilskins who sat smoking in the stern. They recognised him.

"Go it, Donald," they yelled, "you'll catch him yet," and cheer after cheer followed the *Goosander* up the harbour. Donald never turned his head. "Fallin' tide!" he murmured, and his practised eye watched the distance shorten between the *Goosander's* bow and the white water under the *Niobe's* glittering stern. The pitch had been used up and the funnels no longer vomited fire, yet the *Goosander* seemed to be closing the gap as quickly as ever. But the gap between the *Niobe* and the line was closing too. McIntyre could see the wharves packed with a silent crowd of people, and the judge's boat, with a fluttering white flag, just opposite the Government Pier.

Donald had his watch out and was timing marks on the shore. Suddenly there was a yell from McIntyre.

"Look't th' *Niobe!*" All hands looked. The *Niobe's* crew were feverishly heaving something over the rail. "Coal!" said Billy; and coal it was. They were pitching it over as fast as they could pass it up. Donald smiled. "Thut's what a call seenfu' waste!" he said. Carswell was past replying, and Billy had broken out into language. "Conoondrum," said the old man to the spaniel, "he's callin' y' names for fallin' overboard, when y' were only plannin' t' gie them a good feenish!" It was no use; Donald was impregnable. The great calm, bred only of a crisis, had settled down on his soul, and he was supremely happy. Everything came to him with exaggerated clearness, as to a man after a strong dose of coffee. His sense of proportion was perfect. His relation to the world was normal, and the perspective of all things material and immaterial was just and true. He filled and lighted the black pipe with extreme deliberation, and slowly reached out and dropped the match overboard on the lee side. He knew just how the piston was running in the long-cylindered engine, and how the steam cushioned against it at the end of the stroke. He could feel every swirl of steam and its expansion and falling pressure in its complicated course through the steeple-compound ahead. He felt the drive and flow of the water on the blades of the propeller, and the strain on the whirling paddles. He saw, and mentally noted in detail, the fields and hardwood-covered hills beyond the head of the harbour, the blue sky and the sparkling blue harbour itself, and the town sloping up on the north side, with the houses and the church steeples and the trees, and the waiting crowd on the wharves. He felt just how fast the *Niobe* was nearing the line, and just how fast the *Goosander* was nearing the *Niobe*; and he felt the result as a woman feels the result of her intuition. So he sat in the stern with a placidity that was supernal, and enjoyed to the utmost not only the world, but the universe. What could any steamer with a triple expansion engine and one hundred and ninety pounds of steam do in the face of such poised assurance as this? Finally there was but a quarter of a mile to go. The *Niobe* rushed for the line, and the *Goosander* swung out of her wake and roared up beside her. Mr. Montgomery Paul again heard the stuttering thunder of those invincible paddles in his ears, and, without looking round, saw that black, ugly bow crawl up beside him and forge slowly ahead, while he was conscious of the presence of two long, uncomely funnels vomiting black smoke. Then came a great cloud of flying white water and the passing of a high, black stern with the boil of a screw beneath it; then the bang of a gun, the shriek of whistles, the clang of bells and the roars of a cheering crowd. The great race was over. The *Goosander* had won by a length.

The excitement was tremendous, and as the *Goosander* made for the Market Wharf the crowd followed and lined it from end to end. Carswell and Billy Dunn and McIntyre had to stay aboard and explain in detail, but Donald slipped ashore and disappeared. He had a deep-rooted objection to demonstrations.

After sitting with Maisie and Dick on the high bank above the lobster factory and watching the boats go down the Strait, Aleck's feelings had got too much for him, and he had driven into Caribou to see the finish, taking his wife and the children. Donald found him for Mr. Paul, who presented the cheque in person, saying that if the *Niobe* had to be beaten he was glad it was by Donald McDonald, of whom he was beginning to learn something. Mr. Paul at least had the satisfaction of sitting on the wharf and watching the *Mermaid* tie up, while he gave vent to strictures as to the value of oil-fired boilers.

Aleck was determined that Donald should take five hundred dollars, but Donald wouldn't hear of it. Finally Aleck refused to take the colt back except on one condition, which was that he should pay Donald five hundred dollars for him. So Donald was forced to surrender.

That evening down the road to North Harbour drove a very happy family, and behind the wagon trotted a bay colt, whinnying because he recognised the way home. At the same time, round by sea, under the stars, went the only boat since the days of the *Great Eastern* that could boast both screw and paddles. Her crew consisted of an old man, who was smiling at the universe in general — and smoking — and a black cocker spaniel, who was wrapped in profound slumber.

THEODORE GOODRIDGE ROBERTS

Theodore Goodridge Roberts, the youngest brother of Charles G.D. Roberts, was born in 1877 at Fredericton, New Brunswick. After briefly attending the University of New Brunswick, he left school and eventually moved to New York, where he became the sub-editor of the Independent. *In 1898, while serving as a correspondent in the Spanish-American War, he contracted malaria and was forced to return home to Fredericton. Following his recovery, he worked for more than two years in Newfoundland, editing the* Newfoundland Magazine *and working as a freelance writer. During this period he also sailed on a barquentine to the West Indies and South America. With the outbreak of war in 1914, he enlisted in the Twelth Battalion. His distinguished war service included time spent as an aide-de-camp to General Sir Arthur Currie. Although Fredericton remained the centre of his life, Roberts travelled widely and lived with his family in many different places in Canada and abroad. Between 1900 and the late 1930s he published more than thirty books, including the sea novels* The Toll of the Tides *(1912) — published in the U.S. as* The Harbor Master *(1913) — and* The Wasp *(1914). He was also a prolific contributor to magazines. His last years were spent at Digby, Nova Scotia, where he died in 1953.*

"A Complete Rest" was first published in The Canadian Magazine *(June 1905) and is one of several uncollected sea stories that Roberts contributed to the magazine. Like much of his maritime fiction and poetry, it testifies to the lasting influence of his short residence in Newfoundland and Labrador.*

A Complete Rest

The doctor ticked off my symptoms on his fingers. "Irritability of temper. Lack of appetite. Disinclination to work."

I nodded my assent to his analysis.

"What you need," he said, "is a complete rest — months of quiet in the open air. But avoid the haunts of tourists and summer boarders. Avoid excitement."

"I have been reading an interesting article about Newfoundland and Labrador," I said. "How would a trip along those coasts do?"

"The very thing," replied the doctor. "The sea-winds, the quiet nights and days, the seclusion and peace will make a new man of you."

Two weeks later I set out for those peaceful solitudes.

My guide was Mitchell Tobin. He was full of information. What he did not claim to know of the Labrador coast, from Belle Isle to Nain, was what did not exist. His home was in Notre Dame Bay, but his ancestors had come from a verdant island that has given gaiety and raciness of speech to many parts of the globe.

Tobin and I landed from the coastal steamer at Battle Harbour, and there purchased a staunch skiff from one George Jackson, a store-keeper. I wanted to see the country (at least, the fringe of it) in a more leisurely manner than that allowed by the steamer. We were well supplied with provisions and fly-ointment. The season was August. For a whole week we had glorious weather, sailing close along the coast and among the numerous islands during the day, and camping ashore at night. After that a fog set in, and we spent two days under canvas, in the shelter of a grove of scraggy firs, or "vars." Mitchell cheered me with tales of death and disaster due to fog. The number of ships, schooner and skiff wrecks in which he had figured as sole survivor was amazing. On the third morning we awoke to find a clear sky and a visible sun. We lost little time in folding our tent and stowing everything in the skiff. Then we ran up our tan-coloured sail and continued our journey.

"If it be divarsion ye're looking for, to clane t'at fog out o' yer heart, I kin show ye some yonder," said Tobin.

He pointed to a narrow channel between two rocks — a "tickle," in the language of the country.

I looked my enquiry.

"Troutin'," he said; "finest along t'is shore."

"Can you run through?" I enquired.

"Sure," he replied. "I knows t'is coast like t'ey smilin' skippers knows Mother Canty's sheebeen i' St. John's. T'e brook be's bilin' wid trout."

"Good!" I exclaimed, "nothing would suit me better."

He headed the skiff for the narrow channel. She scudded along like a creature of life.

"I knows it like a book," remarked Tobin, complacently, as we darted between the great lumps of rock, and sighted the still water of the little cove, and the mouth of the brook. But his complacency was ill-timed, for the words had scarcely left his lips before the bottom of the skiff smashed against a submerged ledge. I was thrown violently against the tough mast, and the skilful pilot sprawled on top of me. By the time we had scrambled to our feet the wounded craft was half full of water and settling aft, preparatory to sliding off the ledge into the unknown depths.

"Howly Sint Patrick!" cried Tobin, "now ye've did it, ye divil's own lump of a rock."

"Save your breath to swim ashore with," said I.

"Swim, be it," he cried. "Begobs, sor, ye'll have to learn me in a almighty hurry. T'e only way I kin swim be straight down."

The distance between the sinking skiff and the shore was not more than forty feet. I grabbed up my leather knapsack and hurled it toward the land-wash. It lit at the edge of the tide — the wet edge. Tobin heaved a bag of hard-bread after it. Then followed tins of meat, pots of jam, a fishing rod, and everything we could lift. Many of the articles dropped into the water not five yards from the skiff. Others landed well up the rocky beach (especially the pots of jam), and still others lit in shallow water. Then, after taking a firm grip on my guide's collar, and assuring him that I would drown him if he struggled, I slid into the water. Mitchell prayed fluently all the way, despite the fact that his face was under the water as often as above it.

Ten minutes later Mitchell Tobin sat up and looked at the spot on the placid surface of the cove where the skiff had gone down.

"Begobs," was the only appropriate sentiment he could give expression to. I did a trifle better than that; and then we gathered together the articles we had salvaged from the wreck. My companion tried to conciliate me by murmuring audible asides concerning my presence of mind in heaving the stuff ashore, and my prowess as a swimmer. But for fully a quarter of an hour I maintained a haughty and chilly demeanour.

"As you know the coast so well," I said, "please tell me how far we are from the nearest settlement?"

Mitchell seated himself on a convenient boulder and wrinkled his brows.

"T'ere be Dead Frenchman's Bight, about five mile an' twenty rod from here," he said, reflectively, "an' Nipper Drook about t'ree mile nort' o' t'at; and a mile beyand be's Penguin Rock, up Caribou Arm, where o' Skipper Denis Malloney buil' a stage t'ree year ago, an' were all but kilt entirely by t'e fairies, an'—"

"Stow all that," I cried, "and tell me the name of the nearest harbour where we can get a boat."

"Sure, an' baint I tellin' ye."

"Can I hire a boat in Frenchman's Bight?"

"Sure," said Mitchell.

It took us just a shade over four hours to reach Dead Frenchman's Bight, in spite of the fact that Tobin had named the distance so exactly as five miles and twenty rods. We found that the place consisted of about a dozen huts and drying stages clustered around a narrow anchorage. The men were all out on the fishing-grounds, but the women made us welcome. They turned glances of wonder on the mixed condition of our outfit. I told them of the loss of our skiff, and explained our predicament. They shook their heads when I enquired of the likelihood of being able to replace the skiff, and told us that they were not "livyers," but were Conception Bay people, spending the summer on the Labrador for the fishing, and that they had barely enough boats to carry on their business with.

"Does the steamer put in here?" I asked.

"Sure," said Mitchell.

"No, sir," replied one of the women, a strapping damsel with red hair and gray eyes; "she kapes miles off shore hereabouts, because o' t'ey rocks."

She pointed to a string of barren islands several miles to seaward. They were beautiful, but not conducive to safe navigation. I vented my chagrin on Tobin.

We spent three days at Dead Frenchman's Bight, and I got some good fishing in a pond on the barren above the hamlet. Every night we had a dance in the fish store, to the music of a fiddle, an accordeon, and the shouts and whoops of the company. The tramp to Nipper Drook took up a whole morning.

"A long three miles," I remarked. Tobin eyed the landscape with agrieved and wondering regard.

"It do beat all," he said, as if the trail between the two harbours had played him a trick by stretching itself.

In Nipper Drook we found six families of "livyers," or permanent settlers, and a fore-and-aft schooner. The schooner proved to be on a trading cruise, and was northward bound. We boarded her, and I was so charmed with the trader and his stories that I asked him to take me along as passenger, for a consideration. He agreed readily enough. So I paid Tobin his wages and something extra to get home on.

"Home," said he. "Begobs, sir, I'se going back to Dead Frenchman's Bight, to marry t'at girl wid t'e red hair." I gave him my blessing. So long as he went I did not care what he did. I felt that his society stood for an element of excitement unauthorised by my doctor.

The name of the skipper trader was Packer. He hailed from Harbour Grace. He had been in the trade for several years and was doing well at it. His crew consisted of a boy and a man. The boy did the cooking. As Packer always stood a trick himself, and the schooner seldom sailed at night, we were not so short-handed as it sounds. His stock consisted of everything from a barrel of "salt-horse" to a trowser-button, and from a grappling-anchor to a spool of thread. The articles which seemed to be in the greatest demand were oil-skin clothing, packages of tea, tobacco, ready-made boots, and hard-bread. We worked our way northward in a leisurely manner, steadily reducing our supply of groceries and dry-goods, and filling up with cured fish. In the northern bays many of our customers were half-breed and full-blooded Esquimaux. They brought furs and carved ivory for trade.

At Seldom Seen Harbour we gave a dance aboard the *Guardian Angel* (for thus had Packer's shabby little vessel been devoutly named). It was attended by all the youth, beauty and fashion of the place. The belle of the ball was Alice Twenty-Helps, a lady of mixed Micmac and Esquimaux blood. Her hyphenated surname had come to her by way of her Micmac father who had, years before, won fame on that coast by devouring twenty helpings of plum-duff at a missionary dinner. I stepped more than one measure with the fair Alice, much to the envy of Packer and the able seaman. As a mark of my appreciation I gave her a green tin box (it had once contained fifty cigarettes), a clay pipe, a patent-medicine almanac, and five pounds of tea — the last of Packer's stock. In return she presented me with a leather tobacco-bag, cleverly worked in beads and dyed porcupine quills. Next morning, amid the mournful farewells of the Seldom Seeners, we set sail on our return trip to Harbour Grace.

The weather held clear and Packer was familiar with the coast, so for a time we sailed night and day. I took my turn at the wheel and the lookout as regularly as the others. One night I was awakened by hearing Packer going up the companion-ladder. As it was not his watch on deck I dressed and followed him, to see what the matter was. The sails were flapping in just enough wind to puff them out and let them drop. The *Guardian Angel* was rolling lazily in the slow seas. The fog was down on us like a moist snow-drift. Packer was anxious.

"It's these here currents that bothers me," he said, as I joined him on the little forecastlehead.

"Why don't you heave the lead?" I suggested.

"Heave yer grandmother," he retorted. "Man, there aint no soundin's 'round here until you get right atop the rocks — an' then you know all you want to about everything but kingdom come."

"Have you logged her?" I enquired, unabashed.

"Yes, sir," he replied more affably, "an' she's making about three knots on her course. Don't know how fast she's going off it."

"Drifting?" I queried.

He nodded. "But I'm keepin' her nose fer clear water," he said.

Half an hour later the wind freshened a bit, but the fog still clung to us. As I was not on duty I sat down with my back against the harness-cask, just aft of the foremast. I fell asleep and dreamed that Mitchell Tobin and I were aboard a wooden wash-tub, steering for a narrow channel between two frowning rocks. Tobin's face wore an expression of lofty composure. He was steering with a cricket bat. "Can you make it?" I enquired, anxiously. "Sure," he replied, "don't I know every rock along t'is coast by bote names?" Then we struck, and I awoke to find myself sprawled on the trembling deck of the *Guardian Angel*. I scrambled to my feet. Packer grabbed me by the arm. "We're sinking," he bawled. "Hump yoursel'."

I could see nothing, but the roar of surf was in my ears like unceasing thunder. The schooner bumped again, and took a sudden list to starboard. Packer and I were thrown against the rail, and nearly smothered by a great wave that dashed over us. When our heads got clear of the water we heard someone shouting that the dory had been carried away.

"We're aground, hard an' fast," exclaimed Packer. He made a line fast to a stanchion and passed it around both our waists. There we crouched, chilled to the bone and half-drowned, until morning broke gray through the fog. Peter and Mike Meehan were safe. They had tied themselves to the mainmast. The foremast was gone. Above our port bow loomed the cliff, close aboard. Spray flew above us like smoke. The seas that broke over our starboard counter had lost something of their violence. We cut our lashings and crawled forward. The roar of the surf was deafening — terrifying — the very slogan of disaster. I took a grip of Packer's belt with my left hand, not owing to physical weakness, but to a sudden feeling of terror. This passed, however, as quickly as it had come. We lay flat on the forecastlehead and looked over. The bowsprit had been carried away by the fall of the foremast. We could see that the schooner had been driven on to a submerged terrace of rock at the foot of the cliff, and that her bottom and the greater part of her starboard side had been sheered away. We looked aloft, and saw that a deep fissure zigzagged up the face of the rock.

Half an hour later we had a stout line stretched from the stump of the schooner's foremast to a jagged tooth of rock half way up the cliff. Packer had accomplished this after many throwings of the noosed rope. Now that it was securely fastened, Mike Meehan doffed his boots and oilskins and began the perilous climb. He held the rope with hands and knees, and wriggled along face up. At last he gained the rock and threw an arm about the jagged tooth. After resting thus for a minute or two, he pulled himself into the fissure. Then we cheered. He waved a hand and grinned down at us. After a good deal of work, and with the aid of more lines, we got such provisions as were undamaged safely to Meehan's resting place. They consisted of a bag of hard-bread, some tinned salmon, dried fish, and two small beakers of water. By this time the *Guardian Angel* was showing signs of breaking up that were not to be disregarded. We rushed our blankets across and quickly followed them. With two lines, one below the other, we made the passage much more quickly than Mike had done.

The ascent to the top of the cliff was accomplished safely. Sea-birds wheeled about us, flashing and vanishing in the fog, their cries piercing the tumult of the waves. We explored our haven cautiously, and found it to be nothing but a bare rock of about an acre in extent. We could find no wood for a fire, no cave for a shelter. Packer was in the depths of despondency over the loss of his schooner and his season's trade. Mike Meehan seemed content that he possessed tobacco, a pipe, and matches. His young brother, Peter, was clearly in a funk. The fear and distrust of the sea was in his blood. To me it seemed a picturesque and diverting adventure. My chest swelled at the thought of the yarns I would spin on my return to civilisation. Just then I did not count the chances of not returning. The day dragged through. We talked a little, and Mike treated us to a song. Twice we ate hard-bread and drank water. At last the shadow of night fell through the gray fog. We rolled up in our blankets and went to sleep.

Two days later the fog cleared away, and the sun shone on a world of blue and white waters, blue sky and ruddy rocks. Low down on the western horizon the mainland lay pink and purple. Here and there naked rock-islands like our own rose from the intervening water. We found that the *Guardian Angel* had gone to pieces, but that several fragments of wreckage had been washed into the lower levels of the fissure. We salvaged these, and spread them out to dry in the sun. They were soon fit for fuel.

"I guess these are the Strawberry Rocks," said Packer. "The coastal boat 'ill be along in a few days. Her course lays about a mile to seaward."

"So we are sure to be picked up?" I exclaimed, with a note of relief in my voice. The fog had begun to dampen the picturesqueness of the adventure.

"Oh, *we're* safe enough, cookin' our grub an' makin' our signals with the ribs o' the old schooner," he replied, mournfully.

A month later I stepped into the doctor's consulting room. "Hullo!" he cried, "the rest *has* done you good, and no mistake. There's nothing like a few weeks' quiet when a man is run down."

"Nothing like it," I replied, heartily. "You should try it yourself, doctor."

WILFRED T. GRENFELL

Born at Parkgate, Cheshire, England in 1865, Wilfred Thomason Grenfell attended Marlborough College in Wiltshire and then studied medicine in London. Deeply influenced by the American evangelist D.L. Moody, he embarked on a career of service in 1888, joining the National Mission to Deep-Sea Fisherman. In 1892, he was sent to Newfoundland and Labrador to assess the need for a medical mission. The following year, he established a hospital at Battle Harbour, Labrador. For the remainder of his life, he devoted himself to improving the lot of people in the scattered fishing communities of Newfoundland and Labrador. In 1912, the International Grenfell Association was formed. In addition to establishing hospitals, nursing stations, schools, and orphanages, the Association encouraged numerous economic ventures, including cooperatives and home industries. Grenfell promoted and financed his work through lectures and the writing of articles and books. Starting in 1895, he published more than forty volumes, many of which portray the lives of the seafarers of Labrador and Newfoundland. Among his works of sea fiction or non-fiction are The Harvest of the Sea: A Tale of Both Sides of the Atlantic (1905), Down North on the Labrador (1912), and Tales of the Labrador (1916). One of his most memorable works is the autobiographical sea adventure Adrift on an Ice-Pan (1909). He died in Vermont in 1940.

"'Tis Dogged as Does It" first appeared in Putnam's Magazine in August 1909. The next year, it was collected in Grenfell's Down to the Sea: Yarns from the Labrador. Although the story is about Newfoundland mariners, it is unusual for Grenfell, in that it is not set on the Labrador coast.

Wilfred T. Grenfell

'Tis Dogged As Does It

The good fore-and-aft schooner *Rippling Wave* had made a most successful run to her market, which happened this year to be in the Mediterranean. The fact that she had not left the Labrador coast till late in October was no fault of hers or the skipper's; for if there was one ocean-going skipper on the coast known to be more of a "snapper" than the rest, that man was Elijah Anderson. When the fish-planter saw Old 'Lige clewing down his hatches, and trimming the *Rippling Wave* for the "tri-across," he felt satisfied that if his catch lost in value by being late, it would not be the fault of a craft whose record "couldn't be beat," or of a master who was afraid to drive her. If all the tales were true, Old 'Lige had been known to clap on his topsails when other men were lacing their reef-earrings, and so he would give them the "go-by." Many a time, by pressing her, he had got clear of one of those cyclonic storms which are the bane of the "roaring forties" in the late fall of the year.

But this year easterly winds and the foggy blanket they fling over the coast had hidden the sunshine that the fishermen need to dry their catches of fish, and 'Lige had been jammed in and kept waiting for his load, long after he had hoped to be under the sunny skies of the Mediterranean.

But to the *Rippling Wave* as to everything else that waits, the great day had come at last. The cargo was all stowed — hatches sealed down — moorings cast off — the parting jollifications held. She had not even to delay for a tow through the narrow gulch between two islands that had served her for a harbour, in order to wait in the roadstead for a wind that would give her slant enough to clear the off-lying shoals and reefs before dark. A spanking nor'wester had sprung up just as Old 'Lige was ready, and, with flags flying and farewell guns banging, she had cleared with a leading wind through the narrow eastern tickle and was hull down long before dark, leaving good sea-room between her and the outermost shoals.

Day after day, without exception, the wind held abaft the beam, and the miles rolled off like water from a duck's back. Had she been contesting an ocean race instead of carrying a cargo of dry cod, her record would have vied with that of the sauciest racing-machine that has ever attempted the passage from Sandy Hook to the Lizard.

When in due time she hove to under the rock of Gibraltar for orders, her log showed an average of nearly ten knots an hour all through — and she had passed the three-hundred-miles limit in one twenty-four hours, which would have shown a clean pair of heels to the average tramp-steamer.

Ordered to Patras in Greece, she again eclipsed even her own record. She had out-distanced several rivals who started before her from Labrador, and had "caught the market on the hop" — i.e. fish was scarce and therefore in such demand that her cargo fetched splendid prices.

When at last she started on the return journey to her Newfoundland home, after calling at Cadiz for a cargo of salt, no lighter-hearted, happier bunch of men ever trod a good ship's deck. To most of us, in these degenerate days of luxurious floating cities, the prospect of a passage out across the Western Ocean in the month of December, in a ninety-nine-ton schooner, would not be dangerously exhilarating. But the viking stock is preserved in the North lands still, and these men were all Newfoundland fishermen, with the genius for the sea inborn, with minds and bodies inured from childhood to every mood and whim of the mysterious deep; even their baby hands had been taught to hold a tiller and to pull an oar. On the dangerous banks they had served their apprenticeship, till they had learned to fear the perils that beset them no more than we landlubbers fear the dangers of our modern streets. Their finishing course had been in butting into the everlasting ice-floes from the Polar Sea in search of seals, and running home a loaded schooner among the endless reefs of the uncharted, fog-ridden, ice-frequented coast of Labrador. They graduated when, adrift in a dory in thick fog in open ocean, without food or water, they had run for days, "Westward ho!" for the land, some one hundred and fifty miles under their lee; or had wandered in darkness over loose ice astray from their vessels, away out seal-hunting on the Atlantic, till half-frozen and half-stupefied they had been picked up, only to return cheerfully to the same work again, as soon as they were thawed out.

So when once again the *Rippling Wave* dropped the tug and braved the rollers of the wintry ocean, the fact that it was the first day of December didn't cause them even to look at the weather glass, or think of anything but the stories they would be telling of their great good fortune alongside their own firesides by Christmas Day.

But man proposes and God disposes, and there was that in the womb of the future for the crew of the *Rippling Wave* which at that time they little reckoned of. There were lessons to be learned that will have served some of them well when they come to pass the last bar, and "meet their Pilot face to face" on the shore of the great ocean of Eternity.

It is always harder to get to the westward in the North Atlantic than to "run east," for the prevailing winds are ever from southwest to west and northwest. But the *Rippling Wave* was a weatherly vessel, and the fact that by the middle of the month they were only in forty west longitude and forty north latitude did not distress her skipper — though if he would make sure now of being at home by Christmas Day, he could not afford to ease the ship down for a trifle.

The third Friday was a dirty day. The barometer was unaccountably low, and the heavy head sea made pressing even the *Rippling Wave* to windward in the dark somewhat dangerous to the hands on deck, owing to the low freeboard that their heavy cargo of salt allowed them. Old 'Lige was in a generous mood — the success of the voyage had made him more soft-hearted over such details than these men of the sea are apt to be; and, anyhow, Friday is not an auspicious day to take chances. As the Mate went on deck for the night watch, even though an occasional star did show up in the heavens, the Skipper remarked half apologetically to him as he was putting on his oilskins, "You can heave her to till daylight, Jim, if you thinks well."

After one or two seas, more curly than usual, had rolled on deck, Jim did "think well," and till midnight the hands below enjoyed the leisurely motion that these handy vessels assume when jogging "head to it" in a long sea.

Skipper 'Lige had just turned in, and was peacefully enjoying his well-earned beauty sleep, when he felt something touch him on the arm, from which his relaxed grip had but just dropped his favorite pipe on the locker. He started up, to find a figure in dripping oil-skins bending over him.

As soon as he grasped the fact that he was back in the world of realities, he realized that the Mate wanted him on deck to give an opinion as to a strange darkness that seemed to be crossing the ship's path low down over the water. Half a second was enough for him to get his head out of the hatchway, following the Mate who had scurried up before him, and his experience at once told him the truth. "Jump for your life, Jim!" he yelled; "it's a water-spout." The two men had hardly time to fall in a heap down the companion ladder, when something struck the good ship like a mighty explosion.

Over she went—shook—trembled—rose again; and then up—up—up went the cabin floor, both men being hurled against the for'ard bulkhead, which temporarily assumed the position the floor had occupied the moment before. The *Rippling Wave* was standing literally on her head, and it was a question which way she would come down.

But there wasn't time to get anxious about it. Another mighty heave or two, a sudden sickening feeling, and the two men were rolling about in the water on the cabin floor. But the ship was evidently the right way up. "On deck!" roared the Captain, and both men were up in time to know that the crew, who had been literally drowned out for'ard, were also scrambling aft in the darkness to learn what to do next. All lights were out, and everything was awash, for the scuppers could scarcely drain off the water quick enough to clear the waterlogged ship of the seas that rolled over her counter, as she wallowed broadside to it in the trough of the sea.

Knowledge, to be of any value, must be intuitive on these occasions. Instinctively the Captain had rushed to the tiller. The lanyards had broken adrift, and the helm was apparently hard up. Frantically the Skipper tried to force it over to get the ship's head, if possible, to the sea. Alas! the rudder was unshipped and fast jammed. The lower gudgeon was off the pintail, and the trusty *Rippling Wave* found herself free to put her head in just whatever direction she liked best.

Somehow, it seemed that she was endowed with sense, and that she meant to stand by her Skipper. For hazily, but surely, she rounded up in time to prevent herself from filling. The men, meanwhile, had seized the axes, and, almost before 'Lige Anderson had issued his orders, they had ventured for'ard again, to try and clear away the wreckage.

They soon realized that virtually everything for'ard had gone by the board; for the solid spout water had hit the foremast about half way up, and had then broken, falling in countless tons on the devoted deck. For'ard of the middle line nothing was left. The mast, boom, gaff and sails were missing, the rigging, ropes and everything attached. The bowsprit, jibboom, winch and paulbitts, anchors, chains, fore-companion, fore-hatch and galley were nowhere to be seen. The decks were torn open so widely that one man fell through to his thigh between two strips of planking. Much of the bulwarks and stanchions were gone, as were also both the life-boats and jolly-boat, and every drop of water that came aboard poured into the hull, threatening to engulf the ship in a few minutes. Probably what saved her was the fact that some of the torn remnants of canvas were still on deck, or rather in it, for the last of the fore-staysail was so hard driven through the open seams above the foc'sle, that the men were unable to start a rag of it, much as they needed it to cover up some of the other yawning gaps.

With the doggedness that characterizes such men, they had succeeded before daylight in getting out of the waterlogged cabins some nails and spare canvas, and with these they had covered over every large opening. Below the water line the almost solid-timbered vessel was still apparently sound, though the stump of the foremast was unstepped, with the result that its foot, rolling round in the deck gammon, was so thumping the bilge inside that it threatened every moment to smash through the sides. There was enough left of it, however, above decks, to make it valuable for a "jury-mast," and the Mate with two volunteers climbed down into the hold and succeeded in jamming it into an upright position.

In that dark, rolling box, soaked through with the water swashing about in it, not knowing but that at any moment they might go down like rats in a barrel, their task required no ordinary skill and courage. But they managed to accomplish it, fixing the foot of the mast in place with wooden stays captured from the broken rails. The rest of the crew stood to the pumps. Daylight, struggling through the murky sky, revealed a situation that looked hopeless enough.

For forty-eight hours every man was at work helping to jettison the salt and every other available ounce of weight that could be dispensed with, or taking his trick at the pumps, under the stern eye and unflinching example of Skipper 'Lige.

Hour after hour, without a wink of sleep or any refreshment but pieces of hard biscuit that once had been dry, they fought on with sullen strength and energy.

When the galley went, every pot, pan and cooking utensil had gone by the board with it. Not a bit of food could be cooked, nor a sup of drink be heated. There was one thing, however, that these men brought to their aid. Like most Newfoundland fishermen, they were praying men. They knew that praying at such a time is no substitute for work, but they knew also that attitude counts for nothing in the sight of the Almighty, and not one of them had forgotten to "call upon the Lord in their trouble, that He would deliver them out of their distress."

But at last the instinct of self-preservation began to lose its energy, as there came time to think, and they began to realize the apparent futility of continuing the unequal struggle.

It must be remembered that it was the dead of winter. They were in the middle of the North Atlantic. The water was bitterly cold, and they were bruised, wet and exhausted. They were, too, far out of the winter route of trans-Atlantic liners. The chance of being picked up seemed infinitesimal, and it was obvious that with no boat left it was impossible to escape from the wreck. Small wonder that faith and hope began at last to fail!

But all hands worked on incessantly at the pumps, and at the cargo. Hour after hour, watch relieved watch, and the *clank, clank, clank* of the pumps, that alone broke the monotony of silence, was almost enough to drive men mad.

They were apparently making no headway in raising the ship out of the water. They were merely keeping her afloat. But if 'Lige Anderson were to abandon hope it meant abandoning himself, and he was still sane. In the hours between the spells of the pumping, which he shared with his men — hours which he ought to have devoted to rest, — the Skipper had by no means been idle, and he was now able to hearten the rest with three discoveries he had made.

First, the after half of the ship was absolutely sound; so were her mainmast and sails. Moreover, he had been able to rig a "jury"-rudder, which more or less guided the ship. He had set to work with these as a basis to rig a jury-foremast that would carry a small sail. He had dried out the after cabin, and fortified and caulked as far as possible the fore bulkhead, to give a water-tight division from the hold. In this it was possible to get some rest.

Secondly, he had found his logbook and sextant, and though the latter proved useless owing to the sun being continually invisible, it certainly was a source of hope. The last entry in the logbook on the day before the accident led him to the conclusion that he was about fifty miles south of the track of the ocean liners.

Thirdly, from his almanac he found that there was still a forlorn chance that some steamers might still be running by the northern route.

It was difficult to make sure which way the wreck was really moving. But he could now keep her heading somehow to the west'ard, and it was possible that she might still be worked to a position where they could expect to be sighted if such was the case. A more trivial discovery, but one that counted not a little in the hearts of his Newfoundland crew, was an old tin paintpot, with a sound bottom. This Captain 'Lige had managed to clean up, and over the tiny stove in his cabin he had been able to brew enough hot tea to serve out a drink all round. These facts he now thought good to announce to the crew; and, heartened by the warm tea, they stood to the pumps again, as night came on, with fresh faith and energy. Slowly they edged, and worked, and drifted, as they hoped, northwards! If only they could make a hundred miles of northing their lives might yet be spared.

A week had now gone by since the accident, and a settled gloom, close akin to despair, had settled upon the men. As is often the case, however, just in the nick of time a thing happened which, trivial as it may seem to us, meant very much to them. The sun for the first time suddenly shot out thro' the drift about mid-day, and the Skipper was able to get his bearings and tell them that, though they were farther to the westward, they had made at least thirty miles to the nor'ard also. Moreover, he was wise enough, seeing that they were rather more than holding their own, to tell off one man from each watch to keep a look-out from the mainmast head. Though nothing was seen to encourage them, yet the fact that the Skipper believed it was now likely that they would sight something, acted as a fresh charm, and for yet another four days the *clank, clank, clank* of the pumps maintained its even tenor.

The salt was now all out of the boat, and this halved the time that each man had to work pumping. But as day after day passed and no sail was seen, and the ship ceaselessly battled with the angry waters running between a northwest and southwest gale, flesh and blood began to give way; nerve and muscle had been strained to the breaking point.

By the fifteenth morning all faith in the possibility of salvation had so departed from some of the men, that they formally proposed to give up striving, and that all hands should go to the bottom together. Skipper 'Lige was at his wits' end. Violence was out of the question. No man aboard would have minded even death at his hands. His only subterfuge was in continually pointing his sextant at the lowering clouds, in inscribing endless successions of figures in his book, and at last in announcing that he had discovered they had reached their desired goal. Having called them together, he pointed out to them on his well-thumbed chart, that they now lay exactly on the forty-ninth parallel of latitude. A great cross that he had made on it signified the position of the ship. Exactly through this point ran many lines stretching from the Fastnet to New York, intersecting in his picture the spot that represented the ship. "Them there lines," he announced, "be the tracks o' them big steamers. They always races across, and this be the shortest way for 'em to go."

It would not have required much acumen on the part of the audience to detect the fact that the lines on the paper were not as old as the discourse suggested. But men in the condition of these poor fellows are not inclined to be critical. All that was required of them was to move a handle up and down, and the Skipper had staked his all on their not questioning what he told them. They scanned his face narrowly, and saw that he seemed so hopeful that once again the poor fellows returned to their duty at the pumps. "Now we be in the track of the steamers, boys," the Skipper said, "us'll wait right here, sink or swim. Let's keep at it so long as us can stand. They sha'n't call us cowards anyhow." In all this the Mate bravely backed him up. And so again, though the response was feebler than before, the *clank, clank, clank* of the pumps kept on, as the plucky fellows doggedly set their hands to the work.

The morning of the seventeenth day broke with a clear horizon under an oily, sullen sky. The remnant of a ship still tossed up and down, up and down, on the troubled waters. Forward the *Rippling Wave* looked now only like a bunch of weather-beaten boards. Hour by hour, the weary clank of the pumps alone announced that there was any life aboard, and that she was more than a mere derelict on that dreary expanse of waters. Though dispirited and half dead, not one man yet gave in. Now and again one could no longer stand to do his work, yet as soon as he had rested, the faith of the others roused him to action, and he struggled back, even if it were only to fall down at his place at the handles.

It was just 10 A.M. when the watch at the masthead called the Skipper. "Smoke on the horizon to the east-northeast," he shouted. So far gone were some of the men that they took no notice of the announcement; even if they heard, it seemed too wonderful to be true. But in two seconds the Skipper was aloft by the side of the watch, and shouting "Steamer coming, boys; keep her going!"

Little by little the cloud, at first no larger than a man's hand, grew bigger and bigger, till the hull of the vessel was visible like a tiny speck beneath it. There was no need now to cheer on the men. The watch below was turned out to "wear" the ship, that they might, as far as possible, drive across the head of the approaching vessel. The improvised flags, long ago made ready out of bed clothing, were hoisted to the tops, and a pile of matchwood was prepared in a tar barrel on deck to make a good smoke.

The excitement on board can better be imagined than described. But though their eyes were strained to the utmost, they could not make out that the stranger got the least bit nearer, and it wasn't long before 'Lige realized that no help could be expected from that quarter. For the speck grew no larger, and eventually disappeared again behind the wilderness of waters.

The reaction was proportionate to the exhilaration, and an awful despondency fell upon all hands when their hope of safety had again sunk out of sight.

The Skipper's resourcefulness was not exhausted, however, and he spoke to the crew as if he were in the greatest spirits. "You see we'll be all right now, boys," he said. "Our reckoning be just as I told you. Us'll work a mile or two more to the nor'ard, and be home by the New Year if we aren't by Christmas." He took care to emphasize his faith by serving out an extra and earlier dinner, so that, in spite of themselves, not a man slacked at the pumps, and the everlasting clank droned monotonously on.

The afternoon was wearing away, when suddenly once again the eagle eye at the masthead spied smoke. This time it was in the western sky and 'Lige took a bigger risk. Twice as much inside planking as before was torn from the sides of the hold to enlarge the bonfire. So big grew the pile that it could scarcely be kindled without endangering the vessel. As the speck grew bigger, hope grew proportionately large, and without any word from the Skipper, the pulse rate of the pump reached a fever speed. Closer and closer came the stranger. It seemed impossible that she should pass now without seeing them. Evidently she was a small cargo tramp in ballast, and no doubt lightly manned. She was now almost abeam, but still she showed no signs of recognition. Possibly the only man on watch was in the wheelhouse, there being apparently no reason for a special watch. Or possibly the outlook man was smoking his pipe under some shelter from the weather. 'Lige, through his glasses, had long ago learned that there was no one on the upper bridge. That she was an endless time approaching seemed to him their best chance of being seen. For surely *some one* would be on deck to sight them before it was too late. But she passed them by like a phantom ship with a crew of dead men on board; and to this day no one on board knows why.

It was getting dark, and the wind was rising again, with a sea making from the nor'west. The dumb despair that had all along been a kind of opiate, allaying any fear of death, had been rudely removed by the awakened thoughts of home, rest and safety, and by the apparent certainty of at last being rescued. The suspense as the steamer passed by had made the enfeebled men conscious of the bitterness of death, and aroused in them an emotion that was perilously near to fear.

There could be no disguising the fact that the end was very near at hand. The mere pretense of work that they were now able to make was at last permitting the water to gain on the pumps; and finally the relief watch failed to stand to their work. No one was in a mood for speaking now. The Skipper himself silently strode to one of the handles the men had dropped, and commenced mechanically to heave it up and down.

Only a minute, however, did he labor alone. Without breaking the silence, the gallant Mate, whose turn it was to rest, placed himself at the other handle again, and the play at "pumping the ship" went on. There seemed to be no hope. The night promised to be their last on earth. But they were men, and they would at least die fighting, for no man can tell what may be wrested from the fates by a dauntless faith.

The horizon had already faded into the lowering sky overhead, and before the sun rose again, the long-drawn agony would be over, and the bitterness of death passed.

But it was not to be. Suddenly a loud cry from for'ard for the last time stopped the pumps. Sure enough, there was a bright light away to the eastward, now and again bobbing up over the waters. It has always seemed right to Skipper 'Lige that their salvation should have come out of the East. In his own mind, so he says, he hadn't the slightest doubt, then, that all would be well.

It was plain to him that the usefulness of the pumps was at an end, and that his last move in the game of life must now be played. He was always known as a silent man, but on this occasion a corpse would have heard him. The half-dead crew were on their legs in less time than it takes to write it. He had himself but recently come down from the mainmasthead, where he had been fixing fast to the crosstrees a barrel full of combustibles. Now, forcing an unlighted flare into the hands of the Mate, "To the masthead," he roared, "and light up when I do! Up the foremast!" he screamed into the ear of his third hand, above the roaring of the wind and sea, "and take this old can o' tar with yer." For'ard and aft he led the rest with their axes. All were working like madmen, with a strength that was like the final flare-up of a flickering lamp. Soon large pieces of wood had been torn off from the hatches, lockers, rails, bulwarks, and even the decking. They hacked it from anywhere, so long only as the pile on deck should grow in size. But even as they worked the water was steadily increasing in the hold, and every man was conscious that the *Rippling Wave* was sinking under them.

Sometimes — it seemed for ages — the approaching light disappeared from view; yet the axes kept going, and the pile of wood steadily grew. To restrain the crew from setting fire to it during these apparently interminable intervals required a nerve on the part of the Skipper that they themselves no longer possessed. But even at that moment, with death standing at their very side, they were held to an absolute obedience. Their reverence for their indomitable Captain had long since grown into a superstitious fear. As it was, the sound of axe and lever, as once on the walls of ancient Rome, alone broke the deathlike silence every man maintained.

Suddenly, without a moment's warning, a huge black mass rose up out of the water, towering far overhead like some fabulous monster of the sea. The right moment had arrived. So 'Lige Anderson fired his last shot, and lit his flare. In an instant the vessel was ablaze. Fore and aft, aloft, and on the water-line, the ship seemed one roaring mass of flames, which shot high into the heavens above her each time the waterlogged hull rolled heavily to windward. A moment later a brilliant search-light still further blinded the men on her deck, and afforded the pleasure-seekers who were crowding to the rail of that floating palace (for it proved to be a steamer on a trip round the world) such a scene as in their lives they are never likely to look on again. It was a scene well able to bear all the light that could be thrown upon it. For these fishermen had fought a fight worthy of the traditions of the best days of viking seamanship.

The huge steamer turned to wind'ard and stopped short close to them. A loud voice called through a megaphone, "Can you hold on till morning?" There was no hesitation in giving, and no possibility of doubting, the answer. So close were the vessels that every man heard the question, and every throat shouted back the same answer as from one man, "No, we are sinking!" The swash of the fast-gaining water, surging loudly to and fro in the hold, lent emphasis to the reply. Only the voice of Skipper 'Lige once more broke the silence. "We are played out; we can't last till daylight."

Words are poor things at best, but the words that came back this time thrilled them all as words had never thrilled before. "Then stand by; we'll try for you now." The Captain on the bridge had no need to ask for volunteers, though the night was black as pitch by now, and the danger of launching a boat in that rolling sea was a terrible one indeed.

The steamer was a German liner from Hamburg. The perishing men were only common British fishermen. But there is a touch of nature that makes the whole world kin, and the gold-laced Captain bore a true sailor's heart beneath his dapper uniform. Had he listened to the dictates of his own emotions, he would himself have been the first man in the boat. In spite of his brilliant searchlight, the wreck to him looked but the after half of a vessel, as if a ship had been cut in two. Pride in the sheer brotherhood of the sea, that there still lived men that could do the things these men had done, almost led him to throw discretion to the winds, and share in person the welcome danger of the rescue.

But wiser counsels prevailed, and the well-trained life-saving crew that such vessels always carry had already arranged themselves in position by the side of the steel life-boat.

There was no lack of skill, no undue haste, no shortage of tackle. But long ere the boat had reached the water, a heavy sea had swung her into the iron wall of the ship's side and smashed her to fragments. Those on the wreck had witnessed the attempt, and also the failure, and the ominous swash of the water in the hold seemed louder and more threatening than a few minutes ago. Faster the water gained on them as deeper the wreck wallowed in the seas; yet to man the pumps now was not even thought of. The last die had been cast, and, without making any conscious resolution, they simply stood by to watch the issue.

The big ship had forged ahead. By the time she had regained her position, a wooden life-boat was already on its way down from the davits with the men in it. Close to wind'ard of the wreck the Captain manoeuvered the steamer to shorten the distance to row, if by any means he could get a boat launched and safely away. Again every movement was visible from the *Rippling Wave*. The life-boat reached the water. The port oars were out, but before the for'ard tackle was free, a great sea drove her into the vessel's side again. The rescuing party were themselves with difficulty rescued, and their boat was a bundle of matchwood.

All eyes were fixed on the steamer. Could it be possible that they would be discouraged and give up? Even Skipper 'Lige expected to be hailed again, and warned that he must keep afloat till daylight. But the men on the liner were real sailors, and not the faintest idea of abandoning the attempt ever entered their heads. At sea, a thing to be done must be done—and that is the end of it. Cost is a factor that a sailor's mind doesn't trouble itself about, so long as material remains. Anxiety about what loss may be involved is a thing to be left for the minds of landsmen, and harries Jack less than it does a Wall Street millionaire.

The only question with the Captain was, which boat next; as if it were a simple question of which tool would best serve to complete a job that had to be done. A light, collapsible life-boat seemed to promise most. While the ship was again getting into position, this was made ready. The men took their places in her and were almost literally dropped over the side, as the monstrous ship lurched heavily to wind'ard. There was just one moment of doubt, and then arms and shoulders that knew no denial shot their frail craft clear of the ponderous iron wall. Scarcely a moment too soon did they reach the *Rippling Wave*. Her decks were little better than awash, when Skipper 'Lige, the last man to leave, tumbled over the rail into the life-boat. Even his dog had preceded him.

Nor was the wreck left to be a possible water-logged derelict, to the danger of other ships. What was left of the kerosene oil was poured over her as a parting unction and then fired. Before the last man was safe aboard the steamer, however, the *Rippling Wave* mantled like Elijah's chariot in "flames of fire," had paid her last tribute to the powers she had so long successfully withstood.

A line fastened to a keg having been thrown over from the steamer's side, was picked up without approaching too near. With that absence of hurry that characterizes real courage, the life-boat kept off (with her stern to the dangerous side of iron) until each of the rescued men had been safely hauled aboard in breeches of cloth, secured to a running tackle. Even the dog would have been saved in the same way, had he not with vain struggling worked loose from the breeches and fallen into the sea; as it was, before getting the life-boat aboard, the Captain was humane enough to peer round everywhere with his searchlight, in the hope of finding it. The rescued were stripped, bathed and fed, and snugly stowed in beds such as they had seldom even seen before.

From the kindly passengers, more new and warm clothing poured in upon them, next day, than they had ever dreamed of possessing, and the journey to land was as remarkable to them for its luxuries as had been the past fortnight for its privations.

Though Christmas Day had after all been spent on the *Rippling Wave*, New Year's Eve found them in the lap of luxury. At dinner in the grand saloon, to which every man was invited, Skipper 'Lige occupied the seat of honor next the Captain. There was a general feeling that it was a great occasion. Never before had the close of an old year spoken so forcibly of the fickleness of life to many of the others present. After a few seasonable and brief speeches had been made by some of the guests, the climax was reached when the Captain — who, at his own expense, had ordered some dozens of champagne to be served out all 'round — in terse sailor language proposed the toast of the evening. There were few dry eyes among those who drank "To the wives and children of the brave men it has been our good fortune to save."

COLIN MCKAY

Colin McKay was born in Shelburne, Nova Scotia in 1876. The descendant of a renowned shipbuilding family, he followed the sea for nearly three decades, serving on sailing vessels and then steamships, including passenger liners and, during the First World War, the British hospital ship S.S. St. George. Between his stints at sea and after his retirement from seafaring, McKay worked as a journalist, writing for both mainstream newspapers and various labour and socialist publications. As a Canadian Press correspondent, he played a role in promoting the international schooner races between the U.S. and Canada. He also gained some recognition as a contributor of sea fiction and non-fiction to McClure's, Ainslee's, *and other periodicals. By the time of his death at Ottawa in 1939, however, his maritime writings were largely forgotten. In fact, his contribution to Atlantic literature was only recently rediscovered with the publication of the first collection of his sea stories,* Windjammers and Bluenose Sailors *(1993), edited by Lewis Jackson and Ian McKay.*

"The Wreck of the Cod-Seeker" *first appeared in the pulp magazine* Adventure *(June 1913) and was finally collected in* Windjammers and Bluenose Sailors. *One of McKay's most memorable stories, it recounts the harrowing ordeal of two Nova Scotian seamen, James E. Smith and Sam Atwood, in a capsized fishing schooner. For a more recent account of the same disaster, see Allan Easton's* Terror on the Coast: The Wreck of the Schooner Codseeker *(1992).*

The Wreck of the Cod-Seeker

"Have you ever known fear, the stark fear of a slow, lingering, painful, abominable death?" remarked James E. Smith, Fishery-Guardian at Lower Shag Harbour, Shelburne County, Nova Scotia. "I have. Imprisoned in a capsized vessel, gnawed by hunger, tortured by thirst, steeped in a horror of helplessness, racked by a black, blind, bootless rage of resentment against fate, I knew fear, the fear that makes the hair bristle, the saliva in the mouth turn salt and bitter, the perspiration come out in clammy beads on the forehead, the heart almost stop beating." Then Mr. Smith told this tale:

On Wednesday, May 9, 1877, the schooner *Cod-Seeker*, bound from Halifax to Barrington, was running before an easterly gale. Her master was Philip Brown; her crew numbered fourteen hands all told. She was a sharp deep vessel— the first toothpick built in Nova Scotia— and she made wicked weather of it as she slashed through the heavy seas.

A while before nine o'clock the lookout reported breakers ahead. Capt. Brown claimed that the white spaces seen were only the reflections of the Cape Light upon the waves; and he kept her going, though some of the older men criticized him sharply for doing so. I didn't like the look of things, but I was little more than a boy then.

The schooner stormed along, growing wilder in her motions, but as nothing happened I soon went down into the forecastle for a drink. As I reached the foot of the companion, I saw a box containing a picture of my girl and some other treasures shoot out of my berth to the floor, and hastened to salvage my property. That done I went to the cook's water-bucket.

Before I could raise the dipper to my lips the schooner gave a wild lurch and flung over on her beam-ends, and I went sliding to leeward. The light went out; there was a great racket of pots and pans fetching away; a weird lot of noises as the barrels and boxes in the hold rolled into the wing, and brought up against the turn of the deck.

The schooner lay on her side, with her spars flat on the sea, and the water roared into her through hatchways and companions. Getting to my feet I hauled myself up toward the companion, and tried to get out. I might as well have tried to crawl through a sluice-gate. The rush of the water splayed my fingers apart. Soon the bow plunged downward, and the water whelming in with greater force swept me out of the companion.

I fell down on a heap of wreckage on the side of the ship, struck my head against something and was stunned for a space. When I got my wits I was standing up with my feet in the mouth of a berth and against the ship's side, and the water up to my armpits and a raffle of floating wreckage about me.

In a few seconds more I was struggling in a whirlpool of icy waters, beating my hands against the flotsam of the forecastle, unable to see anything or to get a footing. As the ship moved, the flood in the forecastle, rising rapidly, surged back and forth, and once I became entangled in some half floating blankets and nearly succeeded in drowning myself. Like all fishing-vessels she had a large forecastle down in the bows of her, and in the utter darkness I could not tell my whereabouts.

Imprisoned in a Capsized Schooner

For a time I was too frantic with fright to think of getting hold of anything. I only thought of keeping my head above water.

But presently the ship seemed to grow quiet for a little, and I thought of getting a grip on something. Striking out I ran against a wall with an under slope, felt around, realized that it was the deck and, as there was nothing to hold there, I turned about and swam to the other side.

I paddled about for quite a time. But at last, stretching my hands out of the water, I managed to catch hold of the edge of a board

— the face-board of one of the weather bunks. As I held on, taking breath, the water rose and lifted my head and shoulders into the mouth of the berth. I hastily scrambled on to the inner side, then the top side, of the face-board.

While I waited appalled, for I knew not what, I became aware of a moaning sound, and cried out, "Who's that?"

It was Sam Atwood, a young fellow about my own age. He was lying on his stomach on the inner or top side of the face-board of what had been a lower bunk. When the schooner was hove down he had been asleep in his bunk, but somehow he had managed to cling to the face-board, though the mattress and bottom boards had been rolled out into the forecastle. A man can face death better with a friend near him. I grew composed and began to take stock of the situation.

The schooner had settled as the water got in her and, happily for us, the bows were the highest part of her. We learned afterward that she had drowned two men in the after cabin. She was still on her side, but listed a little past her beam-ends, so that her spars sloped down into the sea at an angle of about twenty degrees. If she had been in still water her keel forward would have been a few feet above the surface and a little under aft, while her decks would have been submerged to a line drawn from the weather windlass-bitt to the weather corner of her taffrail; and inside the water would have been at about the same level — that is, the flood in the forecastle would have been about seven feet above the companionway. But of course, as she wallowed in the swell, the bows were sometimes listed much higher out of water and at other times nearly submerged, causing the water inside to rise and fall too.

The way she lay, the round of the starboard bow was the highest part of her, and we were in the after tier of bunks, built against the bulge of the bow. But our position was precarious enough, and neither dry nor comfortable. The face- or side-board of the bunks on which I was lying was only about twelve inches wide, and I had to hold on with hands and knees, especially when she took a roll, to keep from slipping off and falling into the black abyss on either side.

Atwood, lying on the face-board of the lower berth, was in somewhat better position, as he could only slip off one side. About two and a half feet above us was the side of the ship, the round of the bow right under us, usually three or four feet down, was the surging flood, and a litter of floating things. Outside the waves were crashing against the hulk, roaring dreadfully.

Sluggishly she rose and fell to the heave of the swell, and we were afraid she would sink or turn turtle altogether. When the bows were lifted up we could sense the water in the forecastle running aft; and when her bows fell downward, the water would surge forward, back up and whelm into the bunk and over us. At such times we had to hold our breath and cling on to our perches for dear life, or sit up and brace our shoulders against the side of the ship.

After a time she seemed to bring up against something with a violent jerk, and her head was dragged downward, while the water in the forecastle surged afterward.

Mightily alarmed we sat a-straddle on the face-boards, and pressed our noses against the skin of the ship in the angle made by the supporting knee of the deck beam. We found a little air imprisoned there after our shoulders and the backs of our heads were under water. But her bows continued to swoop downward and soon the water was over our faces. I thought it would soon be the end of us. I felt as if my head would burst with the intolerable pressure.

But before either of us lost consciousness something snapped— I thought it was something giving away in my brain. The schooner's head rose swiftly, the water receded and we found ourselves able to breathe again. Oh, but the air was good! Trembling, dizzy, exhausted, we stretched ourselves along the face-boards and rested.

What had happened was this: When the schooner was hove on her side the anchor-chain, stowed in a box on deck, went overboard, and presently, as she swept along with the tide, the end fouled the bottom and dragged her head under water. Then a miracle occurred; the big link in the shackle of the other end near the windlass broke and allowed her head to come up again.

The schooner wallowed on her side. She rose and fell to the heave of the swell, in a heavy, sickening way but she did not roll much. Often we were ducked under; and the noises were frightful; roaring, snarling sound of surf; blood-thirsty gurglings, the dull booming sound of things beating against the skin of the hold. Sometimes I spoke to Atwood, but he was either too stupefied to answer or he could not hear. I lay for a time in an agony of fear. But at last I realized that the ship wasn't going to sink or turn turtle altogether. I suppose her cargo had rolled and prevented her from turning completely over. So presently the sharp fear of being drowned began to give way to a dull horror of our plight.

I was numb with cold, and awfully weary and before long, in spite of the noises, the fear of slipping off my perch, the horror of it all, I dropped off into a doze. And as I dozed I dreamed the schooner was hove down while I was on deck; dreamed that I saw my chum Will Kenney washed overboard and dived after him.

Thirst, Cold and Horror

Then I woke up to find myself struggling under water. It was still pitch-dark and for a moment or so I had no idea where I was. As my head came above the water I struck something hard, and down I went again before I could get my lungs full of air. Half stunned I struggled up again, and rammed my head through a small opening, so small that I could not get my shoulders through. My mouth was just above water. When I tried to struggle through the opening, the thing resting upon my shoulders would lift a little and then press me down till I could not breathe. I struggled frantically, and the harder I strove to keep my mouth above water the more I seemed to be forced down.

I could not imagine what kind of a trap I had got into, and my imagination was mighty active; just as they say of a drowning man. A moving-picture of my whole life seemed to flash before me. Every deed of a sinful nature I had ever done seemed to rise up against me, crowding out all hope of salvation.

At the same time my mind was wildly searching for an explanation of my plight, and at last, when I was nearly done for, it struck me that the thing that was drowning me was the step-ladder of the forecastle-gangway. That was it; the ladder was floating, and I had got my head between the steps. I knew what to do then, but it was not easy to draw my head down and out, for the bevel of the steps held my head as in a trap.

But at last I managed it, and hooked my arms over the floating ladder till I got my wind.

I yelled for Sam, but got no answer. Of course I could not tell what part of the forecastle I was in, but I paddled around and finally, as a sea lifted me, I got hold of the bunk side-board and hauled myself up inside the bunk. Atwood was still sleeping. I touched him, but he did not wake. I got hold of some pieces of boards floating just below me, and propped them across the mouth of the berth so I would not fall through, and soon I guess I went to sleep again.

The Yankee Captain Volunteers

When the schooner was flung on her beam-ends, one dory took the water right-side-up and somehow Captain Brown, Nat Knowles the cook and John Smith managed to get into it. Whether they tried to row back and pick off any of the other men left clinging to the weather-rail I don't know; probably it would have been madness to have tried it in the sea then running. Anyway, they drove before the gale for several hours, and then, after passing through a quarter of a mile of surf, landed on the southern side of Cape Island. How they managed to live through the surf has always been a mystery; but they did and were soon at the house of Pelick Nickerson telling their tale.

Nickerson soon carried the news to Clark's Harbour, and the hardy fishermen of that place were roused from their slumbers to consider means of rescue. The American fishing-schooner *Matchless*, Captain Job Cromwell, was lying in the harbour, where she had come for shelter from the gale, and when told of the disaster her skipper was quite as ready to go to the rescue as the men of the port.

His crew was scattered, but there were plenty of men ready to volunteer. So by the first streak of dawn, the *Matchless* with a picked crew aboard was standing out to sea under double reefs, bound on a mission of mercy. Into the teeth of the gale, putting her bows under to the foremast every plunge, they drove her out to where they expected to find the wreck, and then for long hours they tacked back and forth, straining their eyes into the gloom of the flying mist.

When the *Cod-Seeker* was hove down, the line of men who had been on deck were left clinging on under the rail. They held on there for a while. But when she listed farther-over they feared she would turn turtle. They got up on the side, and rove a life-line between the fore and main chain-plates to hold on by. In this position they were exposed to the scourge of the wind and spray, and now and then a heavier sea, making a clean breach of hulk, would stamp right over them. But they held on, and you may imagine that after daylight they searched the howling seas with eager eyes for sign of a sail.

As the morning wore on the buffetings of the seas, the numbing cold, began to tell on their strength, and along about noon a towering comber bursting over them swept one poor fellow, Crowell Nickerson by name, from the life-lines, and he was drowned before the eyes of his mates, powerless to help him. His body became entangled in some cordage, and hung to leeward.

Naturally this tragedy affected the spirits of the survivors. They watched the towering surges rushing down upon them with a new fear in their hearts, each man thinking that perhaps the next big sea would sweep him to his death. But soon they learned the calmness and the courage of despair. Will Kenney, as a requiem to the dead man to leeward, began to sing:

> *Jesus, lover of my soul,*
> *Let me to Thy bosom fly.*

All men joined in the good old song.

And then, just as they finished the last verse, Will Kenney cries: "Look! Look! A sail!"

The schooner sank into a trough. The men waited, their hearts in their mouths. And when she rose again all saw the sails of a schooner swinging out of the mist hardly half a mile to leeward.

It was the *Matchless* and the men on her had already sighted the wreck. Tack by tack she beat up to windward and then her big seine-boat was manned. It dropped under the lee of the wreck, and the men were picked off by being hauled through the sea with a line about their waists.

The *Matchless* picked up her boat without mishap, and then, because it was blowing a gale of wind with a heavy driving mist making it impossible to see any distance, she was hove to for the night.

Next morning, the weather having moderated, she made sail and at three o'clock in the afternoon stood into Clark's Harbour with the Stars and Stripes flying at her masthead as a sign to those on shore that she had accomplished her mission.

A small boat took the rescued men, Will Kenney, William Goodwin, Jesse Smith, and Jeremiah Nickerson to Bear Point, where the relatives and friends of the crew of the ill-fated schooner had gathered. You can imagine the scenes that marked their return, the joy of their relatives, the frantic grief of those who had waited in vain for their loved ones.

Meantime Atwood and I, inside the hulk, knew nothing of this rescue, and nobody suspected that we were alive. While the gale continued, the seas crashed against the wreck with dreadful roaring sounds, and it was so dark that most of the time we could not discern anything. Sometimes the bows would be lifted up and the waters would recede toward the stern with a roaring as of surf. Again her head would fall off into a trough, and the water would surge forward and cover us completely.

Many times I spoke to Sam, but he never answered me. Afterward he told me that he had spoken to me many times, and got no answer. The only explanation of this I can give is that the awful roaring of the sea affected our ear-drums, as if we had been immersed ten feet in the sea. I had the kind of sensation in my ears that you have when you take a dive.

As Thursday dragged along we began to feel the pangs of hunger and thirst, and our flesh began to feel benumbed, the result of our frequent cold baths. But we dared not move from our perches. In spite of it all I would fall asleep and dream of the disaster, or of home and loved ones — and then awaken with a start to a keener fear and horror of our plight.

That Fevered Hunt for Food

That night the gale blew itself out, the dreadful roaring of the waters began to die away, and Friday morning came fine and clear, though a heavy sea continued to run. After sun-up we were able to see objects in the forecastle quite distinctly.

The light cheered us, and we thought of getting something to eat. At the end of the bunk in which we were lying there was a locker and, getting hold of some sticks, we started to break into the side of it. We broke into one compartment, and found two empty bean-crocks and an old clock. We broke into another, and found nothing, but in the third and last we found five doughnuts, soaked with salt water and kerosene. Soggy as they were we salvaged them and ate them.

Then, feeling thirstier than ever, we looked for some water. A number of barrels were floating about the forecastle; a big hole had been made by the sea in the bulkhead, and they had drifted in from the lazarette. We caught one as it drifted near and, though the way the water was surging back and forth and up and down made it a mighty hard job, we managed to hold it, while I sampled the water in it, using a barrel-pump as a sucking tube. My mouth was so parched that I drank a lot of the water before I could tell that it was salt. We dropped that barrel, and tried all the others we could get hold of, and with the same result. All the barrels that floated had the bungs out, and sea water had got into them.

Tired and disgruntled we gave up the quest, and soon had to face a new trouble. In breaking in the sides of the lockers we had loosed the supports of the bunk side-boards on which we were lying, and the ends were beginning to sag down. We had to do something or we would soon be dropped into the swirling water, and we looked about for something to prop up our perch.

The lazarette door was swinging to the motion of the water, and presently I managed to get hold of it. Then, while Atwood held me, I pulled; pulled the door right through the panels, a feat men afterward said was impossible. We placed one end of this door against the wide-boards of the bunk and, as luck would have it, it turned out to be just the right length to wedge the side-boards back in their places. Then we tore off the door of the flour-locker and, getting this inside the berth, made a platform for ourselves.

Shortly after we finished that job a barrel of biscuits — I could make out the label on it — came sailing in through the hole in the bulkhead, and we became amazingly hungry with the thought of getting something to eat. After what seemed an age it drifted near, and I got my finger on the chimes. But though I held on like grim death and Atwood held me, the surge of water tore it from my grasp, and it sailed back into the hold the way it came and we never saw it again.

Waiting for Death

The ship wallowed heavily in the swell, and the water continued to rise into the bunk, keeping us wet and cold. Now and then the rays of the sun would strike the deck light, so that it would be reflected to the lower side, and there in one of the bunks we could see a shape rolling slightly to the motion of the ship, which we thought was the body of the cook rolled in his blankets. And, of course, that gruesome thought added to the horror of our plight.

The forecastle-companion, which was about eight feet under water, was outlined by a glimmer of light. A good swimmer might have dived out, but we felt too stiff to try it, and it would have been a desperate job; the way the water was surging and swirling. But we wished a fish would swim in and allow us to capture it!

The time dragged along and, as the thirst took a fiercer grip on us, we ceased to feel the pangs of hunger. Our tongues swelled and burned; gripping pains took us by the throat; our muscles ached as if pricked with hot pins. Having swallowed so much salt water, I suffered more than Atwood, and that afternoon I grew so wild I cut the ends of fingers and sucked the blood. But that did me no good.

Night came again. We slept fitfully, dreaming of fresh, cool, sparkling water, and just as we were about to drink we would awake with a start to feel again the burning, gripping pains of thirst, and brood in agony of mind upon the thought that we were doomed to die a slow lingering death of torture. To add to the horror, I became aware that I had no feeling below my knees. I tried to pull off my sea-boots, but my feet were too swollen. It was as though I was dying from my feet up. That night I knew what fear is, the stark, fierce, angry fear of a long-drawn-out and terrible death.

When Saturday morning came we were half stupefied with suffering. Several times we talked of dropping into the water and drowning ourselves. And always the temptation to drink the salt water was strong upon us. But we kept our heads; we hoped against hope that we would be rescued, and determined to hold out as long as we could.

That afternoon the long swell began to subside. The schooner grew quieter, and ceased to duck us, and the fever of our bodies dried our clothes. The fact that the swell was going down brought us face to face with a new cause of fear — the fear that soon there would not be sufficient trough to the sea to cause the main hatch to blow, and give us fresh air.

But we did not worry greatly over the prospect of being stifled for lack of oxygen; we had about exhausted our capacity for fear; we were too sick and miserable generally to be much troubled by the appearance of a new peril.

After Saturday noon it was just suffering and endurance. We seldom talked; our parched throats and swollen tongues made speech painful and our voices sounded weird and unnatural. Nor did we think much. Most of the time we lay as in a stupor. Now and then we dreamed of beautiful ships all around us, all coming to our rescue, and would awake with a start to wonder if we were going mad. We lived as in a nightmare, lost count of time, felt as if we had suffered through eternity. We were growing light-headed.

The Spook of the Derelict

On Sunday afternoon the schooner *Ohio* of Gloucester, Captain Edward O'Dor, was standing up for the Cape Shore when she sighted something black floating upon the waves. Some of her crew took it for a dead whale; others said it was a wreck; and a heated argument ensued. To settle it, the Captain hauled up to investigate. Seeing that it was a vessel bottom-up he sent a boat to try to find out her name, and see if they could salvage anything.

So presently I thought I heard some unusual noises, and roused myself from my lethargy to listen. In a few minutes I heard a sound like the clang of iron on iron; a man cutting at the lanyards of the forerigging with an ax had hit the iron strap of the deadeye.

"There is somebody outside," I said, shaking Sam.

But he showed no interest.

"It's only something washing about the hold," he answered.

"Let's shout, anyway," I said, and yelled as hard as I could: "Help! Help! Help!"

Over my head there was an answering yell of startled fright, then footsteps pounding aft and a voice crying: "She's haunted. Get into the boat, for ... sake!"

And that chap so frightened the others that they piled into the boat and started to pull away. But, after recovering from their fright and astonishment, they grew ashamed of themselves and came back.

106

Meantime I had got hold of a stick and was rapping against the side. Soon I heard raps on the outside. I gave three raps and there were three raps in answer. We kept that up for a few minutes. Then we heard a man walking forward on the outside, and soon a voice called: "In the name of God, are you ghosts, living men or the devil?"

We shouted that we were living men, and asked them to get us out, or we would not be living men very long. The voice asked us questions for a few minutes as if incredulous, and then some of them got to work with axes over our heads, while the boat went back to the *Ohio* for more men and axes.

They worked like Trojans, and cut right through a frame-bolt to make a hole to get at us. When they broke through, the eruption of imprisoned air acted like a whirlwind, and the water leaped through the hole in a solid stream fifty feet into the air. Small sticks which had been floating in the forecastle whizzed by our heads. One man was knocked over as if by an explosion. They told us afterward that the released air gave off a sickening stench.

The schooner settled two or three feet lurching as if she would turn turtle completely, and the men chopped away with redoubled energy. They soon had a hole about nine inches by eleven inches.

Atwood, being slim, was pulled through without trouble, but when I got my head and one shoulder through, I stuck. Four men got hold of me and pulled, and at last when I thought I would be pulled apart I came through, minus my vest and several strips of skin.

A New Heaven — and a New Agony

As I stood looking around I thought of the passage of Scripture which reads, "And I saw a new heaven and a new earth." The sun was nearing the horizon, glowing softly amid a glory of rose and gold. Never have I seen such beauty in the heavens. Of course, I couldn't see the earth, but the sea lay broad, silver-tinted, smiling and strangely friendly-looking.

The schooner which four days before had been taut and trim was now almost bottom-up, lying with her keel six feet above the water and her weather-rail nearly a-wash. Her mainmast was broken off and, far below the surface, I could see a faint shadow of canvas. We thought then we were the only survivors.

Was it any wonder I thanked God for my deliverance?

Captain O'Dor said, "Come, my boy, let me help you to the boat," and took me by the arm. I thought I could walk, took a step and went tumbling. If it hadn't been for the Captain I would have slid into the sea.

Aboard the *Ohio* they had made ready for us. The cabin table was loaded with everything good to eat. But we weren't interested in food; we wanted water by the bucketful. They gave us a spoonful, and that only put an agonizing edge on our thirst. We pleaded wildly for more.

But they had realized our condition, and kept us waiting for about fifteen minutes, and then only gave us another spoonful. After what seemed ages of raging agony they began to give us a spoonful every five minutes.

But the more we got the more we wanted, and the harder we begged and pleaded. Our voices were husky and unnatural and we must have been pitiful objects, for we soon had most of the men in the cabin blubbering like babes. We thought we were moving them and pleaded harder. But we merely moved them out of the cabin, all but one hard-hearted old shellback who stopped to give us the pitiful spoonful of water every five minutes by the clock.

After we had realized the uselessness of crying for more water, and had become quiet, the cook and some of the men returned and cut off my sea-boots. My feet and ankles were badly swollen, and the flesh looked like the flesh of a drowned person who has been many days in the water. The cook began to put potato poultices on them, and in a few minutes the poultice would be baked as if in an oven.

It was six o'clock when we were rescued and we were given a spoonful of water every five minutes up till midnight. But for all that my whole system was still raging so fiercely for water that when at the change of the watches we were left alone for a few minutes I got out of my bunk, crawled to the gangway, got the jug of water and started to drink.

Atwood, lying in his bunk, saw me and begged: "Give me a drop — just one drop. Please — please — just one drop!"

That was too much of a gift. I wouldn't have spared a drop for the world. I drained the jug — and swelled up like a frog.

When the watchman returned and saw what I had done he cried out, "The man's killed himself! He's drunk two gallons of water!"

The skipper and most of the men came into the cabin — to see me die I suppose. But I did not feel any ill effects from that drink and it did not stop the maddening craving for water.

Meantime the *Ohio* was standing in for Wrayton's Harbour, the nearest port to our homes. When we were picked up our position was twenty-three miles sou'west-by-south from Seal Island. By eight o'clock Monday morning we passed Bon Portage, with the Stars and Stripes flying to the breeze, and soon thereafter were lying at anchor in the harbour.

As I was being rowed to the shore I saw the cook of the *Cod-Seeker* in my gunning-boat. Greatly surprised to see him alive I sang out: "Hello, Nat Knowles! Where are you going with my boat?"

The man dropped his oars and went white as a sheet. And no wonder. Everybody had given us up for lost.

Needless to say, when I was carried home my parents were beside themselves with joy. As they expressed it, I was as one risen from the dead. The news of our rescue spread up and down the shore, and was generally received with unbelief. Many people would not believe we had managed to live so long in the capsized vessel, and hundreds came from long distances to see us.

After I reached home I developed a high fever and my feet began to pain me. I had no desire for food; in fact I scarcely touched food for two days. But I was still raging with thirst. I wanted water all the time — milk or tea was no good. I was allowed a glass of water every half hour, but it was four days from the time we were rescued before I got over that awful thirst.

But my sufferings were not over then. My feet pained me terribly, and I couldn't sleep without a narcotic, and then only for a short time. Doctor Clark who attended me said ten drops of the narcotic would kill the devil, but I was so crazy with pain and lack of sleep that I used to cry for a big dose every few hours.

And one afternoon, when mother was out and the spasms of pain were wracking me, I crawled on my hands and knees, got up on a chair, took the bottle of narcotic from the shelf and drank half the contents. Then I navigated my way back to the lounge, crawled half-way up on it and went to sleep. That was the deepest, the best, most blessed sleep I ever had. The Doctor and everybody thought I had gone to sleep for good and all, but I came round in twenty-six hours, feeling fresh and fine. But I continued to suffer great pain in my feet for two weeks, and it was a month before I could walk.

Once More on the Trail

Meantime the *Cod-Seeker* had been picked up by two vessels, the *Condor* and *Dove* and towed into Green Cove break-water and righted. The body of Crowell Nickerson was found floating in her hold; that of William A. Smith badly burned in his bunk with the cabin stove on top of him; and that of Robert Barss in the cabin companion with his arms jammed in the binnacle. After the schooner was righted she was brought home and repaired, and in July I shipped in her again and sailed in her till Christmas, sleeping in the same berth Atwood and I had occupied during our tough experience. Properly ballasted, the schooner proved a good sea-boat. She was out in the great Newfoundland gale some years later, and was one of the five fishing vessels out of a fleet of thirty-five that made port again!

FREDERICK WILLIAM WALLACE

Born in Glasgow, Scotland in 1886, Frederick William Wallace moved to Canada with his parents in 1904. After working for shipping firms for several years, he became a freelance marine writer and illustrator. In 1913 he founded The Canadian Fisherman *and two years later helped to organize the Canadian Fisheries Association, serving as the organization's secretary until 1922. During the First World War he was the sailing master and navigator of a naval "Q" ship before taking charge of the Fish Section of the Canada Food Board. After working in the U.S. fishing industry from 1922 to 1928, he returned to Canada and co-founded National Business Publications Ltd. He also later rejoined the Canadian Fisheries Association. Apart from his work as a fisheries specialist, he was active as a writer of sea fiction and as a maritime historian. Among his many books were the novels* Blue Water *(1907) and* Captain Salvation *(1925), which were both made into movies; the story collections* The Shack Locker *(1916) and* Salt Seas and Sailormen *(1922); and the historical works* Wooden Ships and Iron Men *(1924),* In the Wake of the Wind Ships *(1927), and* Record of Canadian Shipping *(1929). Wallace died in 1958.*

"Running a Cargo" was first published in Adventure *(September 1914) and was subsequently collected in Wallace's* Tea from China and Other Yarns of the Sea *(1926). The story is one of several that Wallace wrote about the wily Nova Scotian fishing skipper Tommy Decker of Decker's Island. As the title suggests, this tale centres on Decker's exploits as a smuggler.*

Running a Cargo

There are several craft of the same name to be found in the Shipping Register, but there is really only one *Quickstep* and she was quick and a stepper to boot. Tom Decker of Decker's Island built her. Tom Decker sailed her and fished in her, and a rough-and-tumble gang of Deckers, Westhavers and Morrisseys manned her. Fishermen characterized her as an able vessel with an able skipper and an able gang ever since her first trip haddocking, when she came in with a market-glutting fare.

Quickstep. Official No. 12,783 Schooner. Built 1898 Decker's Island, N.S. Length 110 ft.; beam 24 ft.; depth 10 ft.; 115 tons gross; 98 tons register. Thos. Decker, Managing Owner, Decker's Island, Anchorville Co., N.S.

So runs the entry in the Shipping List regarding her. A simple record only, but enough for Government purposes. Tom Decker, her skipper, would dilate a trifle more upon his vessel and he never wearied of describing her qualities.

"Yes, sir! Me an' th' boys built that there vessel ourselves down on the Island. There's no scamped work in her, let me tell ye. Hardwood plankin' an' framin' — all picked an' seasoned timber; full o' hanging knees an' galvanized-iron fastenin's o' best Swedish. Her two masts are Oregon pine an' th' finest pair o' sticks on th' coast.

"She kin sail better'n any o' them, even though she ain't one o' them new style round-bow knock-abouts drawed out by yacht-designers. She's a toothpick, but her lines are a dream — yes, sir, a perfect dream — an' she's a ghost for sailin'.

"Handle? Jes' like a yacht. She'll come around on her heel 'thout lightin' up th' jib-sheets; an' for lyin' to, that ain't nawthin' round th' Western Ocean that'll beat her for hangin' to a berth under a fores'l.

"She'll hang to forty fathoms of water for a week while some o' them other jokers 'ull hev drifted a hundred mile. Yes, sir, she's a

Decker's Island product an', like everything what comes from that there Island, she's as smart as they make 'em."

Speak to an Anchorville man about her.

"Th' *Quickstep*?" he will say. "Yes, she's a lively one, all right. She's owned and sailed by them Decker's Island crowd — a proper gang o' ruddy pirates. We Anchorville fellers don't hev no truck with them — they'd steal th' brass-work off a coffin.

"Ye need only t' git ashore in their vicinity t' see how quick they kin loot an' strip a vessel. Why, they've got finer fittin's in their houses down on that Island than ye'll find in a fust-class hotel — sofys, cushions, saloon-doors, mahogany furniture, pianos an' sich-like what they've stole off'n wrecks.

"Th' blame Gov'ment cutter spends most o' her time down there a-watchin' them when th' lobster season's closed.

"Oh, they's a slick crowd all right," he will nod, "an' that *Quickstep* an' her gang is the shadiest bunch on Bank water. Some o' these fine days they'll git caught at their tricks an' none o' us law-abidin' fishermen 'ull be sorry. They're a disgrace to th' country."

In his official orders, Captain Murray of the Government cutter *Ariel* had a standing entry:

"Keep a strict supervision over the Decker's Island fishing-schooner Quickstep. Off. No.12,783. Thomas Decker, master and part owner. Several reports have come to the Department regarding illegal acts on the part of this vessel and her crew. Overhaul and search her whenever possible."

The cutter's commander knew the *Quickstep* well enough and had overhauled her times without number. He also knew what Tom Decker thought of him and the knowledge rankled in the officer's mind, but so far the *Quickstep* was officially clear of any infraction against the law. However, Captain Murray lived in hope.

The *Quickstep* was scarce twelve months water-borne when she fished the last of her Magdalen Island baiting on St. Peter's Bank. With eighteen hundred quintals of prime salt fish stowed in her holdpens, she was ready to swing off for Anchorville market. The gangs, fore and aft, had already seen the tallyboard and estimated the probable stock and share, and after cleaning up the decks and stowing the gear away for the passage, they awaited the skipper's order to put the sail to her for a grand shoot for home.

But Decker appeared to be in no hurry to swing off. While the men were cleaning up, he paced the quarter saying nothing.

"How about it, Skip?" inquired Tom Morrissey, who was at the wheel. "Will I shoot her on a west b'-south course for home? This wind holdin' southerly 'ull give us a good lift to Anchorville."

The skipper glanced to windward and stopped in his steady pacing. "Call the gang," said he to one of the men standing aft.

When the rugged crowd of husky, bewhiskered Islanders gathered on the quarter, he addressed them quietly:

"We got a smart vessel here, boys, an' a crowd what'll hang together. Fishin's all right, but there's easy money t' be made in other things 'sides fishin'. What d'ye say if we shoot into French St. Peter an' lay in a little stock o' rum for th' crowd to home? I bin thinkin' we c'd buy a couple o' hundred dollars' worth o' that French brandy an' make quite a tidy sum out o' it. Them Newf-n'landers run it over to their shore. Why shouldn't we?"

"Where'll we land it, Skip?" inquired a man doubtfully.

"Where else but at home?" answered the other.

"An git cotched by old Murray in th' cutter? It's a chancy, Skip!"

Captain Decker sniffed disdainfully.

"Old Murray an' th' cutter couldn't catch a driftin' trawl-kag. I'll guarantee t' sail circles around his old tea kettle in this packet. Don't worry about that brass-bound bridge-stanchion.

"Come on, now, here's a chanct o' makin' an extry dollar or two. Let's all chip in 'bout ten dollars apiece an' buy some rum. We'll run it inter Jimmy Peterson's place an' he'll buy it from us. We'll clear a hundred per cent. an' no risks but dodgin' th' cutter down home. It's dead easy."

Within five minutes, the *Quickstep* under topsails, stays'l and balloon, was heading N.N.W. for St. Pierre in the French Colony of Miquelon Islands.

These Islands, situated a few miles off the Newfoundland Coast, are the headquarters of the French fishing-fleet; and when the St. Malo, Fecamp, St. Servan and Paimpol "bankers" come across from France they discharge a goodly "ballast" of French cordials and brandy at the Islands. All the Bank fishermen know this, and the thirsty ones are always glad of a chance to run into the French Islands for a cheap drunk.

An American quarter goes a long way in the Miquelons with brandy at five cents a glass — and a beer-glass at that.

"Now, boys," said Decker, when Galantry Head was raised: "We'll jest shoot inter the outer anchorage an' leggo the manila cable. Erne, Bill, Tom an' me'll take th' two dories an' go ashore for th' rum. You fellers better remain aboard!

"'Taint wise," he explained, "for a whole ship's company to git ashore in S'int Pierre with booze sellin' so cheap."

And as he manoeuvred the *Quickstep* into the harbour among the numerous schooners, brigs, and brigantines at anchor, he turned a deaf ear to the audible growls of the disappointed gang.

They let go the anchor abreast of the antiquated French gun-boat detailed by the republic to protect the interests of their colony in North American waters, and the mainsail was hardly down before Decker had the dories over.

"Now, fellers, be good ontil we come off," he said with a grin. "Don't git sassin' them Frenchies aboard th' dreadnaught or they'll be after blowin' holes in th' *Quickstep*— "

"Aye, skip," growled big Bill Westhaver, who had been critically examining the vessels anchored around. "That's advice as would be good for you t' remember. There's that Gloucesterman we met in th' Ma'daleens lyin' to loo'ard. Maybe her crowd ain't forgot th' way you stole their bait at Grindstone—"

"Eh? What?" exclaimed Decker, glancing around in evident concern. "Lord Harry, so it is."

"An' I hev no doubt they'll be pleased t' meet ye," continued the other. "She'd a great bunch o' them wild Judiquers an' Cape Breetoners aboard — fair devils for scrappin' they are. Look out they don't catch ye. There ain't much chanst for a rescue with us away out here."

The skipper paused astride the rail.

"Um, yes, there ain't no doubt but ye're right, Bill. Well, Judiquers or no Judiquers, we come here on business, so let you'n Mike, Wally, Ross, Earle, an' John come ashore along o' me. It might be a good plan fur yez to take some o' them iron belayin'-pins with ye. Shove them down yer boots. No need to go ashore twirlin' them an' askin' for trouble."

When the dories pulled up on the beach-wharf, Decker answered the scarlet-trousered *gendarme* who accosted him.

"Yes! Oui! Schoonaire *Quickstep* Canadien. Just shot in for some provisions. Savvy? Goin' out again soon. No need to report. Stick this silver dollar in yer crimson jeans an' tell me ef Johnny Bosanquet's still doin' business at the old stand?"

"Aw, *oui! Merci, m'sieu! M'sieu Bosanquet* up de street, Capitan! *Cabaret de Pêcheur!* I keep eyes on your doree, Capitan. Lot o' dronk Americaine ashore mak mistake with doree—"

"Any o' th' *Frances Cameron's* crowd ashore?" inquired Decker nervously.

The *gendarme* nodded.

"Oui! *Francois Cameerong!* Their doree over the stone jettee. All up at Pierre Leroux — '*Auberge de Saint Malo*'."

"Then we'll keep clear o' th' Auberge de S'int Malo," muttered Decker as he strode up the windswept street.

At Bosanquet's the purchase was rapidly consummated and Decker made his men hustle the cases of spirits to the dories without wasting time.

"Let's git back to th' vessel now an' to sea afore it comes dark," said he, but the perspiring fishermen demurred.

"Judas! but ye're in a hurry, skipper," growled Westhaver. "There's a drink or two promised us up at Bosanquet's. D'ye think we're a-goin' to' bust our bloomin' hearts out luggin' them cussed cases 'thout somethin' t' cool us off? Be reasonable, skipper."

"An' leave th' dories with all the booze aboard? Not likely."

"Well, tell that ruddy Johnny Darm to keep an eye on them. We won't be more'n ten minutes." Backed up by the others, Westhaver's appeal carried, and after cautioning the *gendarme* to watch the boats, the *Quickstep's* crew made up the street again for the promised thirst-quenchers.

II.

It was Cluny McPherson of the *Frances Cameron's* gang who started the trouble. Cluny was huge, raw-boned and stupid, but he had enough Highland Scotch blood in him to retain a vivid memory of any man who insulted him, for the McPherson strain was strong for revenge.

At the herring traps at Grindstone Island, two months previous, McPherson had been insulted by Tom Decker and consequently the big fisherman had a photographic memory for the skipper's features.

Cluny happened to be in Bosanquet's when Decker and his gang entered for the promised drinks, and without wasting a minute he nipped across to the *Auberge de Saint Malo* for reinforcements. Then the band began to play.

Full of French brandy and the spirit of retaliation, the *Frances Cameron's* crew swarmed into the *Cabaret de Pêcheur*, and Tom Decker turned from the rough bar in time to receive the heft of Cluny's hairy fist on his jaw. Quick as a flash, Decker laid hold of a

117

long-necked cordial bottle and smashed it over the red-thatched McPherson's skull and the latter went down for the count.

With oaths and growls of rage, the twenty husky fishermen congregated in the little room engaged in a battle wherein the Marquis of Queensbury rules had no part — sea-booted feet, belaying-pins and bottles being the principal articles of offense.

Then Bosanquet's assistant — a bull-necked Parisian tough, who had migrated to the Miquelons to avoid an unwelcome migration to Devil's Island — took a hand in the fracas and incidentally took a flying belaying-pin on the temple. The missile, hurled by a brawny arm, smashed into his brain, and the man crashed to the floor like a pole-axed ox. The combatants knew that the brawl had culminated in a tragedy.

"Beat it for th' vessel, boys," roared Decker, making for the door. Two *gendarmes* with swords drawn barred the way, but the mob of men flying out of the door went over them like an avalanche and they rolled into the mud with a clatter of accoutrements and French oaths.

Haunted by a common fear, the opposing factions forgot their differences in the desire to reach the beach, and piling pell-mell into their dories, each gang pulled for their respective vessels with strokes which would have defeated a college eight.

"Sock it to her, son," howled Decker, sweating at an oar. "To th' vessel before we git arrested an' jugged for that shine. Give it to her! One! Two! One! Two! Pull, boys! Put yer backs into it!"

A bullet winged past his ear.

"Th' beggars are firin' at us from th' shore. This is a hangin' scrape! Pull, sons, pull, ef ye ever want t' see Decker's Island again!" And they pulled as they had never done before.

Over the rail of the *Quickstep* they tumbled, and, pausing for a moment to make the dory painters fast, all hands tallied on to the foresail-halyards.

"Up yer fores'l!" roared Decker, running for'ard with the cook's hatchet. "Loose yer jumbo an' h'ist away, some o' yez! Jumbo! Jumbo!

Some o' yez! It don't take all hands to h'ist that fores'l! Weather up yer tail-rope an' up with th' wheel. Judas! Th' ruddy gun-boat is gettin' her mud-hook!"

Ere the sail was fully hoisted, the vessel paid off and Decker slashed the straining manila cable with the axe. The rumble of the steam windlass on the French gun-boat inspired the *Quickstep's* crowd to herculean exertions, and within five minutes from the time they had boarded the schooner the foresail and jumbo were set and the vessel paying off across the gun-boat's bows.

The *Frances Cameron* was also under way and standing out to sea with her foreboom cocked high over the nested dories to a full sheet. Tearing along in her wake, a cable's length astern, came the *Quickstep* with all hands snatching the stops off the big mainsail.

Bang! The gun-boat was talking. Giving a hasty glance over the taffrail Decker saw that she was also under way and heading in the harbour-entrance to intercept them.

"Mains'l! mains'l!" yelled the Skipper. "Up with th' big rag or he'll catch us. Jumpin' Jupiter! I see us all swingin' with our necks in th' bight o' the rope if them Sabots git a-holt o' us. Heave away, bullies! Never mind th' crotch. I'll tend to that."

And while th' men panted and pulled on the halyards, the skipper tended crotch, sheet and wheel at one and the same time.

With six hundred and fifty square yards of extra canvas hoisted, the *Quickstep* began to storm along with five dories romping and tumbling to their painters alongside. To windward flew the *Frances Cameron* under foresail and jumbo — her crowd wrestling with the mainsail and getting ready for hoisting; and to windward of her but a short distance astern was the gun-boat.

"We're goin' to be cotched," panted Tom Morrissey apprehensively. "Th' cruiser's overhaulin' us —"

"Shut yer head, yuh big croaker," snapped Decker. "We ain't caught yet."

Glancing at the course the gun-boat was making, Decker did some rapid thinking.

"We're sailin' vessels," he muttered to himself. "He's a steamer. Ef I was him, I'd git to loo'ard o' the *Frances Cameron* an' jam her an' me up to wind'ard. Will he? I wonder now! We'll hev to haul by th' wind when that headland jams us off from runnin' any further. I jest wonder what he'll do? Um' I see his game now. He knows we gotter come by th' wind soon, so he's edgin' to wind'ard o' both of us. That'll mean he intends to jam us down on th' land.

"Um! Tom Decker, it sure looks as if your goose is cooked. Ye'll either hev t' surrender or run a chanct of pilin' up on th' beach, an' it's jail either ways. What did that stupid swab o' a Frenchman want t' mix up in our little scraps for anyway? . . . . Oh, boys, stand by sheets fore'n aft."

The long summer evening was darkening up for night when the three vessels came to the point of action. To windward lay the open sea and the French gun-boat. Inside of the steamship was the *Frances Cameron* under foresail, jumbo and half-hoisted mainsail with the gaff jammed up against the lee main-rigging.

To leeward, and approaching the *Cameron's* quarter, stormed the *Quickstep* running before the wind under her four whole lowers. Ahead of the latter and on her port hand were the rocks.

To clear the land, both schooners would have to sheet in and haul by the wind, and to block such an attempt the old Republican cutter was edging in as fast as her nine-knot engines would drive her. If they held on, the schooner would go ashore. If they hauled their wind, schooners and gun-boat would meet at a converging line.

The nervous watchers on the *Quickstep* could see the red tassels on the caps of the man-o-war's men as they stood at their stations along the rail. They could also see the breakers on the shore; and the strain was intense.

"Sheet in! Lively, boys, lively!" roared Decker, whirling the spokes over.

Up to windward clawed the gallant vessel and she careened to the weight of the breeze in her sails. The other schooner also put her helm down, but not having her mainsail properly hoisted she lacked enough aftersail to hold her head to windward, and she lay right athwart the *Quickstep's* course.

"Thar's two schooners a-comin' in th' harbour, skipper," hailed a man. And on the information Decker did some Napoleonic thinking.

"I gotter git past that stupid plug ahead an' I gotter dodge that gun-boat. Mister Johnny Frenchman cain't turn very well, now them two other schooners hez showed up, an' ef th' *Cameron* keeps a-goin like he is he'll foul th' steamer."

Aloud he shouted: "Stand by for an American shoot. You fellers aft here all yell with me to th' *Cameron* skipper when we come to weather of him: 'Hard up! Hard up!' Remember that."

The gun-boat had slowed down slightly to leeward of the *Cameron* and was engaged hoisting out a boat. Decker noted every phase of the situation.

"Now, boys, light up your jibsheets."

The *Quickstep* shot up on the *Cameron's* quarter.

"Hold everything for'ard! Now, fellers, all together; 'Hard up! Hard up!'"

The skipper of the *Frances Cameron* was rattled with the predicament he was in. He could see the gun-boat a hundred feet away and just on his lee bow; he saw the rocks to leeward of his beam and also the *Quickstep* on his weather quarter but a good jump from him. His gang, hauling away at the mainsail halyards, were yelping anxious questions at him, and when the startling "Hard up!" reached his ears, he whirled the wheel over without thinking. The action caused his vessel to fall off before the wind, and before he could avert it, his schooner crashed into the gun-boat dead amidships.

"Jump fer yer dories, boys, an' make for th' schooners a-comin' in," bawled Decker as the *Quickstep* surged past. "I'll tell 'em to pick ye up an' stand out again."

It was needless advice, for the *Frances Cameron's* gang were even then pulling out to sea. The schooner had driven her bowsprit clean through the iron plates of the gun-boat's hull and in the various davits and boat-booms of the war-vessel the *Cameron's* foremast and head-gear had become entangled so that both craft were locked together.

"Rammed by a wooden schooner," ejaculated Tom Morrissey with a whoop of delight at the gun-boat's plight. "Waal, what d'ye know about that? S'pose she's so old an' her plates so thin with twenty years chippin' that a knife 'ud go through 'em—"

"Hi-yi! What's th' racket, cap?"

The first of the incoming schooners, a Gloucesterman, was on the *Quickstep's* beam and the skipper was hailing.

"Trouble ashore," roared Decker in reply. "Run in an' pick up them dories what's pullin' out an' shoot to sea again. 'Tis the *Frances Cameron* gang."

"I cotton cap," sang out the other, luffing. "Raisin' hell with the Frenchies, I cal'late. All right, bully, jest watch me nip 'em up."

Decker, however, didn't wait to watch the Gloucesterman "nip 'em up." He knew that the *Cameron's* skipper would be out for his scalp as soon as he got aboard the rescuer.

"Give her th' stays'l, th' balloon an' th' tops'ls," he shouted anxiously. "When that Gloucesterman hears th' story he might be fer givin' us a chase—"

Bang! Bang! Bang! The gunboat was showing her teeth and the *Quickstep's* crowd ducked their heads instinctively.

"What are they doin'?" cried Decker. "Git my glasses, John. Is th' gun-boat clear yet? Hurry! It's gittin' dark."

John, with his glasses glued close to his eyes, stared into the dusk astern. "Th' blame' gun-boat's clear . . . an' here comes that Gloucesterman hoofin' it like the milltail o' Hades with Johnny Frenchman after him—"

"Is th' *Cameron* gang picked up?"

"I sh'd imagine so. Three or four empty dories driftin' about. Th' *Cameron* is driftin' ashore—"

"All right! Git yer dories aboard an' stow that rum in th' kid ontil I git a chanct to think. Lord Harry! What a session — what a session!

Jupiter! I'll hev t' see a lawyer 'bout this scrape ef we git clear. Wonder ef th' *Cameron's* owners kin lay a claim ag'in me for that rammin' business? Judas! What a bluff... an' t' think that it worked. Hard up!' I says, an' he does it — th' silly swab."

And Decker pawed the wheel and chuckled as the *Quickstep* hauled off the land and curtseyed to the lift of open water.

III

The breeze held until the *Quickstep* made the latitude of Sambro; then it dropped flat calm. "Drive her, you!" had been the watchword ever since the flashing lights of Galantry Head had sunk astern, and in the whole sail storming along across St. Pierre Bank, the schooner had eluded her pursuers in the night.

It was a drive which few of the gang would ever forget. Lights doused, a strong breeze, all sail and the lee rail buried in creaming froth, it kept all hands on the alert and nervous with future anxieties.

"I wonder ef th' news of our racket at th' Miquelons has been tellygraft to home," muttered Decker for the twentieth time as he paced the quarter looking for air.

"Why don't ye pull over to that little handliner an' see ef he's got 'ny newspapers?" growled big Westhaver. "He's only jest made th' berth an' ten chances to one he has this mornin's Halifax papers. I'll pull ye over."

"Open one o' them cases an' gimme a couple o' bottles," said the Skipper. "We'll pull over an' see."

A mile's pull over the oily swell brought them alongside the handliner, and the trio smoking around her decks were the first to speak.

"Are youse fellers off th' *Quickstep*? Ye are? Holy trawler. But ye've been makin' things hum. Lord Harry! Th' whole coast is talkin' 'bout ye. Let's see a holt o' yer painter."

"Got 'ny noospapers about it?" growled Decker, none too pleased at the notoriety he was receiving.

"Here y'are, cap. This morning's Halifax papers. How much rum hev ye got aboard?"

Decker looked up sharply.

"Oh, ye know that too, do ye? Sink me. But when a man buys a ruddy long-neck these days th' whole coast knows it. Here's a couple o' bottles. Maybe ye kin drink it an' keep yer mouths shut about meetin' us."

"Thanks, cap, we sure will," answered the handliners in chorus. "Trust us for that. We ain't no Scott Act spotters an' good S'int Pierre's a drink for a king. Come aboard an' give us th' yarn. Th' blame noospapers git things reported all wrong."

There was the suspicion of a breeze ruffling the water and Decker declined the invitation.

"No, thanks, fellers. Got t' be movin'. So long, an' keep quiet."

On the way back to the schooner, Decker hastily perused the papers and his stifled ejaculations had the rowers agog with curiosity. Aboard the *Quickstep* now gliding along to the first of a breeze, the gang lined the quarter and besieged the skipper with a running fire of questions.

"Wait a second an' I'll read it t' ye," snapped Decker. "They got th' whole bill an' a lot more—"

Seating himself on the house, with the crowd craning their necks over his shoulders, he commenced:

"'Strange affair from the Miquelons' (will ye look at th' size of th' print?) Lord Harry! Ye'd think 'twas a ruddy war! 'French Gun-Boat Rammed by Fishing Schooner. Decker up to His Tricks Again.' (What d'ye know about that? Decker must be a hell of a feller 'cordin' to them noospapers. Um!) 'Telegraphic reports from Saint Pierre state that the French Fishery Patrol cruiser *Rouget* was rammed by the American schooner *Frances Cameron* while the cruiser was endeavouring to hold the crew in connection with a shore-brawl. The cruiser sustained slight damage.'

"'The crew of the *Frances Cameron* abandoned their vessel after the mishap and escaped in their dories to a near-by schooner. The

Frances Cameron was engaged in salt fishing under command of Captain Wallace Doyle, and is owned by the Western Fish Co., of Gloucester, Mass.' (Um! that part's all right. We ain't shinin' in that, but here's th' funny part.)

"'Sydney, N.S. The American schooner *Geraldine* put into North Sydney last night and landed the crew of the Gloucester schooner *Frances Cameron* abandoned at Saint Pierre after a collision with the French cruiser *Rouget*. Our correspondent interviewed Captain Wallace Doyle regarding the mishap and learned the following strange story:'

"'It appears that the Canadian fishing schooner *Quickstep*, commanded by Thomas Decker, of Decker's Island, had run into Saint Pierre for the purpose of buying a quantity of spirits, presumably to import to Canada and evade the customs duties, and while ashore making the purchase, the crew of the *Quickstep* along with the crew of the *Frances Cameron* got mixed up in a tavern brawl.'

"'During the *mélée* a resident of Saint Pierre was killed, and both crews, frightened at the outcome of the fight, made for their respective vessels and attempted to put to sea. The French Fishery Patrol cruiser *Rouget* followed the fleeing schooners and endeavoured to stop them, and in crossing the *Frances Cameron's* bows, was rammed by the fishing-vessel.'

"'Captain Doyle stated that it was his intention to heave to and surrender to the French authorities, but the *Quickstep* coming up on his weather quarter crowded him into the cruiser, causing a collision. Appalled by the mishap, the crew of the *Cameron* took to their dories and were picked up by the *Geraldine* and later landed there.'

"'Captain Doyle is emphatic in his assertion that the *Quickstep* was the cause of the accident, and he is also of the opinion that the crew of the latter vessel were responsible for the death of the man in the tavern ashore.' (Th' ruddy gall o' him! What d'ye know about that? We're t' blame fur th' whole thing, by Jupiter!)

"'Upon the information of the *Frances Cameron's* crew, the local Customs Department has advised the Protective Service to maintain

125

a strict watch for the *Quickstep* in connection with the liquor-smuggling.' (Now, fellers, here's whar' th' fun comes in. Listen!) 'Captain Murray in the Government cutter *Ariel* left Anchorville this evening. The cutter is presumably on the lookout for the *Quickstep* with her contraband cargo.'"

The newspaper's account caused the *Quickstep's* gang several emotions, but the latter item made them glance apprehensively around the horizon for the sight of steamer smoke. They were frightened — not the least doubt of it — and for five minutes Decker was bombarded with questions:

"Heave that cussed rum over th' side," cried the gang. "It'll save more trouble! Lord Harry! It's jail for th' crowd of us over that Saint Pierre racket. Ef we hadn't ha' listened t' you an' yer crazy scheme, we'd ha' been home now, 'stead o' being chased by cruisers an' cutters. You got us inter this scrape, now git us out of it."

"To be sure! To be sure!" The skipper laughed grimly and surveyed the men with a sarcastic smile on his dark, strong-lined face.

"Yes," he continued ironically. "I got ye into this scrape, so it's up t' me t' git ye out, I cal'late! Nobody kin suggest any plans but t' heave th' booze overboard.

"Waal, I ain't a-goin' t' heave the rum overboard — at least not ontil I see th' cutter overhaulin' us. Now, it's up to popper t' quiet th' children.

"Ye don't need t' fret over th' S'int Pierre racket. They ain't got no case ag'in us. We niver dodged no arrest an' no warrant was served on us. They can't prove we killed that joker. He was in th' fight as well as all of us, so it's accidental death. We niver rammed the gun-boat — 'twas th' *Cameron*. We kin prove that she wouldn't tack owin' to havin' no sail on her —"

"How about us all a-yellin' 'Hard up!' to her skipper?" asked a man.

"Waal, what ef we did? Are we th' blame pilots o' the *Frances Cameron*? Her skipper won't say a word about that. He don't want that business t' git around. Th' law can't touch us, so don't worry. We're outside th' three-mile limit yet an' safe as a church."

Decker's explanations satisfied the crowd and they dispersed to their quarters swearing that he was "a dog of a feller" and a "downy son of a gun."

While the schooner glided to the south'ard, the "downy one" paced the quarter absorbed in thought.

"Now, Commander Murray is in th' cutter lookin' for us. He knows th' *Quickstep* an' he knows we're bound for Anchorville with our trip. He knows we got liquor aboard an' he knows we'd land it in no place but Decker's Island.

"Now, where'll th' cutter be? Where'd I be ef I was in his place? In behind Decker's Island. He won't come an' meet us, 'cause he'd miss us in the dark. No, Decker's Island is where he'll hang around. He thinks we ain't wise, so he'll lie low, around there an' keep his search-light a-goin' at night with a motor boat or two handy so's they kin nip out an' ketch us ef we try t' skin away.

"All right! We'll hev some fun with th' cutter, an' ef I don't run that cargo o' stingo, I'm a Dutchman!"

Talking to himself and smoking the while, Captain Decker mapped out a plan of action, which to his mind, was a masterpiece of strategy; and after supper that evening he addressed the mystified crowd in the forecastle:

"We'll unbend th' balloon an' foretops'l an' send down our foretopm'st to'night," he said. "That'll make th' *Quickstep* look a trifle different. Some o' youse kin git busy an' make a length o' buoy-line fast to all them liquor-cases in th' kid—"

"What's th' game, Skipper?"

"Do as I tell ye an' ye'll find out. I'm a-goin' t' jig Cap Murray t'morrow night an' ye'll see th' joke then. Now, hez any o' you fellers ever been on th' lobster-ground off West Head?"

"I hev," replied a man.

"Good! Then you'll know where they set them traps off-shore?"

"Yes."

"Then I'll need you for particular business in th' mornin'. In th' meantime you kin rouse all th' bobbers an' floats we got aboard. Cut 'em adrift from our gear and hev' 'em ready. We'll be off West Head at three ef this breeze holds, so ye'll get busy an' send that spar down right away."

IV

Commander Murray of the Government cutter *Ariel* pored over a chart of the coast and addressed his Chief Officer:

"Decker left Miquelon on the fifteenth an' with th' way th' wind has been, he should be off here to-night. We'll steam up an' down th' channel behind the Island there and ye'll see that all lights are screened. Have all hands ready for boarding and the boats out for launching. I'll get Skipper Decker to-night or bust. If I let him slip this time, the Department will have me on th' carpet for sure."

"How about th' searchlight, sir? If we keep it playin' around he's liable to see it an' sheer it off."

"I have made arrangements for that," replied the Commander. "Jones an' Thompson are out in motor-boats stationed at Colson's Point an' Tops'l Head. It ain't a very dark night an' they'll be able to see any vessel standin' in, even if they have their lights doused, for a vessel intendin' to make the Island will have to pass either of these places close aboard. When they sight anything, they'll swing a lantern three times so we won't use th' search-light unless we have to."

The mate smiled approval.

"We'll git him sure, sir," he said, "and ef we make a capture, it'll mean promotion for both of us; you to the new cutter an' me to this one."

The Commander nodded.

"And it ain't altogether th' promotion, John, but it's th' chance of layin' Decker by th' heels. He's dodged me an' made a joke of me so long now that I'd give anything to get my hands on him. You'll remember how he stripped that Norwegian bark that ran ashore off here and also that West Indies' boat.

"We raked his place on the Island for th' loot, but never a sight of it did we get, an' he goes struttin' around Anchorville braggin' about how he did me in the eye. And when he was in th' lobsterin' business — look how he bamboozled me then with his traps out th' whole o' th' close season. Yes! I'm sure anxious to get him."

At midnight the lookouts on the cutter reported a signal from Topsail Head. Out from her hiding place went the cutter, but the sight of four headsails and two wide-space masts against the skyline convinced Murray that it was only a coaster hugging the land.

"That ain't him," said the mate. "That's th' Bayport packet an' Tim Johnson wouldn't smuggle a plug o' tobacco to save his life. No use searchin' him."

At 1.30 A.M. they ran out again on signals. This time it was a fisherman and Murray boarded her in a boat, only to find that she was a La Have banker running in for ice and bait. The crowd of sleepy men who tumbled up on the hail of the watch knew nothing of the *Quickstep* except by reputation. They had not seen her, so the cutter's boat returned.

Just before dawn the shivering mate on the *Ariel's* bridge had a fancy that he heard the rattle of blocks and shackles come out of the darkness. Calling the Commander, he said:

"Seems t' me there's a vessel off there somewheres. I c'd hear her gear shakin'."

"I don't see any lights," said the other, peering into the gloom. "Any signal given?"

"No, sir."

"Look out, there! Have you seen or heard anything?"

"No, sir."

"You must have imagined it," growled Murray. "A man fancies all kinds o' things when he's lookin' for somethin'—"

"But I'm quite sure there's a vessel off there, sir. Open out with th' searchlight. It won't make any difference — it'll soon be daylight."

The Commander turned on the switch and the piercing beam penetrated the dark of the morning.

"Play her over t' th' west-ard, sir," said the mate. The shaft of light swung around and disclosed a long toothpick fisherman lying to the wind off the Island.

"That's him, by Jupiter," ejaculated mate and superior at once, and Murray rang down for full speed ahead.

"I've got him with th' goods this time," cried the jubilant official. "No lights burnin'. He's out for business sure enough. Git that for'ard gun trained on him an' call a boat's crew. He won't git away this time."

Within ten minutes Commander Murray was in the boat and being pulled over to where the fishing-schooner lay illuminated in the glare of the cutter's search-light.

"Schooner ahoy! What vessel's that?"

"*Quickstep*. What's the row?"

"Stand by. We're comin' aboard."

Murray felt that his hour of triumph had come.

"All right, come ahead," growled a voice which the Commander recognized as Decker's.

The officer, followed by four of the cutter's men, leaped over the *Quickstep's* rail.

"Now, sir," said Murray, addressing Decker, "What are you doin' in here with your lights out?"

"My lights out?" cried Decker in surprise. "Surely ye're mistaken, Admiral. Them side lights are both burnin'. Come for'ard an' see for yerself. The cook put fresh ile in them this mornin' so they sh'd be burnin'. Why, swamp me, they're both burnin'. Can't ye see them?"

Murray stifled an oath. The lights were burning all right.

"Darn funny they weren't visible awhile ago," he snapped.

"Warn't they?" Decker smiled ironically. "That's curious. Yer eyesight must be failin' ye skipper — excuse me, I mean Admiral. This is th' grave-eye watch, y'know an' a man's sight gits bad at this time in th' mornin'.—"

"That's enough," rasped Murray. "What are you doin' in here?"

Decker's eyebrows expressed surprise at the question and the assembled gang sniggered audibly.

"Why, Commodore," he said, "we all live on that Island off thar'. What's t' hinder a man goin' ashore for a spell t' see his folks after bein' thirteen weeks to sea? Is that agin th' law? Sure, I just run in to put a dory over an' see th' wife afore makin' for Anchorville with th' first o' th' flood."

"All right, Decker," interrupted the other impatiently. "We'll get to business. I know what you came in here for, so don't lie about it. Where have you stowed that liquor you bought at Saint Pierre?"

"Liquor I bought at Sint Pierre, Lootenong?" repeated Decker. "Where else but under our belts. Sink me. Can't a feller buy a few bottles o' brandy for a little sociable drink 'thout th' ruddy Gov'ment wantin' to know where it is? Come below an' hev a taste. Thar's a bottle or two left."

The revenue officer ignored the invitation.

"I'm goin' to search the vessel. Muster your men in th' waist here. Bo'sun! Off with these hatches an' fetch th' lanterns out th' boat."

For over an hour and a half the Commander and his men raked the *Quickstep* for contraband. The salt fish in the hold were prodded and overhauled; the drain-well probed; bunks turned out; dories hoisted out of the nests; gurry-kid and stays'l-box examined; and a man even crawled among the coal in the lazarette under the cabin floor in the quest.

The search was thorough — so thorough that it was impossible for anything to have been concealed in the *Quickstep* from run to peak without the customs men finding it. Murray knew that Decker had bested him again, for all he could find was two full bottles of cognac in the skipper's locker.

"You ain't a-goin' t' charge me dooty on them two longnecks I hev, Lootenong?" said Decker humbly.

The other felt like a fool and raged inwardly at the fisherman's sarcasm.

"Look here, Decker," he said shortly, "you've had liquor aboard here with th' intention of runnin' it in. Where is it?"

Captain Decker's attitude changed suddenly and there was a strident snap in his voice when he spoke:

"You're makin' accusations, Commander, which I've a mind t' bring ye t' book for. I got inter trouble enough at S'int Pierre 'thout lookin' for more. We come in here, as I've a right to do, an' you say our lights ain't burnin'. They are burnin' as you kin see. Then ye tarn to an' rake my vessel ontil ye know every timber an' bolt in her. Ye found nawthin'. Now, we've wasted enough time in shenanigan. I'm goin' ashore t' see my wife. You git back to yer old squib-shooter afore I give ye the Jonah bounce over th' side for accusin' honest men—"

"Why is your foretopmast on deck?"

"An' why shouldn't it be after carryin' away our topm'st stay? Anythin' else that wants explainin' to yer brass-bound majesty?"

"No," snapped th' other. "You're clear so far. I'll keep my eye on you after this. Bo'sun! We'll get aboard."

"Good night, an' thank ye kindly for th' visit, Admiral," jeered Decker as Murray went over the side. "It's men like you what made Nelson say, 'England expects that every son of a gun will pay th' dooty.' So long!"

"Nothin' doin'," said the disgruntled Commander when he returned to the cutter. "Not a thing to be found. I really don't think he tried to run liquor. He had quite a scrap up at the Islands and he wouldn't look for more trouble."

"Um," remarked the mate when the other had retired. "He don't know Mister Decker. He's a young bird, but he's a downy one jest th' same."

* * *

John Peterson, storekeeper, lobster-buyer, and general agent, smacked his lips over the drink and murmured, "Happy Days!"

"Tell me about it again, skipper, for it's a yarn worth repeatin'. Ye h'ard that th' cutter 'ud be lookin' for ye from th' noospapers ye got from a vessel off Sambro, so what did ye do?"

"Waal, I know'd he'd be around the Island here," replied the wily skipper, lighting up one of Petersen's no-duty-paid Havanas, "so I cal'lated thar' 'ud be no chanct o' landin' th' stuff in th' dories. Then I thought o' dumpin' all them cases overboard with a float tied to them, but that dodge'd be suspicious, as Murray might cotton an' go searchin' for a queer-lookin' float.

"I then thought o' th' fun he'd hev searchin' for such a thing with all them lobster buoys around this vicinity, an' that gimme the idea. He'd never bother pullin' up lobster buoys with a Decker's Island fisherman's mark on them. Yes, says I, we'll dump them in shoal water with lobster buoys tied to each case, for it would be an easy job to pick em up. A case at a time c'd easy be pulled an' landed by a lobsterman in his dory an' nobody 'ud be any th' wiser.

"We had no buoys aboard the *Quickstep* so I planned runnin' in off West Head an' cuttin' some o' their buoys adrift from their gear offshore — leavin' some of our bobbers and trawl-floats in their place so's th' lobstermen wouldn't lose their traps. To make sure we wouldn't be recognized doin' this, I had th' foretopm'st struck in case any one sh'd see us, but thar' was no danger.

"We got all th' buoys we wanted afore daylight an' hauled to sea again, so I didn't bother sendin' th' spar aloft as I sh'd ha' done ef we'd been seen on that lobster-ground.

"I jogged for a spell 'bout twenty miles to the east'ard till night afore runnin' in an' dumpin' th' stingo. I had gunny-sacks over th' lights while we put th' cases over th' side off Colson's Point in five fathom water.

"Man! But ye sh'd ha' seen old Murray's face when I showed him th' lights burnin'. Soon's he come alongside, I had th' cook whisk the screens off them an' he never caught on. Lord! But I sartainly rubbed it into him good that mornin'. He s'arched the *Quickstep* from taffr'l to jumbo-stay, inside an' out—"

"Aye, an' he come ashore an' s'arched this place an' all th' sheds an' barns on the Island," said Petersen with a laugh. "Lord Harry, Captain Tom, but you're a dog. What with yer scrape at th' French Islands an' yer dodgin' th' cutter down here, you've sartainly been goin' some."

"Aye, Petersen, we've sartainly been goin' some. I ain't makin' friends by it, but 'twas excitin' while it lasted. Now, how'd it be ef we sent Captain Murray a couple of bottles o' that S'int Pierre cognac with 'Captain Decker's compliments?'"

ERLE R. SPENCER

Erle R. Spencer was born at Fortune, Newfoundland in 1897. At the age of fourteen, he contracted tuberculosis and was sent to the International Grenfell Association hospital in St. Anthony for treatment. After completing his studies at the Methodist College in St. John's and the Canadian Business College in Chatham, he worked for several years in Calgary. In 1922 he went to Europe, eventually finding a job on Fleet Street in London. For health reasons, he spent his winters in a Swiss sanatorium, where he wrote a succession of novels, including a number of maritime adventure stories set on Newfoundland's southern coast. He died in London in 1937.

The following selection is taken from the first of Spencer's nine novels, Yo-Ho-Ho! A Story of Piracy and Adventure *(1924), a Stevensonian adventure story that portrays rum-running activities out of St. Pierre in the 1920s. According to the Newfoundland scholar Ronald Romkey (see his essay on Spencer in* Essays on Canadian Writing *No. 31, 1985),* Yo-Ho-Ho! *was written not long after Spencer had sailed from Fortune to Oporto, Portugal aboard the schooner* Ronald M. Douglas *under the command of Tom Douglas. In this excerpt (comprising chapters 7-10), Spencer's young hero, Dick Roberts, finds himself involved in a daring attempt by Black Douglas, captain of the* Sea Nymph, *to steal the cargo of a rival smuggler off the coast of New Jersey*

from Yo-Ho-Ho!

Jackson's Cove

Jackson's Cove lies in an isolated position along the New Jersey coast. It contains about a score of fishermen's cottages and harbours a few boats. Ships rarely call there, and when they do so it is usually only for a few hours, perhaps with the object of obtaining water, or to escape the rigors of a sudden gale.

The harbour is formed by a crescent of headland, and can be entered only by a narrow channel. It is spacious enough to hold a hundred sail of ships, being at least half-a-mile across, and more in length.

It narrows towards both ends, so that the basin resembles an oval, rough in outline but true in form. A ship anchored in the centre of it would be completely hidden from the outside world; and Jacobson, with an eye to this and its other advantages, had chosen it wisely as an excellent place in which to get rid of his illicit cargo.

The *Sea Nymph* nosed in cautiously towards the cove on the night of the twenty-second. The moon had fully waned the night previously, and except for a scattered coast-light the gloom through which the ship moved was unrelieved.

It was just the night for the work ahead, as Douglas remarked jubilantly to Jacks. Luck, as he said, seemed to be with them.

The wind, which was unsettled and gusty, came veering off-shore more as they drew in to land. The ship, beating in under mainsail, foresail, and jib, picked up speed as the gusts, which now and then struck her, bellied her sails, and those on the lookout waited eagerly for a sight of the coast. That they were near, they knew, for there could be detected among the other sounds which reached their ears the dull, monotonous boom which denoted seas breaking against the upright cliffs. The crew, tense and excited, were all on deck. Douglas himself had the wheel, and the mate was in the waist of the ship. Rand was in the foretop, and Dick and the

136

cook were on the lookout for'ard of the windlass on the port side. The Portugee and Oscar and the brothers Welsh were at the sheets.

The cook, who had willingly left his pots and pans for the more interesting work going on above deck, peered keenly into the darkness through which the ship had to feel herself. He had exceptionally keen eyesight, and Douglas himself had ordered him to the bow. Twice he had thought he had detected land, only to be deceived. Dick, who was with him, and as impatient as any man on board for things to begin to happen, chaffed him mercilessly. The cook took it in good part. "You'd need stars for eyes," he grumbled. "I never seen a night like it. As black as mud. How we're goin' to get in that cove this night beats me. Now there!" he exclaimed, pointing ahead, "that's land, surely."

Dick could distinguish nothing more than what seemed an impenetrable black pit, and admitted his failure.

"If that's not land," said the cook, "I'll eat my own vittals. Still, we'll wait a minute to make sure."

He had hardly finished speaking when the shout of "Land ho!" rang out from the foretop crosstrees. Rand had caught sight of the mass seen by the cook.

"I knowed it!" exclaimed Cyrus, and echoed the cry.

Hard upon it followed the shout of "Hard a-lee!" Douglas spun the wheel and bawled out to the men to tackle the sheets. The ship, answering to her helm, came round like a top, shuddering from stem to stern as the sails flung the booms from side to side with reckless abandon. Fiercely resisting, they were sheeted home, the decks re-echoing to the confusion attendant upon the struggle.

Then, as suddenly as it began, the clamour ceased. The ship's sails filled, her spars creaked as the weight of the rigging fell upon them, and with an impatient leap she leaned forward on the starboard tack.

Dick and the cook, breathing quickly from their recent exertions, stood side by side staring shorewards. From aft came snatches of orders and admonitions shouted by Douglas to others of the crew. All wondered and waited, not knowing his plan of attack.

The coast became nearer. Five minutes after the ship tacked, the sound of breakers could be heard distinctly, and Cyrus, uneasy at the reckless way in which Douglas was driving the ship in, shouted a warning aft.

A reassuring shout answered him, and a moment later the mate's voice rang out.

"Make ready the boats."

"Dicky me lad, we're off," declared Cyrus. "Man, how he's shovin' her in. He's got the nerve of Old Harry."

The crew unlashed the boats, put oars and rowlocks in them, and set the whips, then, standing by, they waited further orders.

The ship was brought up in the eye of the wind, and with her sheets trimmed down tight, was kept jogging. She was so near the shore that her bowsprit seemed to be in the shadow of the headland looming up just distinguishable against the serried black clouds which massed the sky. When she had practically come to a standstill Douglas shouted out to Jacks to go ahead.

"Hoist 'em out, men," ordered the mate, and with practised speed the two boats were lowered over the rail and floated. The mate, with an eye to what might happen, ran below and came back with four shot-guns in his arms.

"Two in each, Bill," said Douglas, and the guns were placed in the bows of the boats.

Then, when the boats were completely ready, Douglas gave Jacks the wheel and stepped to the edge of the break-deck. "Line up, men," he ordered, and the crew went 'midships on the jump. Not the least enthusiastic of them but was impatient for the order that would send them leaping over the side. "Two miles inside is Jacobson's ship, men," began Douglas, giving a hitch to the waistband of his trousers, "and we've no time to lose if we're going to load two thousand before dawn. Now listen hard, for everything in this depends on every man doing the thing he's told. We'll leave the ship in boats, and row into the cove, creeping up on Jacobson from the leeward side. We'll board him bows and astern; the mate's boat will take the bows, mine will take the stern. The first thing we do on board is to settle the watch; the mate and Oscar will be the two men for that job, and no doubt they'll easy put 'em to sleep; I'll take any one I finds astern. While the watch is being attended to Rube will bar the fo'c'sle companion-way, and I'll fix the cabin. I've made up my mind that's the best way to manage things for all concerned. If there was open fighting some of us would be recognized, and we don't want that if we can help it. It would bring the harbour down on us, too; also it would take up precious time. Three good reasons. My idea is to make a clean job of it and to show a clean pair of heels. If we carries it out as I want to, Jacobson will be two thousand cases short tomorrow and none the wiser for it. Now mind this, men; there's too much depending on this night's work to disobey orders. We'll board her as I say, and the watch will be struck from behind; when the ship is taken I'll leave the mate in charge, and go and bring in the *Sea Nymph*. Do you follow me?"

"Ay."

"Are you ready?"

"Ay, ay, sir."

"Then fall out in order. To the mate's boat, Oscar, Rube, and Joe; to mine, Jim and Rand; cook, you and the boy will be left by the ship."

"Now, by this and that, skipper," burst forth the cook violently, "but I'd rather be boardin' with you. If there's a fight I wants to be in it." He stood before Douglas, his hook poised, his head bare, his legs spread, crouched into the semblance of a fighting attitude, as truculent a figure as ever confronted a man on his own quarter-deck.

"There'll be no fighting, cook," soothed Douglas, "for if there was there's no man I'd sooner have by me than you. But somebody's got to stick by the ship, and the two best suited to it to my mind is you and the boy."

"Orders is orders, skipper," said Cyrus, not trying to hide his disappointment, "and what you says goes. So the ship it is. But I'd give me other hand," he declared passionately, "to climb through the ratlines of the *Hopkins'* bowsprit."

"Well said, cook. Now there's no more time for talk.— Mate, give the wheel to the boy. — Cook. I'm trusting you with the ship. If anything goes wrong, fire a gun."

"Now men, to your boats, and before you gets over the rail, let every one of you take a belaying-pin with him."

The men obeyed, and then tumbled eagerly into the boats assigned to them. Douglas turned to give a last word to the cook. "Keep her jogging, Cyrus," he said; "and watch the wind; there's more of it in the weather. We'll get back to you as soon as we can."

"Jogging it is, sir," answered the cook, and watched Douglas go to the rail and lower himself over the side. There was a rattle of rowlocks as the boats pushed off. Then, "Give way men," sounded the order, and with a few smothered oaths, and a series of splashes as the oars hit the sea, the boats vanished.

Cyrus stared in the direction they had gone for a moment or so, then walked aft to where Dick, who also had not been able to hide his disappointment at being left behind, was leaning against the wheel.

"Well, here we is, Dicky me lad, done out of as pretty a piece of work as a man would wish to take a hand in," he said bitterly.

"We're doing our part here, I suppose," said Dick, who felt the responsibility left upon them.

"Ay, keepin' the old girl jogging. 'Tis ashore I'd wish to be; where there's men's work to be done and the chance of a crack or two."

"Do you think there'll be fighting, then?" asked Dick.

"No, I don't, for Black Douglas is a man as carries a job through the way he plans it. But there'll be a few heads cracked — and there might be more. Think of the moment of climbin' over the *Hopkins'* rails, not knowin' what's before you! A whisper, and the crew would be roused. Anything could happen. Now, curse me, but I could lay many a man by with this hook of mine."

He waved it ferociously in the air, so near Dick's face that the latter shrank back with a half-choked exclamation on his lips.

"Bloodthirsty, you'll think I am," went on the cook, as though the words had to come out of him, so wrought upon were his feelings. "Well, so 'tis. This thing has roused me. There's a power of red blood in me by the feel of it. Me father was a fightin' man. And would you believe it now if I was to tell you how I've seen him break a man's ribs with a hug of his arm? But so 'tis — as true as light. He were a big man, and me brothers turned after him. I was the smallest of the brood, though I'm but three inches under six feet, but not one of 'em ever cared to cross me. 'Twas my hair, they said, the blood of me mother, who was the daughter of Pat Shawn. And well 'tis known that an Irishman do not need inches to be the equal of any fighter livin'. Well, this is neither here nor there, and talk won't bring me any nearer to the ship they're boardin'."

"We'll be boarding her later on," said Dick.

"Ay, when her crew has all been laid by. Well, we've got a job here now to take care of the ship; and that's no light thing. There's work for our heads. But unless I misses my guess, there'll be work for this hook of mine, too, before we're done."

He walked the break-deck with a lurching gait, biting off a full two inches of black tobacco as he did so.

The ship rode fairly easily, although every now and then she shivered with apprehension as a gust of wind swept down upon her. Dick handled the wheel dexterously, preventing her startled attempts to break away from the jogging pace desired of her.

"How long do you think they'll be gone?" he asked the cook, as the work of controlling the ship became more difficult with every succeeding squall.

"Two miles to go and back. Say half-an-hour to board. A smart piece of work would be two hours, but they may be more or less," said Cyrus.

"Did you see the mate put guns in the boats?"

"I did; and a foolish thing it was," commented Cyrus, "for what good would they be on a job like that? But, then, they only took 'em in case Jacobson got on to what was happening and fired on them. One shot, and there would be old Neptune to pay."

"Would we hear it from here?"

"No, the wind is slantin' t' other way."

"There's more than there was," observed Dick, gazing anxiously at the short lop heaving against the swell rolling in to the land.

"And there'll be more," promised Cyrus. "Keep her full, Dicky me lad; but don't let her make any headway. We're near enough the land as it is."

The ship, like a fretting race-horse longing to be free to get away up the course, tossed her head and chafed under the inexorable hands which kept her facing the wind and impotent.

"She's getting a little uneasy. It's a big thing to trust two men to handle her a night like this," said Dick, wiping the flying spray from his cheek.

"It is," assented Cyrus; "and the one thing that takes the sting out of the skipper's orders. Shows he trusts us; and that's more than he does the others. Not that they couldn't sail her, but he wouldn't trust some of 'em alone on board with no one above them; and small blame to him. Black Douglas is no fool. It was a man as planned this night's work."

Dick handled the wheel, moved to a growing excitement, which was not a little due to the cook's attitude and his words. The little man was like a man drunk, with the thought of what was happening in the harbour. He paced the deck with hopping steps, stopping every now and then to saw the air with his hook, and Dick, as he gazed fascinated at the grotesque figure, whose grotesqueness was accentuated in such a wild setting, did not find it difficult to believe more than a little of the cook's own report of his fighting powers.

Away to the land sounded the surf beating against the cliffs, reverberating with a monotonous insistence that held a note of warning. Dick likened it to the sound of a distant drum. To starboard a light flickered like a star as some coastwise steamer ploughed her course. The waves broke against the ship's bow with numerous rippling sounds, which increased in depth as the wind heightened, and enfolding all was an atmosphere as tense as it was black and threatening. The blackness deepened as the sky, heavy with blown clouds, sagged lower, and Dick wondered as he eyed it what it held.

"Rain!" swore the cook, as a splash of water struck his freckled face, and he looked above him. "Ay, a black night it is," he exclaimed; "a fit night for this night's business. Now bend to it, you men ashore there," he shouted, shaking his fist in the direction of land, "bend to it, for, by the ghost of poor John Clifford, there's dirty weather brewin'!"

And, even as he spoke, the heavens thundered a mighty note, and Dick, leaning heavily against the straining wheel, felt the ship shudder from stem to stern as the baffling wind which accompanied the thunder struck her.

Boarders Away

The two boats, each propelled by four oars, found the mile or so to the mouth of the harbour a long pull. Only the foresight of Douglas kept it from being longer still; but when he hove up the *Sea Nymph* he had taken care that she should be to the windward of the cove. For although the wind was blowing straight over the land, the formation of Jackson's Cove made it sweep across it. As it was, the men had a hard pull, for the wind struck slanting-wise on the bows of the boats; and it was with relief that they brought the mouth of the harbour open.

Douglas, eyeing the channel with the thought of bringing the ship in through, realized that it would be nip and tuck, and that he would want good headway, for in the narrow passage the wind was slightly baffling.

Once inside, however, and she would be all right, as there was room enough and to spare if they had to tack. The sea surged along the bald, rocky sides of the channel as the boat pressed through. It was a dangerous gut, and no light guided approaching mariners. Under ordinary circumstances Douglas would never have contemplated entering such a place after night; but on this occasion, when risks were the natural order of things, he thought no more of it than to consider seriously just how it should be done.

Once through the channel, the boats were in quiet water. The wind, broken by the hills rising above the cove, did no more than ruffle the surface of the harbour. Ashore, a few lights gleamed solitarily, and half-way up the harbour, which ran deep, could be discerned one single, isolated light.

So dark was it, that the light seemed as if suspended in mid-air; but Douglas knew as well as if he had lit it himself that it hung from the jib-stay of a ship. He noted with satisfaction how far she lay from the lights which betokened the fishermen's cottages. There would be no danger of any one on shore hearing anything to rouse their suspicions, for the ship was to leeward, and there was sound enough from the rising wind and the uneasy sea outside to swallow up any that might accompany the work which lay before them.

Well inside the harbour he called out a low "avast" to his boat crew, and the mate, seeing the men back water, ordered his to do the same.

"Lay aboard, Bill," said Douglas softly, and the boats bumped gently as the order was carried out. "We'd best board her to leeward," he said; "every man roll a mitt about his oar and take care no sound comes from the rowlocks. Dip softly, and once aboard work fast. Let no man speak above a whisper in case he'd be recognized. Quick and silent is the word. Are you ready, men?"

"Ay," came the answer in guarded tones.

"Then give way."

The boats moved quickly towards the unsuspecting ship. As they drew nearer, the men in them could dimly discern her rigging and the lights in her cabin shining through the glass in the roof. No sound came from her. If there were men on watch they were sitting or standing still, for no one patrolled the deck. Douglas had no doubts of the ship being Jacobson's. No other was likely to anchor in that spot, and as they drew nearer the size of the ship convinced him that she was the one they sought.

A few hundred yards away from the object of their attack the boats separated, with a caution from Douglas to time their boarding. Then with grim faces and set muscles the men in each sent them quickly towards bows and stern, with soft silent strokes that made no more than a dripping sound that was lost in the music of the innumerable ripples of the wind-ruffled harbour.

One to the stern, one to the bow, the boats cautiously approached the low-lying ship, and no voice rang out in challenge. The mate, in the bows of his boat, caught the bobstay about the same time Douglas fended his off the rudder. Each discerned with satisfaction the name which told them that the ship they wanted loomed above them. Then with catlike movements, the men wriggled through the rigging.

As the mate climbed over the cathead, the droning sound of a man humming to himself came to his ears, and he held up his hand in warning to those behind him. From the decklight of the forecastle streamed a yellow glow, and the murmur of voices engaged in argument floated up through. Most of the crew at least were between decks. The man humming to himself so drowsily was, no doubt, the watch, and after a few moments of adjusting his sight to the darkness on deck, Jacks discovered him leaning against the foremast.

With motions to his men to beware of the betraying gleam of the riding light, he stepped forward, pulling at his belaying-pin. As he did so, Oscar, following orders, crept to the port side. The mate reached the man just as he stretched his arms, yawning, and as he was about to turn, struck him heavily, then lowered him softly to the deck. The whole procedure was carried out with no more noise than the dull thud of the hardwood coming into contact with the man's head, and with no fear that he should wake yet awhile, the mate left him and returned to his men, who were close behind him. "The fo'c'sle hatch, Rube," he whispered; "quick now, and no noise."

Rube slipped forward and the mate crept aft. Oscar had found no man on the port side. Together they reached the break-deck, and were abreast of the mainstays when Jacks clutched the Swede's arm. To both of them had come the sound of a dull thud and a grunt of surprise, then silence.

"The skipper," hissed the mate, far from laconic for once; "he's got the other one. To the fo'c'sle, now quick, Oscar, and shove on that decklight. I'll help the skipper bar the cabin. Come with me, Joe."

In less than a minute he reached Douglas's side, just calling out in time to prevent himself from being brained by a belaying-pin. "It's Bill. All's well for'ard, skipper," he said.

"Dark. Thought you was one of the crew. Just one man aft; I got him. Jim is hooking up the cabin now. There'll be Old Harry to pay in a minute."

Almost instantaneously the ship awoke. Muffled cries and the sounds of overturned furniture reached their ears.

"That's them!" exclaimed Douglas. "The shutters have been drawn. By the seven plagues, Bill, the ship is took! For'ard with you and nail them down. Listen," he added, "do you hear it?"

A voice, roaring like a bull, came from the direction of the cabin.

"Jacobson," he gloated. "Nail them down, Bill; nail them down. Smart's the word," he said.

The whole ship was soon resounding to hurrying feet above and below decks. Obeying orders, Douglas's crew did not speak above a whisper, but, except for that caution, they gave free vent to their activities and their feelings, throwing off the restraint of guarded movements now that it was no longer necessary. Below decks, pandemonium was breaking loose. In the cabin Jacobson and his mate had gone mad with rage. Not knowing what had happened— if it was piracy or mutiny that was going on— they were demolishing the cabin furniture in a futile endeavour to break out through the shutters.

Finding their energies wasted on the solid oak shutter and doors, one of them turned his attention to the glass house which gave light to the cabin in whose roof it was set. He swung a chair against it, and there was a crash of glass. Douglas heard the first blow, and, realizing the danger, ordered the house to be covered with canvas, pump handles, and capstan bars. To make sure this could not be moved, a small stream anchor and chain were put on the top of it. So effectually were those below then imprisoned that even their cries were smothered.

For'ard the work had progressed to the same extent. Rube had drawn the shutter of the forecastle and barred it, while Oscar had put the decklight covering on and weighted it down with the greater part of a shackle of chain.

And fifteen minutes after the first men of the boarding-crew had stepped on *Hopkins'* deck, the ship was in their hands.

Douglas, exultant at the ease of the capture, gave a word to the crew, then summoned the mate aft. "I'm leaving you in charge, Bill. I'm off for the *Sea Nymph* at once. By the Lord Harry a pretty piece of work. Keep a man at the fo'c'sle companion-way and a man at the cabin with a belaying-pin each in their hands. Give me Oscar and the Portugee; and whatever you does, Bill, don't let a man get his head above deck. Have the hatches off ready for our coming, and when you sees our lights run up to you, stand by to take our warp. Now good luck to you; and let no man speak louder than necessary."

He leaned over the taffrail and pulled the boat up to the side with a powerful jerk of his arm. It was in moments like this that he showed to advantage. He was a tower of strength, and possessed the driving energy of a dozen men. His influence was magnetic. The men jumped at his orders almost before they were out of his mouth.

Rain and wind struck the ship suddenly, and he spat in disgust. "I expected something like this, Bill!" he exclaimed. "Well, there's one thing; nobody but ourselves will be movin' about to-night."

"It's going to be quite a job gettin' the *Sea Nymph* in," said Jacks. "Do you think you've got men enough to work her, skipper? Say the word, and I'll guard this one myself."

147

"Men enough and to spare," declared Douglas. "I could bring her through anything to-night. Watch out your oars, Joe; stand by to shove off. All clear."

He waved a hand to Jacks, and settled himself in the stern sheets of the boat as she quickly left the *Hopkins* behind. Rain and tobacco juice ran down his beard together, while he leaned forward and urged the two men with him to put their backs into it.

They needed little coaxing to do that, and half backed by the wind, the boat sped swiftly towards the mouth of the harbour.

The Swede and the Portugee, like an elephant and a gnat, pulled in unison. The boat slipped through the channel and out into the open sea.

There the going became a little more difficult. The difficulties increased as the harbour was left behind. Once far enough away from the shelter of the cliffs, and the wind swept down upon the boat with a violent swirl that flung her seawards on the top of a wave which threatened to fill her. After the first surprising gust they righted her, and settled down to the struggle which had suddenly material-ized. For although the boat was being swept to sea, it was not in the direction they wanted to go.

The Swede, who was rowing stroke, put on an enormous spurt and forced the boat's bows towards the point where the distant lights of the *Sea Nymph* rose and fell to the heaving of the ship.

Douglas, at the tiller ropes, became seriously anxious as he noted that they would have all they could do to reach the ship. For it had suddenly dawned upon him that she lay a mile or so nearly to windward. He exhorted the rowers to put their whole weight into their efforts, and leaned forward in the boat as though by sheer strength of will he would force her ahead in spite of the continuous onslaught of the wind. The slowness of their progress exasperated him. Time was precious. His orders became tinged with impatience, although he knew the men were doing all they could. Instead of increasing speed, the boat lost progress. He could tell from the lights which he used as a mark that the boat was practically making no headway at all. Unable to contain his impatience, and not a little alarmed, he took the oar from Joe, and told the Portuguese to steer; then he threw himself upon the oar until it bent like a whip under the strain he put upon it. Oscar pulled against him, and, between them, they forced headway on the boat. Encouraged by this, they both redoubled their efforts. Douglas, who had been assailed by a sudden fear that they might not be able to reach the ship, grunted in relief. If they could keep the boat going, and get a little more to windward, they would make it. They had to make it! He increased the pace of his stroke as he remembered how valuable every moment was. He should have taken more men. Yet Jacks needed them there, too, in case the *Hopkins'* crew got loose. There was nothing to do but make the best of it.

He shouted continually, calling upon himself and Oscar to pull. The wind seemed to laugh at their efforts. All the straining of their mighty limbs went for nothing. The progress made was disheartening, and Douglas, tormented by a dozen reasons for the necessity of speed, worked himself up into a kind of frenzy. So enormous was the strain he put upon the oar that what happened was inevitable— it broke. He gave an alarmed shout that was echoed by the others, and while he tugged at another oar lying near him, the boat was swept back. Casting a swift look towards the *Sea Nymph's* lights he realized they had lost all they had gained, and more.

He put out another oar and literally threw himself upon it. "Oscar — Joe," he shouted above the wind; "must — make it...."

They responded to the best of their ability. Joe left the tiller and added his weight to the Swede's oar. The wind, however, as if to show that hitherto it had been merely playing, swept down in such ferocious gusts that it threatened to tear the oars out of the men's hands, and made it almost impossible for them to control them when they broke water.

The result was the boat was steadily driven back. Despite herculean efforts the lights of the ship, instead of drawing nearer, receded. Douglas, realizing the situation, and stubbornly refusing to acknowledge the futility of their efforts, struggled with a titanic energy to extricate himself and his men from the danger which now fully beset them. A danger, he knew, which threatened to make as naught all the success which had so far attended that night's business.

In a paroxysm of effort his second oar broke. The force of the stroke carried him to the bottom of the boat. He got up, his mouth filled with water, and his heart with rage.

"Put—out—oar," he told Joe, "and pull, man, pull."

The Portugee, as much afraid of Douglas as of the danger resulting from their position, sprang to the oar.

"I'm—going—signal—ship," explained Douglas, beating down the wind by sheer weight of his voice.

He drew a box of matches from his pocket and tore away part of his inside clothing. It refused to do anything but smoulder. He then tried a corner of an oilskin jacket, but the damp with which it was saturated prevented its burning. He spent the whole box of matches in a desperate effort. The men, struggling ineffectually to prevent the boat from being driven back, watched him, and as the effort failed, lifted their voices in an absurd attempt to hail the ship. Douglas joined his shouts to theirs, but the wind snatched up the sound, and before it had penetrated beyond the length of the boat, flung it back brutally in their faces.

The hopelessness of the attempt was impressed upon them. They fell silent, pulling doggedly at the oars. Douglas stood erect in the rocking boat, his beard parted by the wind, his fists clenched, at a loss for the moment how to act.

He realized that not only were they being swept away from the ship, but off shore. Soon they would have difficulty even to reach the harbour. To persist in trying to get aboard the ship with two oars was useless. They must go back and get more help. The delay this would cause might very well mean the total failure of the night's work. At that thought a great rage filled him. To a man of his great physical strength that sense of impotence in the face of an opposing force was intolerable. He shook his fist in the air as though defying the worst the heavens could launch down upon him. Then he sank back on a thwart. Something must be done, and he was about to give an order to turn the boat's head in the direction of the harbour when his hand touched metal. "The guns!" he shouted, and remembered how the mate had placed two in each boat. Swiftly he hauled one out. With half a prayer that the powder and cap had not been damped, he stood erect in the boat. Holding the gun away from him, he pulled the trigger. The powder had miraculously remained dry. It ignited, and a terrific explosion shook the boat. The sound of it, like that of their own voices, penetrated the night a little, then was thrown back in their faces. But a sheet of flame had been emitted from the barrel, and Douglas hoped that it might have caught the eye of Dick or the cook. "They'll be on the lookout, surely," he shouted to his men; "I'll try the other. If that fails, may I burn for ever. I should have taken more men."

He waited a little while to see if the *Sea Nymph's* lights would approach them, and as they remained stationary, he stood erect to make the last desperate attempt. Holding the gun off from him as before, he pulled the trigger. Nothing happened. He pulled it again; the cap exploded, but the powder failed to ignite.

With a cry of rage and disappointment he brought the gun down across the gunwale of the boat, splintering the stock into pieces, and while the men cowed under the weight of the curses he put upon his own carelessness and oversight, he stood in the boat and shook an impotent fist in the face of the storm.

By that time the boat had been swept back so far that even to make the harbour was practically a hopeless task. The *Sea Nymph's* lights sank lower, despite the frantic tugging at the oars, and the wind, flinging Black Douglas's oaths back in his face with insolent contempt, swooped down upon the boat in earnest, raising its voice in a note of vengeful triumph.

On Board the Sea Nymph

When the first rumbling note of thunder sounded, Dick and the cook became seriously anxious: Dick for the ship; the cook for the success of the night's business.

The ship had all her lower sails set, and despite the fact that they were barely drawing, the force of the wind was such that the spars creaked under the strain. It was no longer possible to keep her quietly jogging. She plunged ahead and drifted, alternately, Dick trying his best, with the aid of Cyrus, to keep her as much as possible in the position Douglas had left her.

To ride quietly, she needed to be stripped of at least half her canvas. They dared not lower, however, not knowing what moment Douglas might appear. And when he did come they knew he would not want to waste valuable time in putting sail on the ship in order to beat into the harbour. Therefore they were determined to keep everything standing as long as the ship would ride under it.

Dick, because of his two sound hands, handled the wheel, while Cyrus stood by, telling him when to ease on it and when to keep the ship from getting her head.

It was a lively task which, as rain and wind increased, took all their time. A deep swell began to heave in against the wind; a sure sign, as Cyrus said, of trouble outside. And what with the roll of the swell and the wind lop breaking against it, the sea soon became a white sheet, which every now and then wrapped them in its damp folds. The wind caught up the water in swirling eddies which vanished in wraithlike mists. The ship began to take on a washed appearance, and it seemed positively dangerous for a boat to attempt to board her.

Cyrus and Dick, in oilskins which reflected the gleam of the binnacle light, noted with growing anxiety the turbulence of the sea.

"If they don't come soon," declared the cook, "they'll never get the ship through that channel this night."

"Two hours you said they needed," shouted Dick, shaking the rain out of the brim of his sou'wester.

"'Tis not what they need," bawled the cook in answer, "'tis what they have to do. There's more'n a dirty note in that wind. Ease her a bit....Enough sea now to swamp a skiff, let alone a row boat. I wish they'd hurry up and come. We'll be lucky if there's not a black ending to this night's work."

He drew the back of his hand across his sea-and-rain spattered face.

"Don't you think we ought to take the mainsail off her," urged Dick, as with difficulty he kept the ship's bowsprit facing the white-capped waves. "I can't keep her from making headway— or drifting."

"Keep her as steady as you can. The mainsail stays on her. When the boat comes the skipper will be wantin' to get through that channel as fast as old Neptune will let him."

"She won't be able to carry her mainsail in this wind."

"She'll carry it or it'll blow off her. Black Douglas is no yachting skipper.

"Don't let her get too full, Dicky me lad. By the father who made me, 'tis time they was comin'."

The full booming roar of the wind and sea punctuated the cook's exclamation. "Do you think there's anything gone wrong?" questioned Dick, shouting to make himself heard.

"Who can tell? But by this and that I wouldn't be surprised."

"What will we do if they don't come?"

"We'll run her in!"

"What, through the channel?"

"Ay, through the channel; and if ever you handled a wheel in your life you'll have to handle it then."

"Listen! Did you hear anything?"

The cook turned eagerly upon Dick, and they both cupped their hands to their ears. It was impossible, however, to detect anything but the noises created by the commotion of wind, rain, and sea. "Did you hear anything, Dicky?"

"Nothing."

"Why, it sounded as if it was aboard. Are you sure you heard nothin'?"

"Not a thing."

"It passes me! There 'tis again! Did ye hear, then?" The cook leaned his wet face near Dick's mouth to catch the answer.

Dick simply shook his head, his forehand wrinkled in the attempt to catch the sound the cook had heard.

"Then 'twas for me alone," exclaimed Cyrus, excitedly. "Dicky me lad, there's a death in this, or a man in need of help."

"What do you mean?" yelled Dick, awed by the intensity of the cook's voice.

Cyrus sheltered the sound of his own voice with his hand.

"That call. It come to me before, and always there was reasons for it. Me father heard me brother cryin' for help when he was drownin', and they a hundred miles apart. And once me brother was kept awake all night by a voice askin' him for help. He didn't answer, thinkin' he was dreamin', and the next morning they found me uncle's boat empty on the beach. And twice I've heard it. Once when me father was drowned, and once when a Placentia Bay fisherman was adrift on the Grand Banks. The first time I couldn't answer. The second time I left me ship in the middle of the night and rowed straight to where I'd heard the voice call, and it was dark as pitch; and when I got there I found a dory with a man in the bottom of it. He'd lost his dory-mate overboard, and been drifting three days without food or water. I brought him to me ship, and he lived. It's a thing as runs in our family. Look!"

He jerked Dick's arm excitedly, pointing seawards.

Dick saw out of the corner of his eye a flash of light flame to the starboard of the ship and just a little to the leeward.

"Lightning!" he exclaimed.

"Not it," declared the cook; "that light went up, not down. I'll stake my good hand 'tis our boat in trouble."

For a moment they stood staring intently.

"Our boat?" repeated Dick, as the light failed to reappear.

154

"Ay, I'm sure of it. Dicky me lad, stand by to ease her off."

Dick heard him with incredulous dismay.

"What are you going to do?" he gasped.

"Go down and pick up whoever is in that boat."

"We can never do that alone," protested Dick.

"We'll do it or sink."

"Suppose there's no boat there?"

"I'll take the risk. Stand by!"

Dick, swayed by the cook's certainty, eased over the wheel with a feeling that in doing so he was heading the ship for sure destruction. It seemed impossible that two men could handle her in such a storm.

Freed at last from the maddening necessity of riding futilely in the face of the wind, she fell away with a dizzying rush.

"Slack off the sheets, quick," implored Dick, for the ship, sheeted down, was pressed half under water. Keeping his feet with difficulty he hung on to the wheel, the seas swirling to his knees. He brought the wind more abeam, and she broke water a little.

"Steer for where we seen the light," bawled the cook, and tore frenziedly at the mainsheet. He eased off the mainsail, and the *Sea Nymph*, feeling the force of the wind against the big bellying sail, lowered her head and leaped forward like a mad thing.

Dick struggled for breath, half-smothered by gusts of wind and flying spray. The seas broke over the ship amidships, and, running aft, embraced his limbs to the thighs, sucking at his feet till he had to cling to the spokes of the jerking wheel for support.

He steered blindly for where he thought the light had appeared. The cook, having slacked off the foresail and jibs, ran to the bows, where he stood perilously, his steel hook fastened to the rigging, his hand cupped to his ear. The ship staggered drunkenly, and sunk her lee rail till she was awash to the hatches, and Dick, with a swelling heart, waited for the spars to go by the board.

"No sticks can stand it," he groaned in apprehension, and watched the mainmast bend like a carter's whip. He felt suddenly his youth and inexperience. The ship, he knew was but half under control, and the thought of his responsibility made him exaggerate her very real danger. "We're mad," he gasped, and knew something of fear as the wind threatened to throw the ship out on her beams ends. "If she goes over, she'll never right herself," he thought, and wondered what it would be like to drown in the dark.

He saw the cook in the gleam of the riding light suddenly wave his hand, then come running aft. "Port your helm a little — quick! A boat to starboard," he screamed in Dick's ear, and sawed the air with his hook.

Dick twisted the spokes of the wheel, and as he did so he heard a faint human sound in the midst of all that thunderous clamour. The *Sea Nymph* rushed high on the top of a wave, and the cry was lost.

"I knowed it," screamed the cook triumphantly. "Our boat, for sure. Get to the leeward of them so they can drift down on us. Never mind about the spars."

The ship rushed through the water with the wanton speed of a bullet.

"In the name of God don't run them down!" came Cyrus's cry. "They're adrift!"

Dick by this time was working the wheel like a man inspired. His arms ached with the strain, but otherwise he was proving himself more than equal to the occasion. So imperative was the need of quick, decided action, that any doubts as to his ability to cope with the emergency left him. His nerves suddenly became as hardened as any old salt's. He followed the cook's instructions with minute accuracy, never faltering, though at times the orders threatened to bring disaster upon them all. Guided by the shouts, which began to be heard more plainly, he let the ship fall away a bit, and ran her nearly before the wind.

"Stand by to come about," shouted the cook. "They're well to windward now....Easy does it....Look out, look out — the booms!"

Dick gasped, and, as the ship rounded, ducked the murderous plunges of the main boom. The *Sea Nymph*, like a diver emerging from a header into deep water, came up shuddering in every beam. Her sails tore at the booms and the racks until they threatened to dismast her, or split her apart. Cyrus made no attempt to take in sheet. It was impossible for one man to think of doing it.

"She can never stand it," shouted Dick, and heard his cry wiped from his lips as if it had never been.

"Ship ahoy!" came a voice, and Cyrus flung out a booming answer.

"Stand by — catch our painter," came the voice, which they now recognized as Douglas's. "Port side — hurry!"

The cook ran aft of the mainstays. A rope came whizzing over the rail. He fell upon it, and Dick, leaving the wheel temporarily, went to his aid.

It was well he did so, for the rope went taut with the strain of the heavy boat, and they had difficulty in holding it. Two hitches, however, and she was made fast. Dick ran back to the wheel. The boat lay aboard, rising level to the rail as a sea thrust her upwards. Then on to the deck clambered Douglas and the two men with him.

Recovering his feet with a staggering motion that adjusted his own movements to those of the ship, he blasphemed with the relief of a man freed from a great fear. His first thought, after a word to Cyrus, was for the ship beating herself to pieces.

"Just in time, cook," he gasped. "Thought 'twas all up — oars broke — wind — swept back — fired a gun — thought you didn't see — smart piece of work of yours —"

He broke off and rushed towards a swinging boom. "Hold those sheets, men," he ordered, beginning the dangerous work himself. "Take in your slack. Give me a hand, cook, then take the bow."

In five minutes the booms were tamed and the sails sheeted home.

Douglas ran aft to the wheel. "Get for'ard, young un'," he shouted. "No time to talk now. Won't forget this night's work."

Dick released the wheel and ran for'ard, helped there by a congratulatory thump on the back that sent him staggering to the edge of the break-deck.

"Station your stays," rang out Douglas's voice behind him, and he made for the jib.

The ship fell away and, once more awash to the hatches, leapt towards the harbour entrance, lying almost in the wind.

Dick found himself by the side of the cook, clinging desperately to a cat-head drenched by the spray flung off the bows. His body was afire to his finger tips. Cold, wind, rain — nothing could now damp his spirits. "We did it," he gasped to the cook, as if unable to believe the extent of their accomplishment.

"'Tis proud I am. Did ye hear him — what a man!" Cyrus's voice came in snatches. "He's goin' to run her in under full sail. 'Twill be nip an' tuck. She may lie through— she may not. Stick to your sheet— anything happens, keep your head— all too easy to drown."

"How is he going to find the channel?" Dick fairly spat out his words in an attempt to be heard.

"God knows! He'll feel it likely. He can sail with his eyes shut; another skipper would want two pairs. Breakers— port bow— hear them?"

Dick did. It was easy enough soon to detect the menacing rumble of the surf against the perpendicular cliffs. It grew in violence as the ship drew in. All that could be seen in front was a black void, and where the sea ended and land began no man could say.

A shout came from aft for the cook, and Cyrus made his way there. In a moment or two he was back. "He's not sure of the lay of the land," he told Dick, shouting close to the latter's ear. "Watch for a break in the black ahead. Your eyes may save your life."

He ran to the bowsprit — no man moved slowly on board the *Sea Nymph* that night — and, disdaining a rope offered him by the Portugee, made his way out to the very end of the tapering stick. At times he was shut from sight by clouds of spray, and Dick trembled for the man's life as he saw him disappear time after time as the bowsprit dipped; then he would come to view, still clinging tenaciously to the big jib-stay.

As the ship ran in, the water smoothed a little, but the wind came over the headland as if tumbling from a heaven-pitched cloud.

Cyrus crawled back to the deck and grasped Dick's arm. "Look right ahead. Do you see anything?"

"It's not as black there as on the port and starboard of it."

"I knowed it. 'Tis the channel. — Steady your helm," he called out, and Douglas obeyed; then Cyrus made his way aft. "The channel's right ahead, skipper. She's making dead for it. Will you shove her through, or will we tack?"

"Will she lie in, think you?" asked Douglas, leaning over the wheel.

"There's a chance."

"Then we'll take it. A tack would lose us half-an-hour. To the bow and give the course."

The cook sped away.

"Station your stays, men all. Stand by to run her in, and watch your halyards and sheets."

"Port!" sang out the cook, and the ship ran her head towards what looked like an unbroken line of breakers.

"Port it is."

"Steady all."

"Steady all."

"Starboard a little."

"A little it is."

Dick saw an opening suddenly appear ahead. As the ship shot into it two walls of gloom rose up swiftly on either side. A fathom or so to starboard waves were thundering against an upright cliff. The wind ceased suddenly, then with a roar came baffling. The alarmed shouts of those on board for a moment beat down the tumult about them. The ship fell away a little, and Dick, his heart in his mouth, waited for her to swerve and strike. Then the wind filled her sails again. She steadied in her stride, and with a last shuddering leap shot through into the comparative calm and safety of the harbour.

A ringing cry of triumph came from aft, then a moment later orders followed fast and furious.

"Lower your mainsail — slack the foresail sheet — jibs away— get ready a line — the boat...."

Each man tried to do a dozen things at once. The ship swiftly made her way into the centre of the harbour.

"Lower your foresail — and jumbo — douse everything — lower all, lower all," shouted Douglas frantically as the ship threatened to overshoot the *Hopkins'* berth, and the remaining sails came down with a destructive rush.

Douglas swung over the wheel, and with a skill amounting to genius manoeuvred the *Sea Nymph* within rope's-throw of Jacobson's ship. Ready hands seized the warp thrown and drew the two ships together. The *Sea Nymph* took the *Hopkins'* fenders, checked, backed a little, then came to a stop, and Douglas, expressing his relief and triumph in gratefully-voiced oaths, sprang on to the boarded ship's deck.

Under Cover of Darkness

The first thing Douglas did when he stepped on the *Hopkins'* deck was to look round for Jacks. "Where's the mate?" he demanded of Rube, when Jacks failed to meet him.

"In the hold, sir," came the answer.

"Is everything all right?"

"'Tis, and 'tis not."

"What do you mean?"

"Jacobson and his mate started to chop their way out of the cabin through the bulkhead. The mate and Jim went down into the hold to stop 'em. Barricaded the bulkhead with whisky. While they was doin' it Jacobson fired through the bulkhead."

Douglas gave vent to an exclamation. "Anybody hurt?" he asked anxiously.

"The mate got a nip in the arm. Nothing much."

Douglas, slightly taken aback at this news, turned to the *Sea Nymph*, where the cook and Dick, with Oscar and Joe, were waiting orders. "Tie her up close and get the hatches off," he told them, then made his way to the after-hatch of the *Hopkins* and dropped down into the hold. A lanthorn revealed Jacks and Jim sweating at shifting cases of whisky. "What's up, Bill?" he asked.

"There was old Neptune to pay for a while," informed Jacks. "Jacobson tried to get through the cabin bulkhead; but we fixed him. He'll never get through now."

"Is the fo'c'sle all right?"

"Yes. First thing I did was to make sure of that. I knowed they was the most dangerous. They managed to shove the deck-light off, and one of them got his head up through. Rube cracks it for him, and there ain't been a whimper out of them since. They're beat."

"Nearly got blowed to sea myself," said Douglas, stopping to draw his hand down his whisker. "Broke our oars. As it happened, we had the guns on board. I managed to fire off one of them, and the cook and the boy saw us. They brought the ship down and picked us up. A smart piece of work. It was a near thing, though. Thought it was all up with us for a while." He sighed in relief.

"Well, you pulled through," said the mate.

"Ay. Now, on deck, Bill, and get after the crew. There's work, and plenty of it, ahead of us."

They scrambled on deck. In the light of the lanthorn Douglas noted a stream of blood running down Jacks' arm. "You're hurt, Bill," he stated.

"No. Just a scratch. Bleeds a lot, but it don't run deep."

"Well, tie it up, man. I don't want you weakened yet. Ahoy aboard the *Sea Nymph*!'

"Ay, ay, sir."

"All hands lay aboard the *Hopkins*."

The cook, Dick, Joe, and Oscar climbed over the rail and grouped themselves with Rube, Rand, and Jim.

Douglas spoke to them in terse, jerky sentences, which revealed the desire for haste that gripped him. "Oscar and Rand and Jim will go in the hold of the *Hopkins*. The mate and Rube will stay on deck and pass to me. Joe, the cook, and the boy will go in the hold of the *Sea Nymph* and stow. Smart's the word. And no talkin'. Save your breath for working. Every hour or so the cook will brace us up with a ration of rum. Now then, set to it, men. There's all too little time ahead of us."

The crew went to the places assigned to them, and the gruelling work of shifting the cargo began.

Under the cover of darkness case after case went over the *Hopkins'* rail and onto the *Sea Nymph's* deck, and Douglas, doing the work of three men, passed it down into the hold.

The rain and wind kept up their terrific clamour, cloaking the sounds which went up from the work. The imprisoned crew, having tired themselves out in shouting and struggling for freedom, lapsed into hopeless silence and inaction.

Nothing interrupted the boarding crew, and the work progressed without pause, and at a mighty pace. The four giants — Douglas, the mate, Rand, and Oscar — swung case after case into the hands waiting for them with scarce a quiver of their muscles. But the others sweated under the continuous strain. A high note of excitement gave them added strength, however, and Dick, to whom regular exercise was more familiar than hard manual labour, forgot his aching arms and back in the thoughts engendered by his position, and the daring thing he was helping to accomplish.

In the *Sea Nymph's* hold two tall flares lit up the scene of labour, throwing gigantic shadows of the workers upon the ship's sides and

162

deck beams. The cook, whose hook was doing yeomen service, spoke little, and when he did it was to the point.

The Portugee groaned something about a thirst every hour or so, and then Cyrus would climb quickly on deck and return a little later with a pannikin of rum. Dick refused it each time, but the third time it was forced upon him.

"You're nearly all in. It's harmless, and will put strength into you," persuaded the cook, and Dick, who felt as exhausted as if finishing a cross-country race, gulped down the stinging fluid without further ado. Choking, gasping, at the contact of the burning liquor, he staggered back to his work, feeling a glow of warmth as strength returned to his limbs. Then the work went on. The hold began to fill appreciably. One hundred, two hundred. Each man, as case after case passed through his hands, counted them aloud; and Douglas, through whose hands every case passed, gave vent to characteristic exclamations every time he added another century to the figures he carried in his mind.

If ever his enormous strength and staying power served him well, it did so that night. Standing like some herculean figure of mythological fame, legs well apart, chest thrown out, fists cupped, he caught the cases as they were thrown to him; and not once did he stagger, though hours passed and neither the weight nor the number of the cases lessened. Head bare, sleeves rolled to the elbow, his shirt open at a hairy chest that steamed in the rain, he laboured mightily, shouting encouraging words to those under him, and each time the pannikin was passed to him he drained it.

The mate, whose arm had stopped bleeding, worked side by side with Rube, who struggled to emulate his superior's endurance. And down in the hold Oscar, with a perpetual grin on his great high-boned face, laughed softly as he watched Jim groan, and Rand sweat, as they handed him the cases which, with a machine-like swing of his arms, he threw to the mate and Rube on deck.

"Twelve hundred cases. Put your backs into it, men. Mother of mercy — how it blows!"

The wind howled through the rigging of the ships which chafed against each other restlessly, and Douglas's words ran swiftly on the wings of it.

The mate called down to Oscar and the others in the *Hopkins'* hold, repeating the skipper's words.

Douglas, sliding case after case down the planks which led to the *Sea Nymph's* hold, cheered on Dick and the cook. "Keep it up, boys; keep it up. Stow well but fast. There's twelve hundred aboard. Be careful of the shifting boards, cook."

"Ay, ay, sir," came the answer in gasps, and Cyrus clucked his tongue in his cheek as he passed the words on to Joe.

Hour after hour passed. Midnight went by with none of that calm usual to it. Instead, the scene grew wilder. The ships rolled uneasily, and the lyre-like response of their rigging to the wind sounded mournfully, like a multitude of women wailing.

"Two hours to the dawn, men. Sunrise must see us out of this. Stick to it."

As the others' energy flagged, that of Douglas seemed to increase. Dick, weary and half-blinded with fatigue, barked his knuckles against the clumsy square boxes, and licked the blood from them as a cat licks milk.

"Two hours to the dawn, is it?" groaned the cook; "will there ever be a dawn this day?"

"Fifteen hundred," came the skipper's voice.

"Praise be!' exclaimed the cook devoutly. "Dicky me lad," he added, "pass the pannikin.— Joe ease your back and drink."

The Portugee, nothing loath, drank greedily, and the cook followed suit. Dick passed it by. One drink of that breath-taking stuff had been more than enough for him.

"The wind, she blow," said Joe.

"Aye, a storm."

"Too much to sail, yes?"

"There is. But you heard what the skipper said. This is no place for us once daylight comes."

"I no like it."

"You wouldn't. Pass that planking, Dicky. She'll need shifting boards in plenty when she gets outside."

Dick obeyed, a feeling of apprehension coming over him at the cook's words, which he saw were given voice to with more than usual seriousness.

The note the storm struck was one to quicken the pulse and stir one to a sense of impending disaster. Threatening was the word to describe it. He suddenly realized that the adventure they were engaged upon was more than a romantic episode. There was a grim, realistic side to it. He remembered what the weather had been like outside a few hours before, and knew that the situation had grown worse instead of better. He felt assured from the cook's attitude that to head the *Sea Nymph* out to sea in such a gale was a proceeding which was fraught with a very real danger, and he sought to discover within himself any fear of what might happen. Fear there was not, he decided relievedly, but apprehension—yes. Yet despite it he could thrill to the thought of the impending combat.

There came a stop in the cases descending into the hold, and Douglas's head appeared in the hatchway. "Hold your wind, boys," he said, and disappeared.

Dick lay on his back and listened to the sound of hurried feet overhead. Some note in them made him feel as if every step was a blow upon his heart.

"This is a hard night's work for you, Dicky me lad," said Cyrus, eyeing him solicitously, "and I could wish you could have a spell when we gets outside, but to my mind there's harder work than any of this ahead of us, once we gets to sea."

"I can stand it," said Dick, sitting erect. The doubt of his ability to do so touched that pride which had grown with the recent possession of his manhood.

"Ay, perhaps. All the same— "

The cook did not finish his sentence, but turned over his chew of tobacco and spat voluminously. "What's doing overhead, I wonder?" he said.

Douglas had gone on board the *Hopkins*.

"There's eighteen hundred aboard, Bill," he told the mate.

"Good."

"Dawn will be here soon. We'll take two hundred more. We won't be able to take the lot."

"There'll be but five hundred left."

"Or less. Two thousand, however, is old Dagore's right, and we'll take that suppose the sun is a mile high by the time we does it."

"There'll be no sun this day," bawled the mate, his voice rising with a gust of wind.

"There won't," agreed Douglas, "but there'll be a dawn. Pass the word into the hold. Two hundred more, and hurry it."

The mate did so, and in a few moments the work went on again. I tended when the first suspicion of approaching day lightened the gloom about them.

Douglas, counting aloud the last one as it passed through his hands, voiced his relief. "All hands on deck," he ordered, and the men, pulling themselves together, obeyed willingly.

"Get your hatches on, men. Lay aboard here, all of you.— Bill, what about Jacobson and his lot? No chance of them gettin' free too soon?"

"Not one. They're safe enough till someone comes aboard from the Cove and finds them. And if they do get out before, they'll never follow us. Jacobson wouldn't leave harbour in weather like this."

"'Tis a bit rough outside, Bill," said Douglas eyeing the sky.

"It is. Any other time a man would do better to stay where his anchors hold. But we've got no choice."

"That's so. And the quicker we gets away out of here now the better. Put the foresail on her, Bill, but double reef it first. Do you think that jib will stand the strain of taking her through the channel?"

"I think it will. But it won't last long outside."

"It can blow off her then, and be diddled to it. So long as we gets far enough off to find sea room, I don't care."

"We'll get there quick enough."

"Ay, the wind's off shore. It'll be bare poles before long. Well, set to. Get after the crew, Bill."

The mate made for'ard and Douglas went aft, where he donned a jacket and sou'wester, then took the wheel. The double-reefed foresail was set, every man putting his hand to the work as though fresh from an all night's rest. Dick, to whom a reefed sail was no mystery, stood by. And when the time came for hoisting it, he put his weight on the halyards with the rest of those there, and smothered the graver feelings which accompanied the excitement aroused by the forecasting of danger.

The gloom lightened enough for the channel to be dimly discernible. A glimpse of breaking seas was possible now and then. The set foresail strained and beat its reef ropes in the wind.

"Cast off!" The order came like the flick of a whip, and the ropes which had held the *Sea Nymph* bound were released.

She backed and fell away.

"Up with your jib!"

The head-sail went rapidly into place. As it filled, the ship sunk her head into the water and darted for the channel.

"Station your stays, men all. Watch your sheets and stand by to tackle baffling winds," warned Douglas, and the *Sea Nymph* scudded with frantic haste towards the boiling seas that fringed the narrow entrance to the harbour.

The walls of the channel shot up precipitously on either side. Without a falter the ship lunged through. Out upon the wind-flattened sea near shore she swept like a homing pigeon. Then she struck rough water, staggered at the impact of tumultuous boarding seas, leaped frantically, recovered, and became as a bit of flying spray upon the wings of the storm.

FRANK PARKER DAY

Frank Parker Day was born at Shubenacadie, Nova Scotia in 1881. After attending the Pictou Academy, he worked briefly in the inshore fishery and taught school before pursuing his studies at Mount Allison University, Oxford University, and the University of Berlin. From 1909 to 1912, he was a professor of English at the University of New Brunswick. He then moved to the United States and took a position at the Carnegie Institute in Pittsburgh. During the First World War, he served as an officer in the Canadian infantry, eventually assuming command of the 25th Overseas Battalion. After the war, he resumed his career in Pittsburgh and later taught at Swarthmore College. In 1928 he was appointed president of Union College in Shenectady, New York. During the late 1920s, he became increasingly active as a writer, contributing to a variety of periodicals and publishing three novels and Autobiography of a Fisherman *(1927). Forced by ill health to retire in 1933, he returned to Nova Scotia. He died at Yarmouth in 1950.*

The following selection (Chapter Two) is from Day's second novel, Rockbound *(1928), which portrays life in a fictional fishing community on Nova Scotia's South Shore. At the time of its publication, the book was vehemently denounced by the people of Ironbound Island in Lunenburg County as a slanderous depiction of their community. Others, however, praised the book for its powerful realism. Archibald MacMechan, for instance, wrote that the novel "caught the life of Lunenburg. Absolutely." In this excerpt, Day's main character, the newcomer David Jung, sets out to prove himself to the fishermen of Rockbound.*

from Rockbound

Allas! the shorte throte, the tendre mouth,
Maketh that est and west, and north and south,
In erthe, in eir, in water, man to swynke
To gete a glotoun deyntee mete and drynke

Canterbury Tales

When David woke with a start it was still dark, but he threw off his rough covering and went quickly to the door. Away to the eastward dark mountains of morning clouds lowered, but the offshore breeze had pushed out the fog bank, and the stars twinkled through. As he had never owned watch or clock, he had learned to use the great bowl of the universe as an approximate timepiece. He looked up into the northern sky and saw the dipper, in relation to the pole star, hanging in the position of V on a clock dial, and knew from memories of previous nights that it was between two and three o'clock. There was no time to lose if he meant to show Uriah and the Jung boys his worth. He threw a bag about his shoulders, tied it at his neck with a bit of marline, tore off a thick heel from Anapest's loaf, thrust one half in his pocket for lunch, and gnawing the other half, ran for the launch, his bare feet scattering the dew from heavily bent grasses across the path.

Early as he was, he was none too early! A squat dark object moving swiftly from boats to fish house he knew was Uriah. Casper and Martin were not about yet — Casper, the farmer by instinct, was always last to get his boat off in the morning — but Joseph had shoved the *Lettie* over on her bilge and was greasing her keel. Neither spoke to him. David went over to the *Phoebe*, pushed her over on her side, fumbled in the dark for a stick, which he too dipped in the tub of stinking gurry, and greased her keel so that she would slip easily down the ways. As the seas often run fiercely even on the northern and sheltered side of the island, Rockbound boats never lie at a mooring but are hauled out high and dry as soon as they touch the launch.

Uriah waddled out of the gloom of the fish house with a basket full of herrings.

"Dere's yur bait, an' dere's an extry line, a box o' hooks an' two odd sinkers."

David righted the *Phoebe*, lifted the basket into her, and set it down by the centreboard without a word.

"Got nair a pair o' nippers?" queried the old man.

"I don't need no nippers. I'se fished on de Gran' Banks, an' me hands is tough."

"You best foller Joe; he knows w'ere de big schools o' fish lays dis season ob de year."

David grunted something in reply, but he had no mind to follow Joe or any of them; he would lead or nuttin'; he hadn't fished out o' de Outposts for naught; he knowed where de fish layed well as Joe. He set his shoulder to the stem of the *Phoebe* and started her down the ways. First she moved slowly, then gathered speed, and as his foot felt the chill of the salt water on the last log, she seemed to be flying. With his left hand grasping the jib stay, he gave a mighty spring and rolled in over the port washboard. Joseph, whose boat was already afloat, listened with the malicious hope that he would hear a great splash, betokening that, in the darkness, David had missed the logs set at unaccustomed spaces and been dragged off waist deep by the flying *Phoebe*, as he had seen many a green sharesman dragged before. But David, safely aboard, grasped a sweep and rushed quickly astern to fend her off the ledge and turn her head to the westward; then, darting swiftly forward, he made halliards and creaking blocks sing, and the big brown mainsail rose and bellied to the puff of the shore wind. Astern he rushed to shove his tiller hard aport and rattle in the main sheet till his sail was flat. Up came the *Phoebe's* bow into the wind. Now, setting the tiller in a middle notch, he darted forward again to hoist his jib and belay the halliard, back astern again to haul in and make fast his jib sheet. All his motions were swift and catlike; his bare feet gripped the wet surface of thwart and washboard.

When he had time to look about him, he noted that the breeze was from the northwest and that he could just clear the dull black mass of West Head by jogging the *Phoebe*. Joseph's boat was a hundred yards ahead of him. He tugged at the rusty pin of his centreboard and let the chain go clanking down; it would slow the *Phoebe* up a little, but keep her from drifting to leeward in this light breeze. Joseph made a short tack to the northward to weather the head, but David held straight on.

"Don't go in dere, de water's shoal," bawled Joseph.

But David pretended not to hear and held to his course; there would be plenty of time to come about when the iron centreboard bumped and bobbed up. The *Phoebe* was handy, he knew, for from the Outpost boats he had seen her luff up and come about a hundred times before she turned over with Mark, and he knew her points as a jockey knows the strengths and weaknesses of his rival's horses. He cleared West Head just outside the breakers and passed inside the Grampus with Joseph's boat, in spite of her tack, still fifty yards ahead. He let main and jib sheet run now and stood away to the southeast. With a long-handled gaff he winged out his jib, pulled up his centreboard, and watched to see if he was creeping up on the *Lettie*. Joseph's boat held her lead. The *Phoebe* was fast but crank, and Uriah had loaded her with ballast since she drowned Mark: four hundred pounds of beach rocks lay along her keelson.

"To hell wid ballast, dat makes a boat hard to get up an' off de launch; I'll ballast my boat wid fish," thought David, and stooping he tossed two hundred pounds of beach rocks into the sea. Then the lightened *Phoebe* began to draw up on the *Lettie*, and as David sailed his boat close to the *Lettie's* quarter, to take the quick puffs from her sails, he was soon abreast of Joseph's boat and little by little drew ahead. Now he was leading the Jung boys, first of the Rockbound fleet; Martin's boat showed dimly outside the Grampus, and Casper's trailed far behind. Daylight was coming gradually.

When he was well ahead and well to the southward of Barren Island, he hauled in his sails flat and stood away again to the westward toward his favourite bank. A landsman who looks at the even surface of the sea and whose acquaintance with the bottom is limited to slightly pitched bathing beaches thinks of the seafloor as flat and level. Not so it appeared to the mind of David, who from frequent soundings with a cod line visualized it truly as composed of hills, mountain ranges, deep valleys, sharp cañons, buttes, and wide plateaus. It was futile, he knew, to drop his baited hooks in a valley, for on the tops of the ridges and shallow plateaus lay the cod, waiting for schools of herring and squid to drift over. The finding and exact location of these shallow plateaus called banks by the fishermen seems to the uninitiated, who sees only miles upon miles of waves that look everywhere the same, nothing short of marvellous. They are marked by alignments of distant islands, by cross bearings, and time courses run by the compass.

To his favourite bank in the open sea, southwest from Barren Island and south-southeast from Lubeck Island light, David steered the *Phoebe*, that, lightened of her ballast, heeled over and put her lee washboard under in the freshening breeze. Presently he rounded his boat up, let the jib run, dropped the peak of his mainsail, but held fast the throat, so that the *Phoebe* would ride to the wind, and tossed over his grapnel. Over went his double-baited line, with his sinker he sounded bottom, twelve fathom, and he drew up a fathom to keep his hooks clear of the weeds on the sea floor. He began to saw patiently, but nothing happened; in half an hour he caught only two small rock cod. His heart sank; he could scarcely face Uriah on his first day with an empty boat. He would be cursed for not following Joseph as instructed. What was the matter? He had always caught fish on this bank before. Presently he ran forward, hove up his grapnel, hoisted jib and peak again, and stood farther to the westward toward Matt's Bank.

Again he anchored and tried. This time he was on the fish; ten seconds after his baited hooks reached bottom, a pair of big cod flashed over his gunwale and were snapped into the fish pen. The fish bit fiercely; as soon as the hooks were down came a tug on the line; then, after a few seconds of swift hand-over-hand pulling, gray forms with twirling white bellies showed dimly in the green depths. He gave himself no rest, but pulled and hauled, baited and rebaited for three hours. Once a strange boat drew up to him, and David, with two great cod hooked that twisted and tangled his snoods, let his line rest on the bottom.

"Air a fish?" hailed the stranger.

"A scatterin' rock cod," called back David lying stoutly. When the boat was well away, he pulled up his fish and repaired his snarled snoods. By nine, when the fish stopped biting his fish pens were two thirds full and the *Phoebe* had but a streak and a half clear.

The breeze dropped, and the sun shone warm to dry his shirt and trousers, soaked from the spray of the hand line. He squatted tailor-wise on his bit of deck by the jib stay, and though both hands were bleeding from the run of the burning hand line, he felt happier than he had for many a day. On the sea he was a free man and his own master. The corners of his mouth dropped in his quizzical smile as he thought how Joe, Martin, and Casper would curse when he came in high-line on his first day. And high-line he certainly would be. He drew out his heel of dampened bread and devoured it ravenously, washing it down with deep draughts from the *Phoebe's* water jug that Uriah had stuck in the bows. Uriah was mean and greedy, but he knew how to fit out a sharesman, thought David, and he kept his boats tight.

As he ate and looked about him at the sunlit water and enjoyed the sway of the boat that rocked him as if he were cradled — little cradling had he had as a child — he saw a great swirl and a dozen splashes dead astern to the southward. Then black backs flashed on the surface.

"Playin' pollock," said David to himself. He knew what to do for them. He stuffed the last crust into his mouth, seized his line, cut off the heavy leaden sinker, and, wrapping both hooks with guts torn from a fat herring, let his line trail astern near the surface. Snap, and he was fast to two pollock! Over and over again he repeated the operation, till he dared not lay another fish aboard the *Phoebe*, clear only by half a streak from the gunwale. He tried his pump till she sucked clear. It was a pity to leave those tens of thousands of playing pollock; if an Outposter came near he would hail him. However, no boat neared him.

In the offing far to the eastward, he could see the black specks of Joseph's, Casper's, and Martin's boats bunched near the Rock. It would be a long, hard beat home; the little breeze that remained, puffy and variable, still hung in the nor'west. Far out on the sea rested a thick stratum of fog bank, through which a three-master loomed, with spars unearthly high. He rested patiently, awaiting a breeze, knowing that the wind often hauled at noontime. Before twelve came a draught from the sou'west; luck favoured him that day. He let out his mainsail to catch the quartering breeze and rested happy at the tiller. Then the other Rockbound boats made sail and stood in. By their speed he judged them light; they would be home long before him.

The southwest breeze had caught the fog bank half an hour before it touched the sails of the *Phoebe*, and the fog travelled faster than the boats. Presently the sun sickened, the islands dimmed to a dull gray, and black specks that meant boats were blotted out. David took a course on Rockbound before the fog shut out the island, and kept his ears alert for the sound of breakers. The deep-laden *Phoebe* moved sullenly, her jib flirting from side to side of the stay with a vixenish snap. Now, had David had a draught of rum, or even pipe and tobacco, he would have been comforted, for the stoutest heart is lonely on a fog-shrouded sea.

In two hours time he heard the smash of surf and, standing close in and staring eagerly, made out the black form of sou'west gutter rock. He steered west now, hugging the dim black of the cliff, and dared again to round West Head inside the Grampus, lest he should lose touch with the shore. Then he jibbed, hauled flat, and stood for the launch, letting out a great "Hallo." Uriah was at the launch with the oxen, and, as his prow took the logs, hooked the wire cable into his stem ring.

"Go easy," yelled David, "she's deep."

"I'se hauled out boats while you was yet suckin'," retorted Uriah, starting his oxen with a mighty "Gee Bright."

"How much do ye hail?" queried Uriah as the boat reached the top of the launch.

"Six quintal," answered David proudly. Casper came out and stared in his fish pens.

"Scale fish," said he contemptuously, handling the pollock.

"No dey's not scale fish," said David. "Dere's a few scatterin' pollocks on top, underneat's all big cod."

Uriah said naught to David; silence and absence of complaint were ever his loudest praise, but he had a word to say to Joseph, Martin, and Casper in a corner of the fish house. David hailed more that day than the three brothers put together. In all his years on Rockbound, he never had a better day's fishing nor a greater triumph.

When David had been fishing a fortnight off Rockbound, the dogfish came and drove in the boats from the Rock and adjacent banks. It was no good trying for cod when dogfish were about — even Uriah admitted that — they chased the cod and did nothing but tangle and destroy the fisherman's gear. Still, the boats went out each morning in the hope that the fisherman's pest had vanished; a few unavailing trials, and they returned early. David had hoped for some afternoons of rest and leisure, but that was not part of Uriah's plan, who put him to work tanning nets.

About noon on one such day, Joseph, the sly one, went to Cow Pasture Hill on the west end to stake out his young bull. When he came to the cliff's edge and looked down from the height into the green water, he saw that Sheer Net Cove was alive with herring. They darted to and fro or lay by millions on the yellow sand of the cove's bottom. That could not long be kept a secret, and he knew that the Krauses had their nets and seine laid in their seine boat, whereas the seine of the Jungs was in the upper loft. If the Jungs started to get out their herring seine, the Krauses would see them, launch first, and get round the fish. He thought for a moment, ruffling up his black hair, then ran through the thick spruces on the back of the island, and, bending low to escape observation, dashed across bar and sand beach and made his way into the thick woods on the eastern end. After a moment's pause to catch his breath he came running down the road from the eastern end bellowing: "de herrin', de herrin' is in on de shore in millions."

What a hurry and scramble was there then! Uriah puffed to the loft and tore down the herring seine; down the stairs stamped Casper with an armful of ropes, grapnels, and net buoys; Joseph followed with two baskets of sinker rocks; young Gershom Born ran to and fro, shouting and waving his arms as he gathered up equipment, with Noble Morash following sullenly in his wake; David greased bottoms of seine boats and dories. Do what they could, the Kraus boats were off first, but the Krauses, deceived by Joseph's ruse, pulled madly for the eastern end. Only when they were well out of hearing Joseph said: "Quick now, de herrin's in de Sheer Net Cove an' we kin git dere first."

Casper, who excelled in net fishing, led the fleet of Jung boats around the western end of the island. One man tugged viciously at the oars, and another sat straddling the bows, peering down into the green water, not more than three fathom deep, for the edge of the herring school. Young Gershom Born, the most powerful oarsman, pulled the boat in which Casper was the watcher; David pulled the second boat with Noble Morash in the bows, and Martin, the weakest oarsman, trailed behind with Joseph straddling his bows.

"Here are herrin'! Here are herrin'!" Joseph and Nobel began to shout from the rear boats.

"Not enough yet," bawled Casper from the leading boat. Over the yellow sands the green-backed herring raced in schools so thick and opaque that the sea floor was hidden.

"Shoot here, shoot here," yelled Joseph in his anxiety to beat the Krauses. "Lot's o' herrin' here, ain't it!"

"Not yet, not yet!" shouted Casper.

When the boats came to the mouth of the rocky Sheer Net Cove, Casper raised his hand as a signal to shoot. He took his boat close to the breakers, cast over the end of the seine, tying on rock sinkers with a swift and adroit hand as he paid it out, while Gershom Born, the great blond sharesman, strained at the oars and tugged the heavy seine boat, heavier now with the drag of the seine, westward to sea. Then, at a signal from Casper's hand, he made a sharp turn northward to the right, again a signal, another sharp turn to the eastward, and millions of herring were penned in the cove. The ends of the seine were brought together and tied; now it floated in a great corked circle, the vibrant water within crowded with herrings, a tumult of blues and greens. At the first rush of the imprisoned fish against the outer twine, the seaward corks went under.

"Quick, Dave, quick man, git on de buoys," bawled Casper, "or de fish will git ober de top."

The seaward head ropes were dragged up on the prows of boats to hold up the seine till the white fir-wood buoys could be tied on, and Joseph and Martin ran out moorings and grapnels to north, west, and south, to hold the seine against the rush of the tide.

Still, in spite of the light fir-wood net buoys, the seaward head ropes dipped under, for the seine twine was now white with meshed herring; the smaller fry darted through the meshes and to sea again.

"Quick, now, Dave, wid de nets," bawled Casper. David was everyone's slave; everyone called orders to the newest and lowest sharesman. He did not care for this herring fishing, where there was little chance for individual action: his great moments were when, on the open sea, he was alone in the *Phoebe*. As long as the herring were in, he knew that the boat he already loved because it gave him freedom would lie dry on the launch.

Over the head ropes went dories and seine boats, and the inside of the seine was circled with a fleet of nets that were drawn into a smaller circle. Gershom Born, blue-eyed Viking, hurled in the jiggler, a stone tied with a rope to pieces of white wood. This he flounced up and down, to scare more fish into meshes of net or seine. Noble Morash, the gaunt, black-bearded, silent sharesman, and David darted their spruce oars to the bottom, and when they bobbed from the surface like the sword Excalibur, caught them neatly by the handles, to drive them down again among the frightened fish. Once Noble Morash drove his into deep water, and when the oar handle did not reappear in the usual rhythmic time, he peeped over the gunwale to see if his oar blade had caught in a cleft of the rock bottom. Whereupon the oar handle shot out, caught him between the eyes, and knocked him flat and half stunned into the bottom of the boat. There was a yell of laughter in which David joined. That was a first-rate Rockbound joke to be recounted for many a day. Noble Morash rose, mopping the blood from his nose, and glared savagely at David with his narrow, sinister eyes. He would show the new sharesman if he could laugh at him, even if he wereUriah's kinsman.

"Herrin'! Herrin'!" they screamed at one another as if they had never seen a fish before.

"We got two hundred barrels, ain't it?"

"We got five hundred barrels."

"Chuck in dat giggler."

"Souse her up an' down."

"De herrin's not bin in on de shore like dis fur twenty year."

David caught the spirit and like the rest became a wild fisherman, intoxicated with the great catch of herring, shouting, gesticulating, taking his turn with the heavy giggler, driving down the oars.

Presently the Kraus boats hove up alongside; the Krauses had taken no fish and eyed the Jungs resentfully, though they had not got to the bottom of Joseph's ruse.

The inner net, heavy with fat, gleaming herring meshed from both sides, was hauled now, each end in a separate boat. David and Noble Morash in their boat dragged in head and foot rope and shook the fish into the boat's bottom a half bushel at a time, or tore out those that stuck fast in the twine with a rending of gills and sometimes the loss of a head. When they strode from bow to stern now, they waded knee deep in herring. Lower and lower sank seine boat and dories, till only single streaks were clear. When the net was picked, it was again circled within the seine. Outside giant albacore in pursuit of the herring splashed and swirled the waves into foam.

"Bring in de spare boats," bawled Casper, and in they floated over the head ropes.

David glanced up from his work once in a while to admire the little cove in which these Jungs shouted and toiled unmindful of any beauty about them. It was closed to the eastward, and partly to the northward and southward, by sheer cliffs of slaty black and iron-red rocks, seamed and fish-boned with cracks from some pre-historic fire. The slanting afternoon sun filled these rocks with light and cast deep shadows in the clefts. Above the cliffs ran in a fine curve a narrow margin of green turf crowned with masses of stunted wind-blown spruces crowding like horses in a gale, tails to the sea wind. The cliff-fallen boulders at the foot were clad with raw-sienna rockweed, and among these the green sea washed with a bang and a roar, lashing itself, even on this comparatively calm day, into a fury of foam and creamy lather. It seemed like a dream to David, and that he was dreamer and a part of the dream.

There they laboured together, great shouldered, red faced, clad in yellow oil pants, shouting, gesticulating, pulling on head ropes, hurling the giggler, darting oars, balancing on thwarts or gunwale with all the grace of athletes, tearing out shining fish tangled in brown meshes, wild with greed and excitement, though they had done this a hundred times before. Beneath the yellow dories that were down close to the gunwales the sea, patched in green and black, was vibrant with backs of frightened herring, racing madly about nets and seine in their effort to escape.

Again they hauled the fleet of nets and picked them. The sun was low over Flat Island now, and the boats could carry no more. Reluctantly Casper gave the order to set a fleet of nets about the remnant of the school and to take up the moorings of the big seine, which they dared not leave overnight so close to the shore.

Home they rowed in the twilight, deep-laden seine boat and dories dragging wearily. Uriah was waiting at the launch with his oxen to draw out the boats. From him came no word of praise.

"You got to be quick now, boys," he cried. "It's Saturday, an' I neber works on de Lord's Day, me nor my fader before me." And to David, "Git a snack an' be back quick. Dese herrin' got to be dressed by midnight. Quick, now, we don't want no loafers on Rockbound." This, after he had fished on the Rock before daybreak and tugged at the heavy seine through a long afternoon.

David, with back and shoulders aching, rushed off to his house and tore ravenously at a crust of bread and a piece of salt fish. He would show the old man if he was a loafer; in five minutes he was back at the fish house, just as Joseph was coming down the road. Uriah was waiting for him, Uriah the king, who neither ate nor slept while fish were on the floor.

"You boys is awful slow. Why, in de ole days me an' my brudder Simeon stood on yon beach an' gibbed eighty barrels of mackerel an' never stirred from dere from tree one afternoon till sundown nex' day. Men could work in dem days. Here you, David, look alive, run dat spare dory down de launch an' fill her wid water while I fetches de cattle."

ARCHIBALD MACMECHAN

Archibald MacMechan was born in 1862 at Berlin (Kitchener), Ontario and was educated at the University of Toronto and Johns Hopkins University. In 1889 he became a professor of English at Dalhousie University in Halifax. One of Canada's leading literary scholars, MacMechan was also an accomplished popular historian and increasingly, during the last two decades of his life, devoted himself to the preservation of Nova Scotia's maritime heritage. In addition to collecting documents and artifacts, he produced a significant body of sea stories that were collected in three books: Sagas of the Sea *(1923),* Old Province Tales *(1924), and* There Go the Ships *(1928). He died at Halifax in 1933.*

"The First Mate" appeared in the Halifax Chronicle *(September 8, 1928) before it was collected in* There Go the Ships. *Based on an interview with Captain Nehemiah C. Larkin, the story reveals MacMechan's skill as a chronicler of maritime lore. As Thomas H. Raddall observed in his foreword to* Tales of the Sea *(1947), a collection of MacMechan's sea stories, MacMechan "had the common touch and could meet the simple mariner on his own ground (usually in his kitchen) and in five minutes establish the intimacy which comes of a common love of the sea." MacMechan's own love of the sea apparently began with an 1883 voyage to England on a cattleship.*

The First Mate

The Regina Goes

A life on the ocean wave has been the theme of many a joyous song, but life on board the lightship which is tethered head and tail over the "Lurcher" shoal near Yarmouth is, for green hands and wireless operators, one unending bout of sea-sickness. Hence a considerate Department of Marine and Fisheries allows the crew one month ashore out of every three. In one such period of shore leave, I caught Captain Nehemiah C. Larkin alone in his own house, with his coat off, filling in some government returns. These he courteously pushed aside to tell me his experience in the Yarmouth ship *Regina*.

Let no Biblical or Puritan associations with his Old Testament name mislead. It did not prevent him from being six feet tall, with a handsome, clean-shaven, ruddy face and laughing blue eyes — a typical sailor. Before his hair turned white he must have been as magnificent a piece of manhood as ever trod a deck or kept watch and trick. He told his tale, sailor fashion, with detachment, quiet humour and a wealth of precise detail.

He ran it o'er, at my request, even from his boyhood days. He first went to sea at sixteen in the brigantine *Premier*. After getting his mate's papers, he sailed as first officer in the *Tsernagora* under little Ned Hilton, who died in her hold trying to put out the fire at St. Nazaire. While master of the *Coipell* in the West India trade, he was wrecked.

"She foundered," he said briefly, "and we were all floating around, some one way and some another," which must have been good practice for his next shipwreck.

The *Regina* was a full-rigged ship of 1,212 tons, of Bay of Fundy spruce, built at Tusket in 1873 for the Western Ocean trade, to carry cotton, grain and oil. She was named for the owner's pretty daughter, Regina. She carried a crew of eighteen, officers and men, commanded by big, handsome Joe Bain of Yarmouth, a singing seaman with a rich bass voice, and N. C. Larkin as first mate. In November, 1883, she loaded at Philadelphia with barrel oil and cleared for London on the fifteenth day of the month.

As she was loading, a dispute of some importance arose between the captain and the owners. One of the deck-beams near the main-hatch needed to be replaced; but repairs cost money and all owners object to expense, on principle. The upshot was that the *Regina* put to sea with the old deck-beam; and it proved to be the little rift within the lute, the weakest link in the chain. Once again, the kingdom was lost for a horseshoe nail. Captain Larkin was too loyal to his dead and gone owners to complain of this extra risk. The life of a sailor is all risk, and one more or less hardly counts in the day's work.

It was a bad time of the year, the winds were variable, contrary, and on St. Andrew's Day, late in the afternoon, the *Regina* was far south of her course, lying hove-to on the starboard tack under a single triangular piece of canvas, the main try-sail. Being hove-to means that the ship cannot sail, but is trying to save her life in the turmoil of the storm, by keeping her bows to it. Even so, in the hurricane, she was listed to leeward, and the boarding seas filled her deck. To relieve the vessel of this burden, the crew smashed some of the bulwarks to leeward and let the water pour off as fast as it poured on.

A little before midnight, the wind suddenly shifted to West-South-West, blowing with hurricane force. The effect was to run the ship right into the seas to leeward. It was as if two gigantic hands had seized the *Regina* wrenching her in opposite directions, to twist the fabric asunder. Such a conjuncture looks like the deliberate malice of Nature. The lee seas tumbled in on her and swept the deck. Naturally, Captain Bain tried to get his ship before the wind. The foresail and the foretopmast-staysail were set, but the vessel was lying over so far that she would not answer her helm. The fore-sheet was carried away and the sail was blown to ribbons; even the sails on the yards, though furled in the gaskets, also flogged to pieces.

"We had to cut them away and tried to keep things together as much as we could," said Captain Larkin. "During the night the seas broke the hatch partitions and washed the tarpaulin off the hatch. We got a sail and put it over the hatch and battened it down to the deck as best we could, but it was torn away. We repaired it three times with the same success. Then, of course, she began to leak, and the men were set at the pumps. They were washed into the lee scuppers and were rescued with difficulty.

"It was after daylight the following morning, while all hands were at the pumps, she shipped a heavy sea from the weather or starboard side, carrying away the stanchions and bulwarks from the break of the poop to the forecastle head. It took the forward house off her, broke in the cabin skylight, and carried away the binnacle.

"The *Regina* was what we term a full poop ship; the poop extended from the cabin well forward to the main rigging. Four hundred barrels of oil were stored in it. The two boats rested one end on a sill built on the forward edge of the poop, and the other on a 'gallows.' They were right over the pumps.

"We were at the pumps when this heavy sea hit the ship. It brought down the boat gallows, letting the end of the boats drop to the deck over our heads and smashing the fife-rail and the pumps. But none of us was hurt, to signify. The boat on the port side slid forward out of its lashings, and was immediately smashed up with the other wreckage on the deck. The starboard boat held in the grit, and we succeeded in hauling it aft on the poop. Our largest boat was secured on the top of the forward house and it was lost when the house washed off. That left us with one boat only, the smallest we had."

So the progressive destruction of the good ship *Regina* went on. She was lying on her side, the waves sweeping over her, helpless, for the fury of the storm allowed no setting of sail, nor would she answer to her helm. She might right, if the masts were cut away, an expedient of extremity.

"The vessel was listed so heavily that it was useless to try to do anything with her, so the captain said to cut away."

"Cutting away" suggests to the landsman chopping down the masts as a lumberman fells a tree; but the process is much simpler. By slashing through the standing rigging, the shrouds and stays, on the side from which the strain comes, the masts break under their own weight. But all the axes had gone, when that one wave cleared out the forward house, which is the carpenter's shop. How was the order to be obeyed?

"I had an axe in my room" said Captain Larkin, "which was kept in a becket on the bulk-head. I went down to get the axe and found the water about waist deep. The partitions were partly down; the one that had the axe had been washed out, and just as I stepped in the door, the handle lifted above the water.

"When I reached the deck, the captain said to cut the lines of the lower rigging, mizzen and main. The mizzen-mast broke at the deck and the main-mast about twelve or fourteen feet above the deck. That carried away everything forward, except the lower fore-mast, which remained standing."

The three masts with all their load of spars had crashed over the lee side of the *Regina*, wrenching away the bowsprit and jibboom. All these heavy timbers, with their confusion of trailing cordage, were pounding at the side, but the stripped hull righted. Now, the trim *Regina* was definitely a wreck.

"We cleared away what wreckage we could. The wind began to moderate, but a heavy sea was running."

There was a brief respite for the toilworn, fasting men. They had a moment to think of food and drink.

"The provisions and drinking water were all in a tank just aft of the pumps; and when everything smashed up around the deck, the vessel was full of water and burst up the hatches. The main hatch came off and the oil commenced to come out of the ship, and it spoiled everything. There was a small tank in the wash-room used by the

186

captain, which we used to fill every morning. I asked him if there was any water in it, and he said he thought there was. I said I was going down for it.

"The cabin was partly full of water, and the partitions washing about. He thought a sea would board her any minute. Says he, 'If a sea caught you down there, you would never get out.'

"I told him I would put a rope round me and they could pull me out if I couldn't get out. Says he, 'You may get jammed among the wreckage down there.'

"I told him I would have to take that chance."

Be it noted that taking chances is the first mate's calling, and extra danger is his special perquisite.

"I succeeded in getting the water and a few biscuits that were below the water-line. That was all the water and provisions we had."

In the Boat

On this, the first day of December, the elements relaxed for a little their persecution of the *Regina* and her crew. All hands were gathered aft on the poop of the dismantled hulk, while the captain and the mate drew apart and held council of war. Captain Bain thought that after so much bad weather, there would be a break in it, may be a spell of fine weather. Though they were so far south as to be out of the regular traffic lanes from Philadelphia to London, yet, if they took to the boat, with what little water and provisions they had, they might succeed in getting far enough south to be outside the track of the North Atlantic gales. They stood a chance of being picked up by some vessel making a middling passage to the southward. Such was his argument.

Then the captain asked Larkin's opinion, for the first mate does not volunteer advice to his superior officer.

Larkin did not agree.

"I told him that as our boat was so small and the distance so far; and as we had no way of propelling the boat except by oars our progress would be very slow. I didn't think it feasible. I didn't think we could do it.

"He then turned to the men, and told them what his idea was, and also that I differed with him.

"'We can't navigate the ship any more, and as soon as the oil comes out of her she must sink, as she has stone ballast in her. One man's life is as sweet as another's.'

"And he asked their opinion.

"They all decided with the captain. I said that I still held to my opinion but if they were all going to leave the ship, I wouldn't stay there alone.

"Later in the afternoon, we succeeded in getting away from the ship in the boat, with all hands in her and what little provisions we had, and started rowing to the southward, as best we could direct her. We hadn't a light of any kind. We found that our small boat was making a good deal of water, and with all hands in her, she was overloaded. While some were rowing, others were bailing. I expected to see her capsize at any moment."

So the boatload of castaways endured through the long, black December night, rowing, bailing, expecting every moment the final blow of Fate.

"I remember asking the captain in the night if he could swim. He said he could. I said, if this boat turns over, let's get on the bottom of her. We'll take the last chance."

As uncertain, wintry daylight broke, the shipwrecked men made out a vague shape in the dim distance across the tumbling billows. It seemed a sail, to the north and east, more easterly than their own ship could possibly be, and hope of rescue sprang up in all hearts. But that hope was soon dashed. As the light grew stronger, and as they rowed towards the strange sail, they found it was the poor, abandoned *Regina*.

"The first remark the captain made was that we had better turn round and row to the southward — no use to go in that direction. The

188

wind at this time began to air up again from a south-westerly direction. I suggested to the captain that we try to get back on board the wreck, as it would be impossible for our small boat to outlive any kind of a storm, with so many men aboard. If we could get back on board, we could construct a raft that would give all hands a chance to save their lives."

This time, the mate's judgment prevailed. Captain Bain gave the necessary orders, and the boat got back alongside her mother ship.

"The ropes which we used in getting away from the ship, were trailing over the side. The men got hold of them and hauled themselves on board. The boatswain stayed in one end of the boat and I in the other. We slipped two ropes under her keel, passed the ends over the side, and parbuckled the boat, and so succeeded in getting her on the poop again."

This means that being without davits or falls, the sailors passed ropes round the boat, made one end of each rope fast to bitts on the deck and, watching the favourable opportunity, as the wreck rolled towards it, hauled on the free ropes; and so pulled it on board by main strength. While the ropes were being passed, Larkin and the boatswain ran the risk of being swamped, and the boat being smashed against the side of the wreck; but the post of danger is always the first mate's privilege.

Building the Raft

"The captain and the carpenter started to fix up the boat as best they could. I took the others and started to construct a raft. We hadn't very much to work with. Our tools were all gone except the axe which was lying on the poop where we left it. For sills and the lower part of the raft we used the ship's spanker-gaff and boom. Then we cut the taffrail in sections, which ran round the poop. It was pinned down with iron stanchions an inch and a half thick. We had to cut those rods away with the same axe that we cut the rail off with. Not much of a cold chisel; but we did it.

"The raft was about fourteen feet by eight or nine. There was some small chain, old t'gallant sheets in a locker in the fo'c'sl' head. It would be a grand thing to secure the ends of the raft, which must be made solid if it was to stand the sea at all. If I could only get forward—

"The water was just washing over the main deck as it would over a ledge, but at times there was a lull. I took a coil of rope and made one end fast to a capstan on the poop. I watched my chance, and when the vessel lifted, I ran to the fo'c'sl' head with my rope and made fast. This gave me something to hold on to and get what there was in the locker. Long before this, I had hauled off my sea-boots and oil-coat. I found I could get round quicker in my stocking feet. As I came back, a wave caught me, and the men yelled, 'The mate's gone, the mate's gone.'

"We got oil-barrels out of the poop, emptied the oil out of them, plugged the bungholes, and lashed them securely, two abreast, to the lower sills of the raft and secured them thoroughly. For flooring we took planks which had been used for dunnage on top of the oil barrels. By evening, we had the raft completed; but we decided to remain on board until the morning."

The thoroughness of the job was tested by the unprejudiced winter storm. It stood the test; Larkin's lashings held, and saved six lives.

"By night the wind was blowing a moderate gale, but by next morning it was blowing heavy, with a big sea running. Just at daybreak, the pins in the main-deck came out of her. The whole forward part of the poop came out. While she had a heavy list to port, she took a heavier list, and fearing we would be all broken up with the wreckage, we decided to get away from her as quickly as we could. We launched our raft out, and made it fast to the bitts on the port side.

"There was no decision made as to who were going in the boat or on the raft, but I had made up my mind that I was going on the raft. So I said, 'Those who are going on the raft had better come along,' so I started with two men besides myself. The ship was practically on

190

her beam ends, and, at this moment, I heard the captain call, 'For goodness sake, somebody help us with the boat.' So I turned back to assist them.

"We tried to get the boat aft. In order to get her down between the skylight and the wheel, the stern had to be lifted off the bitts. But with the very heavy list of the ship, it was impossible to get a footing, and it was hard to lift her that high. While we were working with the boat, the wheel standard gave way, taking the wheel and all with it. That allowed the boat to run into the water.

"The captain was pretty well on to the forward part of the boat, and when she plunged into the water, it carried him along; he was holding on to the gunwale. A good many got into the boat, and I called to the boatswain, 'Get the captain in!' He, with another man, got him into the boat. He sung out to me, 'Come on!' I said I was not coming. 'You've got enough in the boat now.'

"They succeeded in getting out through the wreckage, oil barrels, spars and so on. Just a mass of wreckage. I thought the boat would be swamped right there.

"When we first launched the raft, the boatswain, an Irishman from Dublin, grabbed the captain's big, black dog and threw him on the raft, saying, 'We may want your blood and meat before we're through with this job.'

"I looked round for the raft and found that when the vessel made her heavy list, it had carried the whole port side of the poop away, and had taken the bitts which the raft was fast to. Consequently it had gone adrift and was quite a distance to the leeward of the ship. I thought it too far away for me to swim to fetch it, and I saw at that time but one man on the raft.

"I then scrambled up on the outside of the ship (which was the top part) into the mizzen chains, and found that there were five men there who hadn't gone in the boat, — the steward, cook, second mate and two seamen. I said, 'I see only one man on the raft.' The steward said, 'The second man missed getting there. The raft pushed away.

I saw him in the water and pointed to the raft. He shook his head and went out of sight.' That was the first man drowned.

"The captain backed his boat down to the raft and put out all the men but two. He kept two in the boat and made her fast to the raft. As the boat was the lighter of the two, he used the raft as a drag. The men with me made the remark, 'They're rowing back to get us;' but I told them it was impossible to row the boat to windward. We were all six lashed there in the mizzen-chains."

"Lashing" is not what landsmen and uninformed artists make of it. A sailor lashes himself to the mast, or, in this case, to the mizzen-chains, by fastening one end of a rope to something solid and slipping the other end, made into a loop, over his head and under one arm. This secures him from being washed away, but leaves his arms and legs free. He can cut his lashing at any moment. Larkin and these five men were so "lashed" to the wreck, with the billows sweeping right over and half drowning them.

"The heavy seas were coming over the ship and would fairly tear you. Feeling confident the ship would go down in no great length of time, I looked about and saw a piece of the poop off the starboard side that the cabin was on, and I saw Mr. Dog on this piece of poop. He had jumped off the raft and swum back to the ship, but could not get near her on account of the big wash of the ship. He had swum to that piece of poop and succeeded in crawling on top of it.

"I know I said to the men, 'While we are getting washed here, there is that dog standing on that cabin and there is not sea enough to wash him off. If another piece breaks off big enough I am on it.' Just a little after, I heard an extra crash, and looking up I saw the whole starboard side of the poop had gone away in one section. When it first broke, it rushed to the leeward of the ship, and when she lifted, I told the men, 'The whole side of the poop is gone. I am going on it.' When the vessel lifted, I ran along the side of her, and jumping clear, swam down to the poop and got on it. The steward and one seaman saw me, and also succeeded in getting on the poop.

"In a very short time, the ship being higher than this piece of poop, the wind drove her down so that we came back on the quarter. The remaining men said that the vessel had lighted some; they had lengthened the ropes and had got away from the mizzen-chains and were protected from the wind. They thought they had a better place than the piece of poop I was on. They wanted to know if I was coming back. I said, 'No, she will go down.' We went out around the stern and the old *Regina* drove to the leeward of us. As night came on I could still see the ship afloat. The next morning nothing could be seen of her."

On the Raft

As the helpless *Regina* awaited her doom, her crew were in four divisions, the captain's dog on his own private piece of wreckage, the three men lashed to the sinking hull, the first mate with two companions on another portion of the disintegrating vessel, and Captain Bain with ten hands in the boat and on the raft. Let their part of the adventure be told next.

This is the situation.

The boat is made fast to the raft which serves as a drag to keep her head to the seas. There are three men with the captain in the boat, and six on the eight-by-fourteen-foot raft.

About an hour after leaving the ship, the boat capsized, and all the provisions and water were lost. Captain Bain remembered what Larkin had said the night before about getting on the bottom of the boat. He dived out from under, got his hands on the keel, and, by main strength rolled her over. The three men were still clinging to the thwarts. The men in the boat had taken hold of the painter and hauled the boat up to the raft and got on it. First they tried to haul the boat on top of the raft; but to put a twenty-four-foot boat on a eight-by-fourteen-foot raft was impossible. Next, they tried to bail the boat out. This they also found to be impossible. The boat and raft were smashing together, so they cut the boat adrift. Fifteen minutes later, the overloaded raft capsized in the stormy sea. Some of the men were lashed to it, and they were thrown underneath, but the whole of the eleven managed to get out from under and on the top of their frail refuge. The barrels were now uppermost, and the level frame and platform below the surface. Those t'gallant-chains and scientific lashings of the first mate held fast. While the boat was afloat, the two drifted faster than the ship, but after it capsized, the ship drifted faster than the raft. Some strange sort of magnetism seemed to draw the *Regina* and the various fragments of her together. By evening, the raft was close to the wallowing hulk. The captain hailed the three seamen still on board and asked them where the mate was. They told him that he had gone off on a piece of wreckage and must have been drowned long ago. Desperate as were the chances of surviving on the *Regina*, it looked safer than staying with the raft. At least five of the hands thought so, after their two capsizings; and as the raft neared the ship, they jumped for it, and managed to get on board. The eight perished together that night when the *Regina* sank.

In the morning, the wreck was nowhere to be seen. "We were up to our knees all the time," was Captain Bain's report, "and continually drenched with the sea breaking over us. On the third day our sufferings were past describing. One man went mad and we had to lash him, so he could not get at the salt water. About noon on December 6th, we sighted a sail standing towards us. He passed us about two cable lengths off. He hove to, clewed up all his sails except his lower topsails and mizzen-staysail, and lay for about half an hour, when he made sail and left us. It was hard to believe that a man calling himself a sailor could do such a thing, it being fine at the time.

"Another day and night we spent on the raft, with every prospect of a gale from the south-west; but through the special providence of God, at noon next day we saw another sail standing for us, which came to us, and hove to. He put his boat out, though there was a strong breeze and a heavy sea at the time, and came and got us. We were so weak they had to lift us off the raft and into the boat. We were taken on board the barque *Helen Finlayson* of Ardrossan, Captain

Alexander Baker, and everything possible was done for us. It was to the kind and skilful treatment of the captain and his officers that we owe our lives, for we were very weak, and the least mistake might have proved fatal. By the time we arrived at Cork we were all quite recovered."

The Mate Alone

Though Captain Bain and the sailors lashed in the mizzen-chains of the wreck thought that Larkin was lost, he was still afloat on his fragment of deck. Like his captain, he had his eyes on his old ship as the December night gathered down, and, like him, the next morning he looked for her in vain. They could not have been far apart.

"The second night that we were on this raft," said Captain Larkin, "the steward said he couldn't stand it any longer. He was dying and didn't want to hold on any longer. The piece of poop we were on had broken off by a carlin almost as clean as if it had been sawed. There were the fife-rail and bitts at the foot of the mizzen-mast and part of the skylight. He said, 'I will sit down here and hold on to the stanchion as long as I can.' I said, 'I will tie you.' He said, 'No, I want to die,' and he soon washed away.

"The other man started drinking salt water, and he went out of his head. The first I knew of it he began asking how far we were from some place, — sounded like Tron-yem. Then he said, 'What's the use of staying here starving? No use staying here. I was down there and saw the table spread. I looked in the window and there was every-thing on the table.' He said this in broken English; he was a foreigner. He said, 'Salt water don' taste too bad.' I said, 'You're not drinking salt water.' It was impossible to keep from drinking some, as we were under water part of the time. Then I thought I didn't know what he might do, so I reached round and took his knife out of his sheath. Before morning he died. I was feeling pretty hungry but I said, 'I'm not going to eat you.' So I cut the lashing and let him go overboard. Then I was alone.

"Some time in that night or in the early morning, the wind moderated, so that if the boat was anywhere handy she would come to me. A little while after we drifted away from the ship, a white table-cloth floated out from underneath, and I grabbed it. The steward said, 'That's no good to keep you warm.' I told him the idea was that if there was a heavy rain we could catch the water and get a little to drink. On the second morning, I decided that if the boat was anywhere handy, they could come and get me. So I took the knife I got from the seaman and a belaying pin from the fife-rail, and with these tools I worked off a little of the moulding on the inside of the skylight. I lashed the strips together with some rope-yard and attached the tablecloth to this flagpole, and fastened it up on the bitt. I thought the boat might see it, if it was any ways handy. This raft of mine was not the best place in the world, and I wasn't anxious to stay there alone.

"Quite early in the forenoon, I sighted a sail to the westward. In a short time I could see that it was nearing me. Just how the sail was heading I couldn't tell until I got hold of the jibs. Then I saw the vessel was heading for me, or just a little north, most of the time. As she got near, I judged they also had had bad weather, and everything was being broken up. I had the impression that every one was busy. The mate would have his men at work, and I thought the chances of anyone seeing me would be pretty small. The captain might possibly be on deck, and the man at the wheel might possibly be gazing round. So as the vessel came nearer, I got up on the bitt and raised the table-cloth in my hand to make it that much higher, and I held it up till the vessel was quite close to me. I could see men moving on the deck. By and by, they put the helm up, and I thought they saw me and that the captain intended to let his vessel come round to the wind and drop down alongside of me. When I saw that, I let my flag go, thinking it was no more good. At the last minute, the vessel hauled on her course again. I looked for my flag, but as soon as it struck the piece of poop, it washed away.

196

"Then I wondered if it was possible to make anyone hear. I tried to sing out, but there didn't seem to be any power in my throat. Then I thought it might be eight o'clock, and that they had shifted watch. But they had seen me, and the captain did what I thought at first he would do.

"When I was first discovered, it was eight o'clock, and the starboard watch had gone below. The vessel had double forecastles, the doors opening to the side of the vessel. They had all turned in but one man, and he was sitting in the doorway, smoking. The wind was on the quarter, blowing much harder than I thought. The vessel went down in a sea just as I happened to lift on one, and this man got the flutter of that table-cloth. He said, 'There is something down there with a white flag flying.' The steward looked and said, 'My, there is a man down there,' and ran aft to tell the captain. As soon as he came out on deck and glanced at me, he began to do what I had expected, that is, come up into the wind and drop down alongside of me. He put his glasses to his eyes, took a second look at me, saw the bitts and thought there might be a whole hull there submerged. That was why he put the ship on her course again.

"His men were not in very good shape; they had malaria. It took him some little time to get volunteers and lower his boat. He got a little vial of water ready because he didn't know how long I had been floating round. He intended to give it to the men in the boat for me, but he must have been a little excited, for when he went up into the main-top to see where I was, and give the boat's crew directions, he forgot about the vial. As the boat came to me, I said, 'You can't come in there,' and I jumped in and swam to it. The boatswain, an old Welshman, in charge called, 'Don't throw your life away!' But I got alongside, and they picked me up. I was bareheaded, in my stocking-feet and shirt-sleeves.

"The vessel was the barque *Barroma*, Captain Hughes of Liverpool, England, loaded with cotton from Charleston, S.C. He was a kind and thoughtful man, as getting the vial of water showed. I told him about the *Regina* and the boat, probably to the S.E. of him, and he hunted round all day for them, but did not find them. We did see a wreck, Norwegian built, with no men on it.

"I was landed at Liverpool a little before Christmas."

ARTHUR HUNT CHUTE

The son of a Baptist minister, Arthur Hunt Chute was born at Stillman Valley, Illinois in 1888 and grew up in Halifax and Wolfville. A graduate of Acadia College and the Newton Theological Institution, he served with the Canadian army during the First World War until he was invalided home in 1917. After his recovery, Chute became a journalist and author, dividing his time between Wolfville, Bermuda, and New York. In addition to contributing to a wide variety of British, American, and Canadian periodicals and newspapers, he published a memoir of the war, The Real Front *(1918), and five sea adventures:* The White Ships of Judique *(1923),* The Roaring Forties *(1924),* Mutiny of the Flying Spray *(1927),* Far Gold *(1927), and* The Crested Seas *(1928). Chute's promising literary career was cut short in 1929, when he died in a plane crash in Lake Manitoba, near Reykjavik, Manitoba.*

"The 'Bluenose Bucko'" was first published in The Canadian Magazine *(April 1929). The story is likely based on Chute's experiences as a young man on board a lumber-carrying barque, the* Snowden. *Following an eventful month-long voyage from Halifax to Queenstown, Ireland, Chute received his able seaman's certificate, which, according to his father, "he prized more than if it were a parchment from some great school of learning."*

The "Bluenose Bucko"

John Robertson, M.A., a divinity scholar with honors had been ordained to a little church in Falmouth, Nova Scotia, a village a-hum with seafaring activity.

From the start everything went ill with the Reverend John and his nautical parish. The young parson could find no point of contact with his congregation.

"'E's got too much trekle and molasses in his gospel for me," protested Captain MacKenzie, the presiding elder.

"What he needs is a breath of the 'Roarin' Forties' in his veins," burst in Job Laurence. "That's what made old Parson McNeil so much respected by the boys. We all knowed that he could lay out on a top-sail yard-arm and pass a weather reef-earing in a Cape Horn snorter. But this here Robertson feller is all book learnin' and uselessness."

"I believe ye're right, Job," said Captain MacKenzie, "'e'll be no good for this parish, nor any other, until he gets out of the clouds and comes down to earth."

It was agreed that the unacceptable parson must be eliminated. But how? Robertson himself came to the same conclusion. But he did not like to back out admitting defeat, so parish and parson stuck together a little longer, while each fervently prayed to be rid of the other.

An unforeseen event, suddenly, and happily, ridded Falmouth of the incubus of its undesirable minister. A new clipper the *Orion* had been launched from North's shipyard at Hantsport that fall. Robertson attended the launching, and saw the fair ship slide down the ways into a cresting sea, little thinking what fate she held for him.

There, off the Horton's Bluffs, at the mouth of the Avon, lay the *Orion*, riding at her anchor, a thing of sentient beauty. She was owned by the Dimmocks of Windsor, and they appointed as master,

Captain Bill MacCumber of Chiveree, to command her on her maiden voyage.

Captain MacCumber, on taking over, sent to Halifax to the shipping office for a crew. There were two famous houses on Water Street, the "Rialto," and the "Alhambra." The Rialto was served by a boarding house runner named Barney Upgate, an Irish packet rat, grown tired of the sea.

To Barney's tender mercy was entrusted the shepherding of seven erstwhile able, but at that moment most unable seamen. Barney was to take this variously intoxicated gang up country as far as Hantsport, where he was to deliver them aboard the *Orion*.

To handle a shanghaied crew from the crimp to a nearby ship is one thing; to take that crew for fifty miles by rail is a task demanding infinitely more resource.

Late at night, when the train arrived at Falmouth, his seven appeared to be in a comatose state, and Barney retired to a rear car for a drink with Music Murphy, who was escorting another helpless gang. It only took a minute, but that minute was enough for one seaman to shake off his lethargy, and bolt through the car window. Barney was just in time to see his heels.

Running out of the car he beheld the fugitive disappear into the night. Just then, the train began to move. In the darkness Barney almost bumped into a broad-shouldered figure. Quicker than thought, the boarding-house runner dealt the upright one a blow in the back of the head, and as he collapsed, grabbed him, and tossed him onto the platform of the now moving train.

As Barney rolled the limp figure into a seat, he noticed with consternation that he was clothed in clerical garb. A shanghaied parson seemed like tempting Providence, but the runner, full of Dutch courage, reflected: "It ain't no difference who I starts out with, or who I ends with, so long as I deliver seven coves, I'm Jake."

The crew of the *Orion* arrived at the beach in a number of hay-wagons. Most of them were laid out like corpses.

"Looks more like a gang of stiffs for the morgue, instead of the fo'castle," said Mr. Wallace, the second mate.

"We'll give 'em the morgue, all right," exclaimed Mr. MacDonald as he delivered his complement of men. Barney Upgate delivered his chit with a trembling hand. The Bucko glanced at it and grunted, "Seven."

Mr. Wallace counted Barney's complement and announced, "Only six here, sir." Despite Barney's vigilance another hand had escaped.

"Where is your seventh?"

"Gone," answered Barney helplessly. "Faith and it ain't me that's to blame, Captain!"

"We'll show you who's to blame. Pitch that gentleman's son in disguise aboard with the rest."

Before the astonished Barney could gather himself, he was pounded into senselessness, and pitched across the thwarts beside an inanimate heap, which had formerly been the Reverend John Robertson, M.A. of Falmouth. Both were dead to the world when they arrived at the *Orion*. They were hauled over the side in buntlins, and stowed away in their respective bunks.

Bang! Bang! Bang! A capstan bar thundered against the fore-hatch with reverberations to wake the dead. Slumberers and inebriates alike were startled back to life.

"Come on," bellowed the Bo'sun, "lay aft all hands, an' step lively while yer at it. If there's a soldier below, he'd better forget it quick, or he'll get a lump o' coal at the hells instead of a coffin."

Bang! Bang! Bang! sounded again, eloquent of the welcome that waited on deck for a possible loafer.

Sprawling figures that had been yawning in their bunks, at the challenge, catapulted onto the deck. Yes, this was a Bluenose ship all right. Every man with a realization of Bluenose ways came up with a jump. Sore or sleepy, shipped or shanghaied, drunk or sober, they answered at the double.

As the others jumped for the fore-hatch, Barney waited behind to rouse John Robertson. To his consternation, the parson lay insensible, in spite of the rudest shaking. Regarding the pallid face, there came to Barney an unspoken dread. He gaped about, but the forecastle was now deserted. With horror he started for the deck.

The muster aft was proceeding in the usual manner, when a laggard from the forecastle burst through the crowd, rushed past the mates, and entered the cabin alley-way. At the cabin door the steward blocked the way.

"What yer want 'ere?"

"To see the Captain."

The tone of resolution caused the steward to give and the next minute Barney Upgate was face to face with Captain MacCumber.

The Captain, who had just come aboard, was clothed in Sabbath attire of beaver hat and long black coat. Said Barney afterwards: "Struth, I thought it was another Holy Joe I'd tumbled into. Sure, he looked more like a preacher than a skipper standing there in a square mains'l coat and a long hat wid a rake aft."

The skipper was the first to speak. Taking off his frock coat and beaver hat he exposed a gorilla head, on a pair of massive shoulders. Barney felt a cold shiver run down his spine, while he regarded the sudden transformation that accompanied the shedding of that meeting-house attire. The Captain was a deacon in the Baptist Church at Chiveree. But all the soul-saving and sanctimony vanished from his aspect, as he faced about. In a twinkling, he passed from a Christian Baptist Deacon, to a barbarian master mariner.

"What are ye doin' butting into my cabin, ye dirty packet rat?"

"Beg pardon, Cappen, I ain't meant to do no buttin' in, but it's a case o' life or death. His Riverence is dyin' up there in the fo'csle, right now. In the name o' the Blessed Mary, Cappen, come quick, before it's too late!"

"His Reverence! I've met liars from Paradise Alley before, but his Reverence is the biggest yet. You want to tell me you've got a parson down forrard, and just as we're getting under way? You think I ought to come about, and take him back to the parsonage, eh?"

"Struth, Cappen, there's a dying man forrard, who'll be gone, if we don't get 'im something quick."

"Get out of here, and muster the crew. I'll take a look at your malingering mate later, and I'll wager beforehand that there's nothing ailing him but an overdose of 'White-eye.' And remember, my man, I'll keep an eye on you for your impudence, butting into this cabin.

"Don't stand there looking at me!"

For the saving of his skin Barney literally went flying through the cabin alley-way. He lost no time finding his place, first upon the foretopgallant yard, then at the capstan, till the anchor was hove short, then aloft again.

The canvas was set fore and aft. The inner and outer jibs were run up, and the sheets hauled to windward. The main and after yards were braced to the wind, while the *Orion* began to take on the appearance of some great white-winged seabird, fluttering before her flight.

As she began to gather way, the Ensign was dipped, and Old Man North, from the Horton Bluffs saw another of his new born clippers starting for a voyage round the Horn.

While they wore out of Minas Basin, all hands were kept on deck getting ready for sea. Toward the end of the forenoon watch, Captain MacCumber, on a tour of inspection, came forward and disappeared down the fore-hatch.

When he entered the fo'csle, he was greeted by the strangest sight of all his thirty years of seafaring. In one bunk was a dead

Irishman, sitting up with a death smirk on his face, a short pipe in his mouth, a sou'wester pulled down across his eyes, his whole make-up most artistically arranged.

Old Shanghai Burke had played some grim jokes, but this was his grimmest, shipping a corpse to pay off an ancient score with MacCumber.

In the other bunk lay the unconscious parson. Such a combination was too much, even for Captain MacCumber to face alone.

"Mr. MacDonald!" he bellowed.

At his bidding, the Mate came clambering through the fore-hatch. For the first time, the Mate beheld his Skipper nonplussed.

"I've seen some dirty ones, but this here is the worst yet, a stiff and a parson shipped wi' me as foremast hands."

"What do ye expect, when ye order a crew from a place like the Alhambra in Halifax.

"While on the sea I be,
     From Hull, Hell and Halifax,
     Good Lord deliver me!"

"No good runnin' down a port because of its crimps."

"Well, what do ye think we'd better do? Put back to Parrsboro for a couple of new hands?"

"Put back be damned. I'll make them boardin' house runners pay for their dirt, there's the one we fished out o' the river last night on top of a hatch combing, and there's the other one who came abuttin' in my cabin this mornin'."

"I thought you only took them two to work ship down the Bay."

"I may have thought so first, but not now, with these two Alhambra jokes wished on me."

When John Robertson opened his eyes the forecastle was in semi-darkness. He sat up and peered in the uncertain light to behold a waking nightmare, an ominous figure was bending over him holding a black bottle. At first sign of consciousness the attending figure drew back with a contemptuous grunt, disclosing pale scowling eyes, and an implacable face, charged with brutal force.

Beyond the dread figure of the Skipper, Robertson beheld the Mate and the sailmaker engaged in sewing up a corpse in a piece of canvas. As Hell-fire MacDonald attached a couple of large blocks of holy stone to the feet, the parson let out a shriek of horror.

"Where am I at?"

"You're aboard the *Orion*.

"Well, I hope you'll put me ashore soon. Where do you land?"

"On the west coast of South America."

"What?" Robertson almost jumped out of his bunk. "But you must put me ashore."

"Yes, at the end of the voyage."

"But you don't know who I am. I'm the Reverend John Robertson, M.A."

"Aboard this vessel, you'll drop them handles. Here, you're a man before the mast. Now then, rouse out of that bunk, and get out on deck."

"I couldn't possibly. I don't feel able."

"Well, we don't take ships out and bring 'em back by doing just what we feel like. We think o' the ship first, and our carcass last. Because you call yourself a preacher means nothing to me. There are all kinds o' preachers. When the voyage is ended I'll give you a discharge telling what kind of a preacher you are, whether a man of God, or a whitened sepulchre. So rouse out now, quick!"

Robertson still looked dazed.

"I'm sure I can't. I'm sure I can't move, Captain."

"There ain't no such word asailin' wi' me," answered Bully MacCumber, dropping his meeting-house tone, and coming back to that voice which was the terror of the Western Ocean.

"Mr. MacDonald!"

The first Mate left his gruesome task, and crossed the forecastle.

"Mr. MacDonald, you are to take this new hand into your watch. He says he's a parson. I want you to make him into a sailor. I want you to start right now."

"Aye, aye, sir. I'll make him into a sailor, or I'll make him into mince-meat.

"Now then, you in the bunk there, pile out quick."

"But you didn't understand, my head's all in a whirl. I must have a rest before I'm fit to do any work."

"Rest! You look as if you've never had nothing else but rest. Come on, up ye go."

The next instant, the giant mate pitched the recumbent figure from his berth, and with another couple of heaving lifts, sent him sprawling onto the deck.

"Now, then, you Holy Joe, ye ain't in no doxology-works, aboard the *Orion*. Get off your prayer handles and sweep down the waist, after that you can clean the brass."

For the parson, the whole world seemed to be swinging and heaving. Was he in the midst of an earthquake? or had he become the inmate of a mad-house? One thing, however, remained real. Merciless and pitiless at the rope's end the Bucko drove him on, pouring forth an endless rain of taunting rebuke.

"Hi there, don't play with that broom like a house-maid. Handle it like a sailor.

"Don't know how, eh? I suppose ye're one o' them eddicated idjits who knows everything, and can't do nothin'.

"How did ye ever live so many years, and learn to do so little? You're just about as much account as a paralytic laying in bed and sippin' gruel.

"Well, God'll surely punish me, if I don't punish ye fer growin' up so useless."

No sooner was the sweeping completed, than Robertson was initiated into cleaning brass work. After attending the capstan, and bell, on the forecastle head, the Mate exclaimed: "Now then, lay aft on the poop, and polish the binnacle."

This language was incomprehensible to the Greek and Hebrew scholar. But he dared not question, and picking up his gear he came aft as directed by the Mate's hand.

They were already in the Bay of Fundy, the *Orion* close hauled was shoving her nose into a tideway sea, mantled in flying spray to weather, while along her lee scuppers the seas were boiling white.

In the distance could be seen the Nova Scotian shore, sheer, black, foreboding, rising from a solitary ocean, grey and cold. Robertson shuddered as he gazed at the drifted snow along that bleak, bleak shore. Small wonder that the Bluenose breed, cradled thus, was a breed of iron!

At that moment, Robertson's utter inadequacy came over him like a drowning sea. With mincing steps, and sinking heart, he picked his way aft, keeping to weather to avoid that wicked water that boiled and foamed through the lee scuppers. Thus he came up the weather ladder, all unconscious of his sacrilege of sea custom, in profaning the side reserved only for the over-lords.

Bully MacCumber, pacing up and down the quarter, at his appearance, was seized with a sudden hyprophobia.

Without a word, the Captain blocked his progress. Robertson blinked apprehensively, like a bird held in fascination by a serpent's eye. There was a moment's trembling impotency, then he saw Kicking Bill MacCumber leap into the air, and for the second time, his memory faded in a flood of shooting stars.

When he came to, he was lying in a heap at the break of the poop. The Skipper was pacing up and down as unconcernedly as ever. But the Mate was there to drive home the lesson.

"Hit first and talk after is the style aboard a Bluenose hooker. Don't ye go up that weather side no more, that side's for officers, to leeward there is for the crew. Now then, up ye go and get on with yer polishing."

Whatever weakness may have held Robertson down was swiftly overcome by the toe of Hell-fire MacDonald's boot. As he dragged himself up in abject wretchedness, he caught a glimpse of Barney Upgate toiling with careless abandon far aloft.

Like a seabird's scream, there came faintly the sound of a lusty chorus, while the packet sailor sang on his eerie perch. For Robertson here was a vision of what one should be. What was the good of him, with all his scholastic distinction; winner of the Edinburgh Bursary, and helpless as a child? In that moment, Barney Upgate appeared to the parson as a flashing picture of the man beyond his dreams. Unconsciously, within, a resolution formed itself, "Some day I'll be like him."

When Robertson dropped down into the forecastle for supper, he encountered hell with the lid off, smoldering with base profanity, reeking with the mingled stench of booze, tobacco smoke, musty underclothing, and rancid oil skins; down there it was rank enough to turn the stomach of a camel.

Barney Upgate was holding forth in loud defiance: "S'help me, I've eaten gut-rot in me day, but this here's the bloody limit. Calls that bully, does he? I calls it an old horse that stopped on the way to the glue-factory."

"Well, what else would ye expect on a Nova Scotia or New Brunswick vessel?" chimed in a wise shellback. "N.S. on the counter, means no supper, and N.B. means no breakfast. This is the skinflint line, all right. Rip the heart and guts out o' ye on deck, and starve ye to death below. Bluenose Bucko's what ye call it. We're in for it."

"Ain't me that's goin' to take it, lying down," snapped Barney.

"I went up to show the old man what they served us from the galley.

"Smell it, says I. And the next thing I know he ups and kicks me off the quarter, as if I was some useless slob, like his Riverence, what's just come through the hatch there."

In grieved tones Barney continued to hold forth, while he did so, glowering across at the pale face of Robertson who had retired to his bunk, against whom Barney had taken a violent revulsion.

"Wished I'd never seen that Holy Jo," he muttered to friend Murphy. "But for him, I'd be in a warm bed on Water Street. That Parson's the guy I gotta thank for this!"

"Aye, and he's turning up his nose at ye, right now," confided Murphy. "Just look at him, will ye?"

Robertson had been an aristocrat socially and intellectually. His superior attitude was all right in the college cloister, but it did not go in a Bluenose fo'csle. Thinking that he was being regarded with condescension Barney's sullen resentment flamed into white heat.

"Who ye lookin' at?"

"Are you referring to me, my friend."

"Yea, ye, ye useless slob o' a Holy Jo, what d'ye think ye doin' in that bunk there?"

"I'm resting."

"Well, out o' that wid yez. We ain't goin' to stomach the likes o' yez lolling around in this here fo'csle, while yer betters is settin' up. It's bad enough to have a stiff like yez wished on us as a watch-mate. Someone's got to pull twice as hard on de halliards just because yer wished upon us. Us sailors'll have to do yer dirty work on deck. But we're goin' to make ye do our dirty work below. Ye're Billy Ducks aboard this hooker."

"What do you mean to imply by 'Billy Ducks'? That's a new word for my vocabulary."

"Aw, cheese it, cut de gruff, shake a leg der, and rustle de grub from the galley, after supper swab down de mess gear and sweep out dis f'csle. What d'hell do ye mean by comin' buttin' in here for, anyways?"

"I don't know how in the world I came here. It certainly was not of my own volition."

"Don't youse gets smart, now. Didn't I tell yez to quit callin' names?"

"Your vernacular is not quite comprehensible to me, my friend."

"I ain't no friend o' yours," screamed Barney, working himself into a paroxysm. "Thinks yourself better than anybody else, eh! And ye! Yer nothin' but a dude, a Holy Jo dude at that. But you won't turn up your nose at us no more, or I'll bash yer face in fer yez."

Barney's remarks intimating that they were despised by this useless watch-mate brought forth a general chorus.

"He's a blamed soldier, that's all."

"A featherbed soldier, wished on to us as a bloody watch-mate."

"Couldn't rustle the grub fer his own belly."

"Couldn't pull the fleas off a wet tarpaulin."

"What's the good o' him, anyways?"

At the general outburst, Barney deemed it expedient for an attack. Expressing the ill-will of all his mates, he leaped upon the hated parson, who went down at the first blow, while Barney satisfied his brute nature by kicking him around the fo'castle, and finally driving him with a halting limp to the galley, as the fo'csle flunkey.

The longed-for rest came at last, the rest for which every aching bone and outraged muscle clamored. Tumbling in, boots and all, the parson slept like one who would never waken. It seemed to him that he had just closed his eyes, when he felt the bo'sun shake him into consciousness.

He looked up stupefied and dazed, but there was no grace for hesitating.

"Come on, ye bloody soldier. It's yer trick on deck."

At the change of the watches, the mate started in with a half-hour's sweating up on sheets and braces. In the toiling mass, men trampled on the parson's feet, others jabbed him with their elbows, but in spite of himself, he was carried along with the swinging lilt of a halliard grind.

Once, while they were all toiling at the lee fore brace, the parson thought that his time had come. They were bending their backs at the brace, when the *Orion* went over on her beam end, and the solid green sea broke inboard over the lee rail.

With that engulfing mountain toppling down upon him, Robertson opened his mouth to scream, and as he did so drank his full of choking brine. Everyone was taken clean off their feet. Those near the rail with only a little slack on the brace were held down so that the sea broke clear over their heads.

Under that engulfing sea, the parson prepared to give up the ghost. But, to his amazement, the watch-mates came out alive and kicking. While the mate, who fished him from his swimming pool, ejaculated:

"The sea makes ye hard, me son."

A few minutes later, all hands were sweating up again, the mate calling out his orders to "Heave," and "Belay" as though nothing out of the ordinary had occurred.

Shaking hands with Death, in this nonchalant manner, was amazing to John Robertson; he had attended funerals, but this was his first experience of snapping fingers at a funeral.

As eight bells struck, to set them free for their rest below, the old man who had come out on the poop sang out to the mate:

"Hold on to yer watch for a moment, mister."

While they paused, Robertson, standing in the waist, heard an old shellback say: "There's a regular whistler, coming."

Gazing far off to weather, he could see the water black with a squall of wind, preceded by a wicked-looking line of creamy foam.

In a moment everything was in an uproar.

"Let go your royal and top gallant halliards!"

"Stand by yer clewlines!"

"Haul down yer outer jibs!"

"Let go yer staysail halliards!"

In the first rush aloft the parson hesitated, crouching like a frightened thing at bay, but the toe of a boot suddenly sent him leaping for the ratlines.

"Come on, ye Holy Jo! Up ye go. Up wi' ye now!"

With a buckle at his heels, Robertson was driven aloft, and out onto the main course, where he hung on for dear life.

It seemed incredible that he could have gotten there, but between death through beating, and death through falling, he chose the latter, though the minute the man-driver turned his attention elsewhere, he was in a panic.

When the roaring squall struck them, Robertson tasted a terror in the wind, more terrible than the terror of the drowning sea. He could hear nothing but the deafening crash of slatting canvas, of thumming shrouds and stays, and the seething of foam to weather.

With the yards whipping at every jump it seemed that every man must be catapulted into the sea. Fighting with the billowing mainsail, Robertson had his fingernail torn clean away. At the agony of excruciating pain, he cried aloud, but crying and sobbing, he continued clawing and fisting in mortal combat for the breath within his nostrils.

That first trip aloft always remained in the parson's mind as his first glimpse of real fighting. There in horrific flashes he came to see something of the meaning of naked fists against a naked ocean.

The *Orion* sailed steadily southward. Twenty-five days after leaving the Bay of Fundy she was on the Equator. On the fifth week out, she fell in with the trades setting a fast pace for the Horn.

In the first squall off Cape Sable the crew had been so slow that the old man was forced to stand by and see his light-weather sails blown to tatters. But he swore that thing would never happen again. "Belaying-pin soup," and "marlin spike hash" had done their part,

213

until now the crew were smart as paint, in whipping the canvas off her, and the Captain was able to risk carrying on to the last minute.

The strangest metamorphosis of all was that wrought in John Robertson. He had come aboard pale-faced, soft-handed, flabby-muscled, short-winded, a caricature of what a man should not be.

On his first day, from the abysmal depth, he had looked up and seen the vision of Barney Upgate on the royal yard. Then and there his sub-conscious nature had registered a decision, "Some day I'll be like him!" Every day thereafter he had continued to advance toward the stature of a real man.

As time passed, his pallid countenance had begun to take on a bronzed and healthy glow. Alow and aloft he attained surprising nonchalance. His stiff gait gave place to a swinging lilt, while he came to know the joy of muscle-hunger, jumping to the end of a weather-brace with a veritable yearning to "eat it up." From being the last, Robertson came to be the first to answer when his watch was called, the first to lead the way in a head-long racing for the topmost yards. To see him lay out on the point of honor on the weather-end was to cause even the old bear of a first mate to exclaim: "Well done!"

On the voyage south, Robertson achieved first, a real manhood, and second, a real enmity.

Having wronged the parson, like his kind, the packet-rat now blamed him in turn for his own sorry predicament. In the hard-bit life of a Bluenose hell ship, Barney continually muttered: "I'd be back in Water Street takin' it aisy, if it hadn't 'a' been for that psalm-singin' puke of a Holy Jo."

In time, Barney became insane from brooding over his imagined wrongs. There was too much of the sly-fox in his make-up to come out into the open. But day and night he nursed his grudge, secretly biding his time.

In the night watches below, brooding over his wrongs, he would climb out of his bunk, and with the slush-lamp dimly burning, he would come over and gaze at the sleeping Robertson. The sight of that loathed face would put him into a paroxysm.

"Why not do it now?"

Then a snort, or a groan, from a sleeping watch-mate, would cause him to jump back, as though eyes unseen were watching.

In a covert manner, Barney made several attempts on the parson's life. Finding him alone, one night, on the fo'csle head, he stole up in the darkness and brained him with a marlin-spike. He was starting to heave him overboard, when the mate, on his way forward, frightened him away.

Robertson was later discovered unconscious sprawled out in the snow.

On one occasion, at supper, with a burst of rage, Barney suddenly smashed the parson's pannikin into his face, exclaiming:

"Get that Holy-Jo-coffin-plate smirk o' yours out o' me sight, or I'll rip the tripes out o' ye!"

Robertson did not attempt to retaliate, but the crew exchanged knowing glances, as much as to say, "We told ye!"

Speaking to his friend, on the side, Murphy exclaimed:

"By God, it's comin' out again, Barney. Ye can't hold yerself much longer. If ye're that bad, now, God knows what ye'll be when ye get the Cape Horn fever in yer veins."

"Before we weather the Horn!" Barney paused for breath, "damn ye, Murphy, he and me'll never get 'round the Cape Stiff alive. This bloody hooker won't hold us both, that long. One of us is goin', either him or me!"

The *Orion* had run her southing down to the foul weather zone, in the Roaring Forties round the Horn.

The hungry giant wind came swooping on. The clipper laid over to it, her windward rigging strained and screaming, her every stitch of canvas drawing full.

Louder and louder the high winds roared, and still the skipper carried on. His was a new vessel and all the challenge therewith. Out of the forests at home, John North had fashioned a clipper. Now, out of the gales, it remained for Captain MacCumber to fashion a queen.

The old man had a weakness for carrying sail as long, and sometimes longer, than spars and rigging would warrant. Mr. Wallace, the second mate, shook his head dubiously, while the watch below grew jumpy, from the strain of the awful driving.

"He's tempting Providence too far," wailed a grizzled shellback.

The wind piped up until a regular gale was brewing.

"Most of her canvas should come off now, or else it'll be ripped off," muttered Mr. Wallace. Then, caution ruled him.

"Stand by your main royal halyards."

"Let go your royal halyards."

The royals were down for good. Another tremendous blast laid her far over, the breaking crests a lather of foam to windward. Sky and sea alike were breathing uneasily like a rising giant.

The Skipper came on deck, looked around, shook his head and muttered, "Guess I might as well drop the last of the flying kites," at which he shouted at the full pitch of his lungs:

"Mister, send down your main royal yard."

Already, at the bending of the heavy weather sails, all other lofty gear had been sent down. With a touch of bravado, Bully MacCumber had carried his main royal, to flaunt that soaring stick as it were in the very face of the mountain greybacks of Cape Horn.

Mr. Wallace heard this order with relief. At his word Barney Upgate was already on his way to carry out the old man's bidding.

With a snow squall whistling about his ears, and the clipper jumping into the big seas to her knightheads, Barney raced aloft with cheery shoutings.

In woollen mitts, sea boots, and monkey jacket, John Robertson stamped about upon the deck and watched the *Orion's* finest sailor swinging through high spaces, a fellow to the wheeling albatross. To see this rugged, brawny Jack toiling unconcernedly at his perilous task made it easy to forget his sins in admiration for his courage.

"Splendid fellow! Splendid fellow!" said Robertson, with tingling pride, following with understanding eye every move of his daring ship-mate.

After removing the lee and weather lifts, Barncy unparalleled the yard, and heaved it into a horizontal position, so that it swung suspended by the giantline. This done he clambered down to the lower end of the swinging yard to guide it clear of the rigging, and gave the signal to lower away.

The man on deck tending the giantline, let go with a run. Barney lost his hold of the rigging, and the suspended yard was tossed outward, the unfortunate sailor clinging helplessly to the end.

His sudden predicament was not pleasant to contemplate. To lower away on the giantline, with the yard out of control and swinging to leeward, would be to drop him into the sea. To heave to with the pitching vessel, would be to risk smashing him against the mast.

Even the imperturbable MacCumber shuddered under his long pilot cloth watch coat, as he gazed at the helpless dangling figure.

"He's gone!" he exclaimed aghast, at the first vicious plunge.

But no! There at the end of the swinging yard, grasping to the foot-ropes, Barney was hanging on for dear life.

Captain MacCumber put hands to mouth to bellow forth an order, but as he did so observed a figure already dashing aloft. The runner struggled over the futtocks heel and toe, up the top-mast cross-tree and into the very teeth of the wind where his hair was blown like ribbons.

"Who's that Mister?"

"That's the parson."

"Praise God, but can't he go."

"Yes, yes, I believe he'll do it."

While the Captain and crew watched with upturned faces, Robertson attained the top-gallant yard. Pausing there, he took a gasket, made a bowline, passing it round the upper end of the royal yard, then getting into the rigging opposite he bent over for his task of life or death.

"I'm coming," came the reassuring yell to the imperilled sailor.

"For God's sake, hurry!"

A moment later Robertson slipped his bowline, hauled it taut, and began steadying the swinging yard into the rigging.

This feat was all but accomplished, when the *Orion* heeled over before a sudden gust, tearing the yard from his grasp, while again it pitched away to leeward.

By this time, through endless wriggling Barney had gotten a leg around the foot rope and grasping the spar had gained a safer position. From the end of the swinging yard, he sang out cheerily: "Take a turn wi' the gasket round the riggin'."

Robertson accepted the tip, and hand over hand began to haul in once more, this time passing the rope around the shroud to hold what he had gained.

As he hauled away Barney exclaimed: "Sure, yer Riverence, and why did the likes o' yez ever do this fer sich a dog as Barney Upgate."

"Because you did so much for me."

"Why, what else could I 'a' done. 'Twas me that shanghaied yez aboard this hooker."

In his surprise, Robertson almost let go the rope on which he was hauling. Barney verily expected in the next minute to be precipitated into that watery grave, from which he was just being delivered.

The parson held fast. But for the first time in his life he swore aloud.

"Well, I'll be damned!"

"Why don't yez drop me? I got yez in for all this hell. Why don't yez drop me?"

"No fear," and the next instant, with a last heave, Barney was pulled into safety. As he stood beside his rescuer in the rigging, the poor fellow was still nonplussed.

"Sure, an' won't yer Riverence curse me now fer what I've done to yez?"

"No, but I'll bless you though. You did the best thing for me that anyone could ever do. Will you be my friend, Barney?"

"Faith, and I'll be that forever, Matey."

Matey!

Saul of Tarsus was changed to Paul on the Damascus Road, and there, aloft on the edge of the great West Wind Drift, there likewise "His Riverence" had changed his name.

ACKNOWLEDGEMENTS

Theodore Goodridge Roberts' "A Complete Rest" first appeared in *The Canadian Magazine* (June 1905) and is published by permission of John Leisner.

The excerpt from Frank Parker Day's *Rockbound* (Garden City, N.Y.: Doubleday, Doran, 1928) is published by permission of Donald Day.

FURTHER READING

Most of the sea-related writing by the authors represented in *Atlantic Sea Stories* remains out of print; however, during the past 25 years or so a number of maritime works by these writers have been republished. The following listing identifies titles that are currently available.

Frank Parker Day
Rockbound (Toronto: University of Toronto Press, 1988), with an afterword by Gwendolyn Davies.

Norman Duncan
Selected Stories of Norman Duncan (Ottawa: University of Ottawa Press, 1988), edited and with an introduction by John Coldwell Adams.

Way of the Sea (Ottawa: Tecumseh Press, 1982), with an introduction and bibliography by John Coldwell Adams.

Wilfred T. Grenfell
The Best of Wilfred Grenfell (Hantsport, N.S.: Lancelot Press, 1990), edited and with an introduction by William Pope.

Adrift on an Ice Pan (St. John's: Creative Publishers, 1992), with an introduction by Ronald Rompkey.

W. Albert Hickman
Canadian Nights (Freeport, N.Y: Books for Libraries Press, 1971)

Colin McKay

Windjammers and Bluenose Sailors (Lockeport, N.S.: Roseway
  Publishing, 1993), edited and with introductory essays by
  Lewis Jackson and Ian McKay.

Archibald MacMechan

At the Harbour Mouth (Porters Lake, N.S.: Pottersfield Press,
  1988), edited and with an introduction by John Bell.

Theodore Goodridge Roberts

The Harbor Master (Toronto: McClelland and Stewart, 1968),
  with an introduction by Desmond Pacey.

Erle R. Spencer

Yo-Ho-Ho! (St. John's: Creative Publishers, 1986), with an
  introduction by Ronald Rompkey.

Frederick William Wallace

Wooden Ships and Iron Men (Belleville, Ont.: Mika Publishing,
  1985)